WEDDING CAKE CRUMBLE

This Large Print Book carries the
Seal of Approval of N.A.V.H.

A CUPCAKE BAKERY MYSTERY

WEDDING CAKE CRUMBLE

JENN McKINLAY

WHEELER PUBLISHING
A part of Gale, a Cengage Company

GALE
A Cengage Company

Farmington Hills, Mich • San Francisco • New York • Waterville, Maine
Meriden, Conn • Mason, Ohio • Chicago

Copyright © 2018 by Jennifer McKinlay Orf.
A Cupcake Bakery Mystery.
Wheeler Publishing, a part of Gale, a Cengage Company.

ALL RIGHTS RESERVED

Wheeler Publishing Large Print Cozy Mystery.
The text of this Large Print edition is unabridged.
Other aspects of the book may vary from the original edition.
Set in 16 pt. Plantin.

LIBRARY OF CONGRESS CIP DATA ON FILE.
CATALOGUING IN PUBLICATION FOR THIS BOOK
IS AVAILABLE FROM THE LIBRARY OF CONGRESS

ISBN-13: 978-1-4328-5110-1(softcover)

Published in 2018 by arrangement with The Berkley Publishing Group, an imprint of Penguin Publishing Group, a division of Penguin Random House LLC

Printed in the United States of America
1 2 3 4 5 6 7 22 21 20 19 18

For my very favorite girl, my niece Kiersten. Bright and beautiful inside and out, you are one of the shining lights in my life, and I'm so glad I get to be your aunt. I can't wait for our next adventure together — try not to get hit by a bike next time! Love you forever!

ACKNOWLEDGMENTS

When I started the cupcake series, I was sure that I would get three books out of it and then the party would be over. Cupcakes were a fad, I thought. Surely, it couldn't last. But now here we are at book ten! Ten! Can you believe it? I want to thank all of the readers who have been along for the ride since book one. Without you, Fairy Tale Cupcakes would have closed a long time ago. I also want to thank my team — the people who help me and nudge me and give me pep talks when required — Kate Seaver, Christina Hogrebe, Roxanne Jones, and Jeff Fitz-Maurice, the terrific artist, who gave this book such a wonderful cover. I couldn't do what I do without all of you. Thank you all so very much.

ONE

"Here comes the bride," Melanie Cooper sang as she held a bouquet of multicolored snapdragons in front of her as if she were walking down the aisle.

"Practicing for your own wedding?" Angie DeLaura asked her.

"No, just yours," Mel said, then she smiled. "For now."

They'd been best friends since they were twelve years old, so it was no surprise that Mel would be Angie's maid of honor when Angie and their other childhood friend Tate Harper tied the knot in just one week.

Today, Mel and Angie had left Fairy Tale Cupcakes, the bakery they co-owned, in the capable hands of their employees while they ran around town, finalizing payments to vendors and making sure everything was a go for Angie and Tate's big day. At the moment, they were paying for Angie's flowers, calla lilies, with their stems wrapped in aqua and pewter ribbons.

"Annabelle? Hello!" Angie called. She rang the bell on the counter and peered at the back room. "What do you suppose is keeping her?"

"No idea," Mel said. She admired the brilliant yellow petals on a huge sunflower. So pretty.

"Okay, so after we pay the florist, who's next?" Angie asked.

Mel put the snapdragons back in their display bucket and checked her smartphone, where she kept her to-do list updated.

"We need to pay the photographer and the caterer." She glanced at Angie. "Are you really having them make Jell-O? 'Because crème brûlée can never be Jell-O'."

" 'I *have* to be Jell-O,' " Angie said. For emphasis, she tossed her long, curly brown hair over her shoulder.

"*My Best Friend's Wedding,*" they identified the movie quotes together and then laughed.

Since middle school, the three friends, Mel, Angie, and Tate, had shared a love of sweets and movies. Now as adults they tried to stump one another with random movie quotes, and in the case of serving Jell-O at their wedding, Angie chose it deliberately.

10

She wanted Tate to know she was his comfort food, his Jell-O, which he had always loved, much to Mel's cordon bleu dismay.

"Do you think we should leave and come back?" Angie asked Mel. "Maybe she's on her coffee break and forgot to lock the door."

"Maybe." Mel frowned. She didn't want to admit she was starting to get a hinky feeling in the pit of her stomach.

Annabelle Martin's flower shop sat in the heart of Old Town Scottsdale. Despite the small size of the space, it was full to bursting with blooms, both real and silk, as Annabelle's talent with flowers was legendary. In Scottsdale, Arizona, a wedding was just not a wedding unless Annabelle did the flowers.

"But even if Annabelle stepped out, why isn't anyone else here? Doesn't she have four assistants?" Mel asked.

Angie nodded and Mel saw her big brown eyes get wide and Mel knew she was thinking the same thing that Mel was. Angie swallowed and in a soft voice, she said, "Maybe something happened to her?"

They stared at each other for a moment. Over the past few years, they had suffered the misfortune of stumbling upon several dead bodies. Given that Angie was one week from saying "I do," it would just figure if they found a body now.

"This can't be happening," Angie said. "Not now."

"Don't panic," Mel said. She blew her blond bangs off her forehead. Being a chef, she kept her hair nice and short to keep it out of the food, because nothing said *"Ew"* like finding a hair in your frosting.

"Don't panic?" Angie cried, her voice rising a decibel with each syllable. "Why would I panic? It's only a week until my wedding, you know, the most important day of my life to date."

"Breathe." Mel squeezed Angie's arm as she scooted past her and around the counter. "I'll just check in back and make sure everything is okay."

A curtain was hanging in the doorway to the back room. She knew from being here before that the back room housed all of Annabelle's supplies as well as a kitchenette and her office. It was a tiny space and she had to turn sideways to maneuver through the packed shelves.

Vases of glass, steel, and copper; baskets; ribbons; glass marbles; florist wire in all sizes and colors — all of it — was stuffed onto the shelves until they looked as if they'd regurgitate the goods right onto the floor.

Mel shimmied her way past until she cleared the shelves and reached the worktable in back. A couple dozen purple irises were scattered across a sheaf of floral paper as if someone had just left them out of water and gasping for air.

Annabelle loved flowers; they were her passion. Mel couldn't imagine that she'd have just left these here to rot. Mel felt the short-cropped hair on the back of her neck prickle with unease.

Where was Annabelle? What could have happened to her? Mel closed her eyes for a moment, trying to dredge up the courage to circle the table and see if Annabelle was there, lying on the floor, unconscious, bludgeoned, bloody, bleeding out even as Mel stood here shaking like a 'fraidy cat.

"Hello? Annabelle? Are you here?" Mel called.

There was no answer. She opened her eyes. She was just going to have to see for herself. She took a steadying breath and stepped around the worktable. She glanced at the floor. It was bare. The breath she'd been holding burst out of her lungs as the sound of a toilet flushing broke through the quiet.

Mel whipped around to face the back hallway just as Angie came barreling through the curtain into the back room.

"Any sign of her?" she asked.

"Maybe," Mel said. She stared down the hallway, listening to the water running in the bathroom. Please, please, please, let it be . . .

"Well, doesn't that just figure?" Annabelle asked as she strode towards them. "It's quiet all morning and then the second you go to the bathroom someone shows up."

"You're okay!" Mel cried. Impulsively, she threw herself at Annabelle's big-boned frame and hugged her tight. "You're not dead."

"Oh, honey." Annabelle hugged her back. "You need to calm down, maybe take a vacation or something."

Mel let her go with a nervous laugh. "Ha, you're right. I must be working too hard."

Annabelle fluffed her close-cropped curls and then turned to Angie with a hug and a smile. "And how is our bride? Seven days to go! Are you ready?"

"More than," Angie said. "I'm excited for the wedding but I'm even more excited to have it over and be Mrs. Tate Harper."

Annabelle clasped her hands over her heart and sighed. "Of all the events I arrange flowers for, weddings are my favorite. Yours aren't here yet, but come on, I'll show you what I just got in."

Annabelle scooped up the irises and put them in water and then led them to the front of the shop. While she and Angie oohed and aahed over some of the fresh flowers, Mel took a moment to get herself together. Clearly she had some issues if her first thought when Annabelle hadn't been available was that she was dead. Seriously, what was wrong with her?

She had been around an inordinate amount of death over the past few years. She wondered if perhaps it was her own fault. Maybe she found all of these bodies, maybe bad things happened all around her, because she went looking for them. The thought disturbed Mel on a lot of levels.

"Did that daisy do something to offend you?" Annabelle asked.

Mel looked at her in question and Annabelle pointed to Mel's hands, where just the stem and one petal were left of an orange gerbera daisy. Mel had been systematically stripping the petals off of it without realizing.

Snatching off the last petal, Mel said, "He loves me. Phew!"

Angie looked at her as if she thought Mel

was drunk or crazy or drunk and crazy. Mel shrugged. Annabelle gave her a concerned look and took the stem out of her hands and threw it in the trash.

While Angie paid Annabelle for her flowers, Mel picked up the petals and then paced up by the front of the shop. She didn't trust herself not to destroy any of the lovely arrangements and kept her hands in her pockets just in case.

With a wave, they left Annabelle and her flowers to head to the photographer's studio. It was across Scottsdale Road, on a small side street, nestled in amongst the trendy restaurants and art galleries.

"Okay, what gives?" Angie asked as soon as the door shut behind them.

"What?" Mel asked.

Angie widened her eyes and said, "Come on, you know what. You started shredding flowers in there. What was that all about?"

"Nothing. I just had this random thought," Mel said. "It was silly."

"Good, then you won't mind sharing."

Mel pursed her lips. Angie was a badger. There was no way she was getting out of this.

"Fine, if you must know —"

"I must."

They paused at the corner to wait for the

crossing light.

"I just thought it was weird that my first instinct when Annabelle wasn't readily available was that she'd been murdered. I mean that's weird, right?"

Angie squinted at her. "There's more, isn't there?"

Mel blew out a breath. "Okay, it also occurred to me that maybe, just maybe, the fact that I am always looking for something bad to have happened is what makes it happen."

The light turned and the walk signal lit up. Angie opened her mouth to speak, closed it, then took Mel's arm and pulled her across the street.

Once they stepped onto the curb, she looked at Mel and said, "Now, that is nuts."

"Is it?" Mel asked. "I mean, isn't there a whole philosophy that says whatever you put out there comes back to you?"

"So, you think that by putting out thoughts of dead bodies or worst-case scenarios, that's what makes them happen?"

"Yeah . . . maybe . . . no . . . I don't know."

"Listen, we've definitely had some crazy stuff happen to us since we opened the bakery, but don't you think it's because we work in a service industry with a whole lot of different people with all sorts of bad and good things happening in their lives?" Angie asked. "I mean, how many weddings, birthdays, retirement parties, etcetera, have we baked cupcakes for and nothing bad has happened? Quite the opposite, in fact — the person has had the greatest day ever."

She began walking and Mel fell into step beside her.

"You're right," she said. "Maybe I just have a little post-traumatic stress going because the bad when it's bad is so very bad."

Angie nodded. "I'm sure that's it, but since my wedding is coming up in a matter of days, why don't we hedge our bets, and you just keep picturing happy things in that head of yours."

"Like puppies and kittens?"

"Yeah, or go big with unicorns and glitter bombs," Angie suggested.

Mel laughed. Angie was right. She needed to chillax. Probably, she was just nervous about the wedding. She was maid of honor, after all, which carried a lot of responsibility. Not that she thought Angie would pull a runner, but it was Mel's job to get her to the church on time, dressed appropriately, and to be prepared to crack some skulls if anyone interfered with her best friend's wedding.

"Okay, glittery unicorns it is," Mel said.

"That's my girl." Angie paused in front of the photographer's studio, pulling out her phone to check the time. Mel glanced over her shoulder and noted that they were right on schedule. Excellent.

Blaise Ione, the photographer, was a friend of Tate's from his days in the high school marching band. After graduation, Blaise had gone to art school and lived in New York City for several years, but when his aging mother needed him, he'd come home to Scottsdale to be nearby.

Blaise was a hardcore hipster and wore his short hair bleached white and paired it with his large Andy Warhol glasses, striped skinny pants, and pointy-toed shoes. He was exuberant, enthusiastic, and always made Mel laugh. She knew the wedding was safe in Blaise's hands.

Although it was a small space, Blaise made the most of it with huge portraits decorating the black walls, and mid-century modern furniture that made a statement as well as being a place to sit. Through the window, Mel studied one of the chairs, which looked to be molded out of cement. The statement she got was, *This is uncomfortable, so move along,* which, knowing Blaise, was exactly what he wanted it to say.

Angie pulled open the door and a gong sounded somewhere in the back of the space. Leave it to Blaise to have an unconventional door chime.

"Blaise? Hello?" Angie called out.

Mel moved towards the wall to study the portraits. Blaise had done Tate and Angie's engagement pictures and they were spectacular, managing to capture the longtime friendship that had morphed into romantic love between the couple.

Mel's favorite shot had been taken in black-and-white in an old movie theater. In it, Tate and Angie were sharing a bucket of popcorn, the red and white stripes on the bucket the only pop of color in the photo, as they gazed at each other with all the love in their hearts. It made Mel water up every time she saw it.

Oh, and here it was on the wall! Blaise had added it to his display. Mel felt her throat get tight.

"Hey, I didn't know he was going to put that up," Angie said as she joined her. "That's my favorite."

"Mine, too," Mel said. "Wow, it keeps hitting me that in a few days you'll be married to Tate."

"I know, right?" Angie grinned. "Say it again, it makes me dizzy."

"In a few days you'll be married to Tate." Mel laughed and hugged her friend close. "I am so happy for you both."

"Thanks," Angie said. "Man, I can't believe I spent all those years thinking he was in love with you."

"Idiot." Mel's voice was teasing when she said it, and Angie laughed and said, "Yep."

They sighed and then glanced around the studio. There was no sign of Blaise. They glanced at each other and Mel shrugged.

"Blaise, hello," Angie cried out. "It's Angie, your favorite bride."

Silence greeted them. Mel felt the hair on the back of her neck begin to prickle. No, no, no! She wasn't doing that again. She pictured a unicorn prancing through the studio. It didn't really help.

"Probably, he's in the bathroom," she said.

"Yeah," Angie agreed. "I'll just poke my head in the back."

"Okay," Mel said. Under her breath, she began to chant, "Unicorns and glitter, unicorns and glitter, come on, unicorns and glitter."

Angie got halfway to the back and turned around. "Come with me."

Mel nodded. She followed Angie to Blaise's office in the back corner. It had no windows that looked into the studio, just a

21

door painted with black chalkboard paint where people could scrawl messages for him. Several messages in different colored chalk were there now, including one in bright blue that listed Angie's name and the time. So he had been expecting them.

Angie knocked on the door. There was no answer. She rapped again. Still nothing. She reached down and grasped the handle, turning it and pushing in the door.

The office was a cluttered mess with papers and proof sheets and pop-art tchotchkes littering every surface. A life-sized self-portrait of Blaise was on the wall opposite and Mel almost greeted the picture instead of the man.

"Blaise, hey, are you napping on the job or what?" Angie asked.

Blaise was in his office chair, with his back to them as he faced his very large computer screen. The screen saver was on and the pattern was undulating all over the display. Mel followed it for a second, but then realized that Blaise sitting in front of the computer while the screen saver was on was wrong. So wrong!

"Blaise!" she cried.

She stepped around Angie into the room to get a look at the photographer. He was sitting upright, staring at the computer with

22

vacant eyes, his lips tinged with a faint shade of blue. Mel reached out to touch his hand. It was icy cold. There was no pulse. No rise and fall to his chest.

Blaise Ione was dead.

Two

"You were supposed to be thinking of unicorns and glitter bombs," Angie said. She pressed against Mel's side as they both studied the body of the man before them.

"I was! Like a mantra in my head, I swear."

"Oh, poor Blaise," Angie said. A sob bubbled up and she went to touch his hand but Mel intercepted her. They needed to keep him exactly as they'd found him for the police.

She hugged her close, trying to calm her own shaking as much as Angie's. She could feel her heart pounding hard in her chest and it was hard to breathe.

"We need to do something," Angie said.

"Yes, we need to call the police," Mel agreed. A glance at Blaise and it was clear what had killed him. A camera strap had been twisted around his neck and was still lying there, resting on his collarbones like a choker. Never had the term been more literal.

"Let's go call Uncle Stan," Mel said.

She put her arm around Angie's shoulders and ushered her out of Blaise's office and into the studio. She pushed her onto the hard concrete seat and Angie put her face in her hands and began to cry. Mel kept one hand on Angie's shoulder, trying to comfort her while she thumbed through the contacts on her phone looking for her uncle's number.

Her fingers were shaking and she fumbled her phone. Sucking in a deep breath, she tried to steady herself as she found Uncle Stan's number and pressed call. Not for the first time it occurred to her that it was handy having an uncle who was also a local homicide detective.

"Mel, this had better be an invitation to your mother's for pot roast," Uncle Stan answered on the third ring.

"Sorry, no," Mel said. She blew out a breath. Her voice was shaky and she tried to pull herself together enough to continue. "I'm at Blaise Ione's photography studio over in Old Town, and he's, well —"

"Dead," Uncle Stan said.

"Yes," Mel said, thankful that her uncle

could voice the word she was struggling with.

"Are you safe?" His breathing changed and Mel got the feeling he had started to run.

"There's no one here except me and Angie, if that's what you mean," she said.

"Are you sure?"

Mel scanned the tiny studio. Other than Blaise's office there was no other room except the bathroom in the back. She gave Angie's shoulder a squeeze and walked across the room to check the bathroom. She might have been nervous, but she had the feeling the place was empty. She doubted that whoever had strangled Blaise had lingered to use the facilities.

She pushed the door open and jumped back just in case. No psychopaths leaped out at her, so she flipped on the light switch using the back of her hand. The room was empty.

"No, no one is here," she said.

"I've got a patrol car on its way," he said. "Stay on the phone with me until they get there."

"Okay."

She walked back to stand beside Angie. Angie glanced up at her, looking crushed and a little lost. Neither Angie nor Mel had known Blaise as well as Tate had, but they had both been fond of him. Mel couldn't help but think of his poor mother. She was going to be devastated.

Mel could hear the sound of a siren coming from her phone. Uncle Stan was obviously doing his best to get here as fast as he could. Still, she felt her heart beat *hurry, hurry, hurry.*

She was in desperate need of a hug, and no one gave better ones than her Uncle Stan. Her father's younger brother, he was built in the same Cooper male mold as Mel's dad, who had passed away unexpectedly over ten years ago.

There was nothing polite about Cooper men's hugs. They were big, meaty bear hugs that made even a tall girl like Mel feel safe and protected. One of the many reasons Mel had fallen in love with her fiancé, Joe DeLaura, who was also Angie's older brother, was that he could give the same type of no-reservations-all-in-don't-worry-I've-got-you sort of hug. At the moment, however, Uncle Stan was all business.

"Tell me what happened," he said.

Mel recited the events of the past fifteen minutes while watching the door, willing a patrol officer to appear. She really wanted to hang up and call Joe now.

Angie rubbed the tears off her face and took her phone out of her handbag. She stared at it for a moment and then blew out a breath.

Mel watched as she opened her contacts and pressed Tate's number. They exchanged a look of shared misery while Angie waited for Tate to pick up.

Angie cringed when Tate's voice came through her phone, sounding delighted to hear from his bride. Angie closed her eyes. Her voice was gruff when she spoke.

"Tate, I have some bad news," she said.

A movement by the front door drew Mel's attention and she saw a female patrol officer walking towards the entrance. She gave Angie's shoulder another quick squeeze and went to greet her.

"Uncle Stan, there's an officer here," she said.

"Don't hang up until you let him know who you are and that I'm on the phone with you," he said. "In fact, put him on with me."

"It's a her," she said. "It's Lisa Kelley."

"Good, she's the best," Uncle Stan said. "Hey, does she have Cupcake with her?"

"Cupcakes?" Mel asked. "Why would she have cupcakes?"

"Not cupcakes — Cupcake," Uncle Stan said. "Lisa was moved to the canine unit.

Her dog's name is Cupcake."

"Really?" Mel asked. "That's ridiculously cute."

"Don't be fooled. She's a four-and-a-half-year-old Belgian Malinois, and she can take down a three-hundred-pound drug dealer on the run in less than ten seconds."

"Well, okay then," Mel said.

"Put Lisa on the phone," Stan said. Then as an afterthought he added, "Please."

"Will do."

Mel reached the door before Officer Kelley and pushed it open. Lisa kept her dog tight at her side as she stepped into the studio. Mel watched Lisa do a visual sweep of the room. Cupcake made a low whimper in her throat and Lisa patted the dog, letting her know she heard her.

"She smells the body," Lisa said. "She's not a cadaver dog, but still the smell must be alarming for an animal that has three hundred million olfactory receptors in her nose."

Mel nodded. She had no idea what to say. They were standing in the midst of a crime scene, which was bad enough, but the fact that it was someone she knew and liked made her heart hurt and her stomach twist.

Lisa seemed to understand. Her dark brown hair was pulled back into a bun at the nape of her neck and she glanced at Mel and then Angie through her rectangular-framed glasses. Mel suspected she didn't miss much. Lisa gave Mel a rueful look, and said, "I much prefer seeing you when you come into the station with cupcakes."

"Same," Mel said. "But I'm glad you're here." She held out her phone. "Stan wants to talk to you."

Lisa took the phone, but before answering, she asked, "Are you two all right?"

Mel nodded. "We're okay." She gestured towards Blaise's office. "The owner of this studio, Blaise Ione, he's . . . he . . . you'll find him in there."

Lisa nodded and lifted the phone up to her ear. "Hey, Stan, it's Lisa."

Mel could hear Uncle Stan barking instructions while Lisa listened, a wrinkle creasing her brow. Mel couldn't tell if it was concern or annoyance. Uncle Stan could be a wee bit overbearing.

"Yes, I can do that," she said. "Right away."

Mel glanced back at Angie to see how she was holding up. She was weeping again and having a hard time talking. Mel took the phone from her hand and lifted it to her ear.

"Hey, Tate, it's Mel," she said.

30

"Mel, are you both okay?" he asked.

"Yes," she said. "Officer Kelley is here from the Scottsdale PD and Uncle Stan is on his way."

"Good, that's good," he said. His voice cracked. "I'm on my way, too."

Mel knew it was pointless to try and talk him out of it. Blaise was an old friend of his and Tate's bride was here in a puddle of tears. Of course he was coming. That was the sort of man Tate was.

"Be careful, Tate," she said. "I know how hard this must be for you, but I'm with Angie. There's no rush."

"Got it," Tate said. His voice was gritty and Mel suspected that was all he could get out.

The call ended and she handed the phone back to Angie. Angie dabbed at her nose with a tissue she'd pulled out of her bag. She glanced up at Mel and handed her one, too. Mel felt the dampness on her cheeks. Huh, she hadn't even realized she was crying. She took the tissue and blotted her face.

"What if we did this?" Angie asked. Her voice was just above a whisper and Mel had to lean in close to hear her.

"What?" Mel's eyes bugged. She looked at Angie as if she'd hit her head on the concrete chair. "What do you mean? I'm pretty sure I'd know if I strangled someone with a camera strap."

Mel glanced over her shoulder to be sure that Officer Kelley and Cupcake had gone into Blaise's office to check on him. She could only imagine what Lisa would think if she heard what Angie had said.

Angie twisted her fingers in her lap. "I just mean that we were talking about looking for bodies when Annabelle wasn't in her shop right away, and, frankly, I had the same instinct here, too. When Blaise didn't greet us in front like he usually does, it was my first thought, and then sure enough he's dead. It's like we're bad juju or something."

"No!" Mel insisted. "No, you were right before. Think of all the great events we've done where people have been so happy. I refuse to believe that our paranoia got Blaise killed. It's just a coincidence, a horrible, horrible coincidence."

"Why don't I believe you?" Angie asked.

"Because you're overly emotional right now," Mel said. "Blaise was your friend and this is a shock and you're getting married in a week and of course it's too much to take in."

Mel looked at Angie and forced herself to maintain eye contact. She was lying. Something felt wrong about this situation, really wrong.

Their appointment was written on his chalkboard. It was clear to the whole world that they were to be here in this place at this time. Was Blaise's death planned for when they arrived, or was Mel the one being paranoid?

She had to be. It had to have been a random happenstance. Like a burglary gone wrong. Although, she couldn't imagine why anyone would rob a photography studio, never mind harm Blaise.

From what she knew of him, he was a great guy. Quick with a smile and a joke and he was a heck of a photographer — he knew how to make portraits intensely personal. Her gaze moved over the engagement shot of Angie and Tate. It was heartbreakingly perfect.

"I just don't understand," Angie said. "Why Blaise? How could this happen?"

Feeling utterly useless, Mel shook her head. "I don't know."

"Mel. Angie." Uncle Stan charged into the studio with the ferocity of a lion protecting his pride.

He didn't slow down but barreled across the room. He reached for Mel and hugged her close, as if that was the only way he could be certain she was okay, and then he scooped up Angie for the same. His hug grounded Mel in a way nothing else could.

Ever since her dad, Charlie Cooper, had been called to the all-you-can-eat catfish fry in the beyond, Uncle Stan had taken over his role of doling out the bracing hugs. Mel was ever so grateful. She watched as Angie hugged Uncle Stan back, and she could tell that she felt the same way.

"You're good?" Uncle Stan asked Angie, swiveling his head to include Mel in the questioning.

They both nodded, despite the fact that their red-rimmed eyes made liars out of them.

"We got here maybe twenty minutes ago," Mel said. "The door was open, no sign of anything being disturbed. Blaise didn't answer our greeting, so we checked his office and found him —"

"Strangled with a camera strap," Lisa finished for her. She crossed the room to stand beside Stan. "If you could come this way, Detective, I'll show you the scene."

Uncle Stan glanced at Mel and Angie and they both nodded, letting him know they were fine.

"I'll have Officer Kelley come back out and take your formal statements," he said.

"There's no reason for you two to linger here."

"Thanks," Mel spoke for both of them.

Lisa and Stan disappeared into the office while Cupcake sat just outside the door like a sentinel, and Mel felt her stomach twist, knowing the scene that would greet Uncle Stan. He was a pro. If anyone could handle it, it was him.

The door was yanked open and Tate hustled inside. He looked wrecked and Mel felt her heart pinch. Angie jumped up from her seat and launched herself at him. Tate caught her close and hugged her hard, then he set her on her feet and cupped her face, checking to make sure she was all right.

"I'm okay," Angie said. She knew him well enough to know he needed to hear it.

Tate nodded and glanced past her at Mel with the same seeking expression.

"I'm okay, too," Mel said.

Tate nodded and hugged Angie close again. When he released her, he kept his arm about her and Mel wondered who was anchoring whom.

"How bad is it?" he asked.

Mel and Angie exchanged a look, and then Angie said, "It's pretty bad. Oh, Tate, he was strangled with his own camera strap."

Tate's eyes went wide. "I have to see him.

35

I have to know —"

Mel understood. This was his friend, and there was some sort of code or loyalty that meant Tate couldn't flinch away from seeing what his friend had suffered.

"Uncle Stan is in there," she said. "He'll need you to give him Blaise's mother's name and number if you have it. He's going to have to go and break the news to her."

"I'll do it," Tate said. "Or at the very least I'll go with Stan when he does it." His voice wobbled a little. "It's the least I can do."

"I'm sure he'll appreciate that," Mel said.

Tate gave Angie one more quick squeeze before he strode across the room to join the police. Tate was tall and thin with thick unruly brown hair. A former money magician, he had left the world of corporate investment to work full time on the bakery's franchise operation. So far, they had opened up bakeries in Nevada, Connecticut, California, and Florida, and were currently looking at opening one in Washington State.

It was still new and scary for Mel, but with Tate at the helm, things had been going smoothly and the money had been crazy good. Mel was still trying to adjust to having discretionary income, i.e. mad money. With Tate's plan for world domination with cupcakes in full swing, she figured she'd best get used to it.

"Poor Tate," Angie said. "He looks wrecked. I don't know how he's going to be able to face Blaise's mom. Blaise was her only child; he was her whole world."

Mel blew out a breath. She couldn't imagine. She knew how her mother felt about her and her brother, Charlie Jr., and his two sons. If anything happened to any of them, it would devastate Joyce.

"Was Blaise seeing anyone?" Mel asked. "I know he was single at your engagement party, but maybe he'd met someone since then."

"Do you mean someone who knows what's going on in his life and can clue us in?" Angie asked. "Or someone who might be angry with him enough to kill him?"

"I feel like strangling someone with their camera strap is a particularly angry way to murder them," Mel said. "I mean, to use his own equipment; it was either a weapon of convenience or it must bear some significance in another way."

"I'm the least photogenic person who ever lived," Angie said. "And I have the chubby-cheeked, unibrow, squinty-eyed pictures to prove it, but even I never felt the need to strangle the photographer."

Her voice wobbled and Mel knew her

friend was struggling to keep it together and not cry again.

"Which is why I'm thinking it has to be someone in his life who has a grudge," Mel said. "If only we could see his client list, then we could talk to them —"

Angie's eyes were round. She was making slashing motions across her throat. She began to clear her throat really loudly and Mel tipped her head to the side, trying to figure out if she was having a fit or a delayed reaction to the murder or not.

"What's the matter?" she asked. "Are you okay?"

Angie flapped her hands in the air and Mel looked to see if there was a fly buzzing her.

"Sheesh, Cooper, she's trying to warn you that someone is listening," a voice spoke behind Mel. "Even I got that. A bit slow on the uptake, aren't you?"

THREE

Mel didn't have to look to know to whom the voice belonged. It was Detective Tara Martinez, Uncle Stan's partner, and the woman who hated Mel's guts because Tara had a thing for Mel's fiancé. Great, just great.

Mel turned around slowly. "Hello, Detective Martinez."

The short Hispanic officer was in street clothes with her badge clipped onto the waistband of her slacks. She looked polished and professional while Mel felt as if she'd just crawled out of her own hamper.

"Hi. Where's my partner?" Tara asked.

"He's in the office with Bla— the victim," Mel said.

She gestured towards the other room and Tara glanced at her hand. It was her left hand, the one that displayed her engagement ring. Tara stared at it until Mel shoved her hand behind her back, feeling self-conscious.

Tara's gaze met Mel's for just a moment and the look of hurt in her eyes made Mel suck in a breath. Tara was taking her engagement to Joe pretty hard, and Mel felt bad about that but not enough to deny her own joy.

Tara walked towards the office but paused beside Angie and said, "I heard he was a friend of yours. I'm very sorry for your loss."

"Thanks," Angie said. "I . . . we . . . we're all a bit shocked. He was a good man."

"We'll find out who did it," Tara said. "I promise."

Angie's face crumbled in her grief and Tara patted her shoulder before joining Uncle Stan, Tate, and Lisa in Blaise's office.

Feeling drained, Mel sat on the edge of Angie's uncomfortable chair. She could have sat on her own seat, but she felt the need to be close to someone to buffer the upset that was ricocheting through her like a rogue pinball.

Angie must have needed it, too, because she leaned her head on Mel's shoulder and let out a long drawn-out sigh. Mel put her arm around her friend. Mel wasn't sure how long they sat like that. The muted conversation from the office gave her no idea as to what was happening. Cupcake, the dog, never moved but sat silently at attention, her ears twitching occasionally, the only indicator that she was mindful of what was happening around her.

Tate came back and Mel moved seats. Tate promptly picked Angie up and sat in her seat holding her on his lap. His eyes were red and his face pale. Grief was etched in the fine lines at the corners of his eyes. He rested his cheek on the top of Angie's head and Mel knew he was taking comfort in her closeness.

The door opened and Mel turned and felt her heart leap in her chest. Joe! She was halfway across the room before she realized she was moving and she was in his arms and hugging him close without ever re-alizing that she'd grabbed him.

He pulled her close and his mouth was right beside her ear when he whispered, "Hey, cupcake, it's okay, I've got you. I'm here."

A half sob, half chuckle bubbled out of her before she could stop it. Joe leaned back to see her face. His dark brown eyes looked concerned as he studied her face.

"What is it?" he asked. "I came as soon as Stan called. Are you okay? He said you weren't hurt."

His hands swept over her as if assuring

himself that she was all right.

"I'm fine," she said. "It's just . . ." She glanced at the police dog still sitting at attention. "Cupcake is *her* name."

Joe looked from her to the dog. "Seriously?"

"Yeah." Mel nodded. Her throat was tight. "Sorry. I might be a teensy bit hysterical right now."

"It's understandable," he said. He pulled her in tight and placed a kiss against her temple.

This. This was why she was going to marry this man and become Mrs. Joe DeLaura. He was her rock. When everything was chaotic and crazy, Joe knew exactly what to do. And right now, it was to hug her and tell her that what she was feeling was totally legit. He didn't try to fix it, make it go away, or diminish it. He just let her feel.

"Better?" he asked after a moment.

"A little," she said. She sniffed and used the tissue wadded up in her hand to make one more swipe under her eyes and nose. "I'm worried about Tate, though. He's known Blaise since high school. He was more than just a wedding photographer for them."

Joe glanced at the portrait of Tate and Angie on the wall. His lips moved into a grim line. His gaze shifted to the couple, who hadn't moved from their sad huddle.

"I'll go see what I can find out from Stan," he said.

Mel nodded. As a prosecutor, Joe was privy to information in ways that Mel never would be. Before he could walk away, she grabbed his hand and gave it a squeeze.

He glanced at her and Mel said, "Tara is here, too."

Joe raised his eyebrows. "Should I be concerned about that?"

"Only in that she has a thing for you," Mel said.

"Says you," Joe said. He shook his head as if he didn't know where she got her crazy ideas. Mel could have pushed the point, but this was not the time nor place.

Instead, she said nothing as she watched him go and confer with the others. Lisa passed him on the way, with Cupcake at her side. They exchanged greetings and Cupcake sniffed Joe's pant leg and then moved on.

"Listen, I have another call," Lisa said to Mel. "They need Cupcake to sniff out a possible drug house. Stan said he'd take your statements. You guys going to be okay?"

"Yeah, sure," Mel said. "We'll be fine."

Lisa accepted the lie, giving Mel a quick

half hug on her way out the door. Cupcake followed her handler without looking back. Mel wished with all her heart that she could go with her.

"Let me see if I've got this," Marty Zelaznik said. "You went to the photographer's studio to pay him, but when you got there he was dead."

"Yup." Mel twisted the pastry bag in her hand. She was making specialty cupcakes for an anniversary party where the husband wanted bacon and/or bourbon flavored cupcakes but the wife wanted lemon cupcakes with lavender frosting and/or black forest cupcakes. Instead of arguing, the couple had decided to go with his-and-hers cupcake towers and order all four flavors.

Mel figured this was probably why their marriage had survived twenty-five years. Clearly, they had the art of compromise down. Personally, she had been delighted when the wife requested the lavender frosting. It took Mel a couple of tries to get it just right but she was pleased with how it had turned out. In fact, the lemon-lavender combo was so tasty she was considering making it a specialty item on the menu. Sort of like the McRib sandwich or the bacon crust at Little Caesars.

"What is it with you two?" Marty asked, bringing her attention back to him. He clapped his hands on his bald dome and his bushy eyebrows rose up to his forehead. "You just had to find another body, didn't you? I was almost in the clear. The girls were about to call off that shark of a lawyer and leave me be. If they get wind of this, I'm doomed."

Mel lowered the pastry bag and stared at him. "Really, Marty? A man is dead. A friend of Tate's, and your biggest concern is that your daughters are going to find out that we ran across a body and decide you're a few eggs short of a dozen?"

"You're missing the bigger picture here," he said. "My daughters, Nora and Julie, are still convinced I'm off my rocker."

"But you passed your psych eval," Mel said.

"They don't care; they still think this place is —"

"A hell mouth," Mel said.

"Yeah, pretty much. They're just looking for a reason to make me move back to the Midwest and live in some old person's home, so they can keep an eye on me and my money."

"I take it they haven't warmed up to Olivia?" Mel asked.

Olivia Puckett was Marty's girlfriend, and his grown daughters had taken an instant dislike to her. That was likely the only thing Mel agreed with them about, but for Mel it was more that Olivia owned a rival bakery than whether she was good for Marty or not. As far as Mel could tell, Marty and Olivia had been happy together, which was saying something given that Marty was well into his eighties and Olivia could be a handful.

"No, they haven't, and discovering another dead body isn't going to help," Marty said.

"It wasn't just a dead body," Mel said. "He was an old friend of Tate's, so you can't look at it through the filter of how his murder affects you."

"You make me sound very petty and selfish when you put it like that," he said. He crossed his arms over his chest and glared. "You know it's not that simple."

Mel heaved a sigh. He was right. She wasn't being fair, but at the moment Angie was home, no doubt crying her eyes out, while Tate was with Stan, telling Blaise's mother that he was dead, and even worse than that, he'd been murdered in his own studio.

"I know, Marty," she said. "I'm sorry. I do realize that your daughters are worried that

46

we're a bad influence on you and that Blaise's murder will not help convince them otherwise, but there really is nothing we can do to keep it quiet. Someone strangled Blaise with his camera strap. It was grisly."

Recalling Blaise's vacant eyes, the strangulation marks around his neck, and the cold feel of his skin beneath her fingers made Mel shiver. She inadvertently squeezed her pastry bag and purple frosting shot out, hitting Marty in the apron with a splat.

"Sorry," she said.

Marty took the bag out of her hands and put it on the table. Then he used a wad of paper towels to clean off the bib of his apron. He nudged Mel into a seat at the table and went over to the coffeepot they kept in the corner and poured her a piping-hot cup of coffee. He put in the exact amount of sugar and milk that she liked before he set it down in front of her.

Mel squinted at him. How had it happened? Marty, who had shown up here two and a half years ago, looking sad and bedraggled in a baggy cardigan sweater and a toupee that looked more like road kill that wasn't quite dead, had become such an integral part of their operation. She could barely remember a time when the octogenarian hadn't been her main counter person.

Now his daughters, Nora and Julie, were trying to take him away because they thought he was crazy to be working here in his eighties. What they didn't understand was that he was happy.

Unbeknownst to Mel or any of the others, Marty was loaded and his daughters lived in fear that he planned to fritter it away on what they called "his little bakery friends." The only person they disliked more than Mel and the bakery crew was Marty's on-again, off-again girlfriend, Olivia Puckett, who owned a rival bakery called Confections.

Presently, Marty and Olivia were struggling with the fact that Marty had never mentioned to her that he was a millionaire. Mel could understand both sides. Marty didn't want someone after his money but Olivia was furious that he hadn't trusted her with the information after they moved in together. In short, they were a hot mess.

With Angie and Tate's wedding coming up fast, Mel was just hoping the chaos could be contained so as not to damage the day Angie had been waiting for her whole life.

"It'll be okay," Marty said. Mel wasn't sure if he was talking her into believing it or himself. "If we could just keep it quiet, you know, not make a fuss, not draw attention to ourselves by sticking our noses where they don't belong, that might keep the whole incident off their radar."

"I don't see why we would have anything to do with it," Mel said. "I mean, we only found him. It's not like incidents before where he was a customer, or someone the bakery was working with in an official capacity."

Marty blew out a relieved breath. "Good, that's good."

"Of course, it might come out when Angie and Tate hire a new photographer and people talk about what happened to the old one."

"No, I've got that covered," Marty said.

"*You've* got it covered?" she asked. "Marty, you can't take Blaise's place and do the pictures for the wedding. He was a pro."

"I take a good picture," he protested.

"Sure, if you like the whole severed-head look," Mel said.

"What?" He looked offended.

"When have you ever taken a picture that actually included anyone's head on their body?" Marty opened his mouth to protest but she interrupted and said, "Or without

49

blocking their face with your thumb?"

"Well, I thought it was really nice of me to volunteer my services, but if you're just going to nitpick, I'll go back out front," he said.

"Marty, we need someone who can take a professional picture," Mel said. Then she bit her lip, realizing she wasn't at her most tactful.

"Well, that's gratitude," he snapped, and pushed through the swinging doors back to the front of the bakery, where he'd left Oz, Mel's other main employee, manning the front counter by himself.

Mel put down her coffee cup and reached for the pastry bag. She was just lifting it when Marty's head reappeared around the swinging door.

"And just so we're clear, I wasn't talking about doing the photos myself. I figured Ray DeLaura probably knew a guy, so I placed a call," he said. "But your confidence in me really warms my heart. Not!"

The door swung shut after him, moving back and forth until it came to a stop, and Mel stared at it for a moment. Ray? Did he really say he'd tapped Ray DeLaura for a replacement? Oh, hell no! Joe would have a stroke.

Ray DeLaura was the black sheep of the

DeLaura family because every family has to have one. If Joe was the mediating peacemaker of his six brothers, Ray was the instigator, the troublemaker, the wild card. If he hired a photographer for the wedding, it would likely be the same person who took his mug shot at the local police station.

Mel debated calling Joe. But then again, he had his hands full already and maybe Ray would surprise them. Maybe when he said he knew a guy, he actually knew a guy who was qualified.

Needing distraction, Mel got back to work on the cupcakes. The purple frosting lifted her spirits just a little bit, enough to keep her moving at any rate, and as she loaded up a tray to store in the walk-in cooler for delivery later, she convinced herself that Uncle Stan would figure out who had harmed Blaise. Her throat tightened up, but she swallowed past it.

Deep in the cooler, Mel didn't hear the back door open, so when she stepped out, she gave a small yelp to find Angie sitting at the worktable, surrounded by three of her brothers, Tony, Al, and Paulie.

"Ah!" Mel jumped and put her hand over her heart. "Give a gal a warning shout, guys."

"Sorry," Tony said.

51

Being the nerd inventor of the family, he was fiddling with some small electronic device. To Mel, it looked like a sort of house arrest anklet. That couldn't be good. She raised her eyebrows at Angie, who was puffy eyed, red nosed, and pale looking.

"Oh, Ange," Mel said. "I thought you were going to stay home for the rest of the day."

"I was," she said. "But I had to make some more of the payments for the wedding." She paused to hiccup and then continued, "So I figured I'd do it over the phone. I called the limousine service . . . and —"

Angie stopped talking. It was as if her voice had given out and she couldn't form the words. Mel studied her face. She glanced at the brothers. They were all looking at their sister as if they didn't know what to do. Growing up with seven older brothers, Angie really wasn't much of a crier, so when she did leak out of her eyeballs, the boys were understandably paralyzed by the sight.

"Can someone tell me what happened?" Mel asked. She was fighting to keep her voice even and not sound impatient. It was a struggle.

Al cleared his throat. "The limo company wasn't answering their phone, but when Ange did get through, she found out that the driver they'd hired was —"

Al stopped. Just like that. As if his voice had vanished, too.

"Was what?" Mel cried. "Double booked? Sick? Missing? What?"

"Dead," Paulie said. "Bludgeoned to death with a tire iron."

FOUR

Mel's legs gave out and she sank onto the nearest stool. Angie let out a wail that sounded as hysterical as an abandoned kitten on an iceberg in the Arctic.

"Dead?" Mel repeated as if it were a motion requiring a second.

"Yeah," Tony said. "They found his body last night outside the company's garage. It looked like a robbery, so the police have been investigating it as such, but now —"

Mel blinked at him, waiting for him to finish his sentence.

He glanced back down at the gadget in his hands.

"Now what?" Mel asked Angie.

Angie scrubbed her face with her fist and sucked in a steadying breath. "Now they think it might have been murder and that it has something to do with Tate and me getting married."

" 'They' being Uncle Stan?" Mel asked.

"Yeah, he seems to feel that it's too coincidental and that there is someone out there with a grudge against Tate or me and they're trying to stop our wedding."

Mel shook her head. "Not to state the obvious, but wouldn't it be easier to go after you or Tate directly?"

The brothers collectively gasped.

"I didn't say I wanted that to happen, just that it would be more expedient than murdering everyone involved in their wedding," Mel said.

"That's what I said," Angie agreed. "But Uncle Stan and Tate were pretty freaked out, so now I have them." She hooked her thumb at her brothers. "They are going to watch me right up until the ceremony to make sure nothing happens to me."

"What about Tate?" Mel asked. "Who's watching him?"

"Stan has assigned plainclothes policemen to watch all of our vendors and Tate," Angie said. Her voice wobbled and she looked at Mel and said, "I can't believe this is happening."

Mel rose half out of her seat and hugged her friend. "We don't know that it's directed at you two. It could still be coincidence."

"Not to be negative," Tony said, "but my calculations on the probability of this being a random happenstance are fifty to one."

Mel would have asked him how he arrived at that conclusion, but math was not her gift and he'd likely offer up some complicated algorithm that would just make her feel dumb. Tony was the only person she knew who actually did math equations for relaxation. Weirdo.

"But everyone loves you and Tate," Mel said. "Who could possibly want to stop your wedding?"

"Christie Stevens's family," Al said. "Her father has hated Tate since she was murdered and I wouldn't put it past that guy to hire some muscle to ruin Tate's life in revenge."

Mel's eyes went wide. Tate's former fiancée had been murdered a couple of years ago. She hadn't liked Christie but she'd never wished death on the woman. Besides, her murder had been proven to have nothing to do with Tate. Why would someone be out to get him now?

Mel paced the kitchen. She didn't like this. She didn't like it at all. As much as she disliked Tony's stats, the coincidence was unsettling. Then she had a disturbing thought. She glanced at Angie and wondered if she should say anything. Maybe it hadn't occurred to her yet, but then again, if plainclothes officers were being assigned to everyone attached to Tate and Angie's wedding —

Mel didn't get the chance to take the thought any further.

The doors to the kitchen slammed open with a bang. Tony and Paulie assumed fighter's stances, while Al wrapped his arms around Angie and dragged her to the floor.

"What the hell?" Angie cried. "Al, get off of me!"

"I can't work like this!" Oz cried.

He stomped into the kitchen and Mel noticed a petite little redhead with delicate features right on his heels. Oz whipped around and bent low so that they were eye to eye, or more accurately in Oz's case, eye to hair, since he wore his bangs over his eyes all the way to his nose.

"This area is off-limits!" he barked at the woman.

For anyone else, this would have been a terrifying sight. Oz had a lip ring, tattoos all over his arms, and when standing straight he was easily six feet, four inches. The redhead did not look impressed in the least.

She crossed her arms over her chest and glared at him with flinty gray eyes. "Where you go I go."

"Argh!" Oz roared. He spun around and

57

looked at Mel. "Help me."

"I wish I could," Mel said. "But since I have no idea what the problem is it's hard to know where to jump in."

"The problem is her!" Oz roared.

The redhead took her badge out of her pocket and was holding it on display for everyone to see. "Officer Hayley Clark. I've been assigned to keep watch over Mr. Ruiz."

"Oz, the name is Oz," Oz corrected her.

"Whatever you say, Mr. Ruiz," Officer Clark said. She glanced around the kitchen and Mel got the feeling she was looking for access points from outside and doing a risk assessment.

When she noticed Al, still holding Angie in a huddle, she bent low and asked, "And who do we have here? Do you need help, miss?"

Al let his sister go, and Angie struggled back into her seat. She huffed out a breath and looked at Officer Clark and then at Mel. "Why can't I have her? She'd be so much less annoying than these three."

Mel shrugged.

"Officer Clark, this is Angie DeLaura, the bride, and these are her brothers Paul, Al, and Tony," she said. "I'm Melanie Cooper, Stan's niece, and part owner of the bakery."

"You're Mel?" Officer Clark asked. Mel

58

nodded and Officer Clark gave her a thorough once-over. "I've heard a lot about you."

Between Uncle Stan and Detective Tara, she doubted it was anything good.

"I take it you've been assigned to Oz because he's the official baker for Angie and Tate's wedding," Mel said.

"Exactly," Officer Clark said. "Detective Cooper doesn't want to take any chances that there may be another . . . incident."

"This is ridiculous," Oz protested. "I mean, look at me. No one is going to come near me."

"Able to stop a bullet with your bare hands, are you?" Officer Clark asked. "Or maybe you can distract the assailant with some of your pretty baked goods."

Mel saw a telltale red streak up Oz's cheeks under his fringe of hair. She wasn't sure if it was embarrassment or anger, but either way, he was her employee and she had his back.

"Officer Clark, may I speak with you for a moment?" she asked. She jerked her head in the direction of the bakery.

The woman glanced between her and Oz, then she pointed at Oz and said, "Do not leave this room."

He looked like he was about to argue, but

Paulie picked up the rubber frosting spatula Mel had been using and popped it into Oz's mouth. Oz gagged and then mumbled something through the frosting, and Paulie gave him a bug-eyed look.

"You don't argue with the Five-O, man."

Oz raised his hands in frustration, but he didn't say anything else.

Mel pushed through to the bakery, where Marty was helping two older ladies pick out their cupcakes. She paused to frown at him. He was wearing a cowboy hat with a red bandanna around his neck. It didn't go with his navy blue bakery apron and she wondered if she'd missed one of the town's Old West days or something.

She stared a bit too long and as his gaze met hers his please-the-customer smile slid into a look of worry. Mel gave him a tight smile and led Officer Clark to the far corner of the bakery.

"About Oz," Mel began.

Officer Clark braced her feet and crossed her arms over her chest. For a petite thing, she sure threw up a good impression of a brick wall.

"Is there any reason to think he might be a target?" Mel asked.

"He's making the cake for the wedding, isn't he?"

"Yes, but —"

"No buts. Detective Cooper was very clear that anyone involved in the goods and services of the wedding was to be monitored twenty-four-seven until the big day," she said.

"But is there any reason to think that Oz in particular has been targeted?" Mel persisted. If anything happened to Oz, she knew that none of them would be able to live with it.

"I'm not at liberty to discuss the case with you," Officer Clark said.

Mel blinked. "But it involves me."

"Not really," Officer Clark said.

"What do you mean, 'not really'?" Mel asked. Her voice was getting higher with her agitation and out of the corner of her eye she saw Marty's face whip in her direction. "These are my people. The bride and groom are my best friends, Oz is my employee, and I went to high school with Blaise. How can you say it doesn't involve me?"

"Because as far as we can tell, you are not a target, and since you're not a target you have nothing to do with this case, so I will not be discussing it with you," Officer Clark said. She spoke slowly as if intentionally giving Mel time to absorb every word. "If you'll excuse me, I need to get back to my assignment."

She turned on her heel and marched back to the kitchen.

"Uncle Stan told you to say all that, didn't he?" Mel shouted after her. "Well, you can tell him it is so my business and I'm not just going to sit back and —"

Officer Clark pushed through the doors into the kitchen without even acknowledging Mel's tirade. Rude.

The ladies left and the bakery was quiet for the moment. Mel saw Marty watching her from under his bushy eyebrows.

"What?" she snapped.

He raised his hands in a surrender gesture. "Nothing."

"It is my business," Mel said.

"Whatever you say, boss," he said.

He was being way too calm for her normally cantankerous employee. He gave a booth in the corner side eye. Mel glanced over to see two men in casual attire sitting there. She glanced back at Marty.

"What's with the ten-gallon hat?"

"Disguise," he said.

"It's not going to work," she said.

"I know, but those two goons keep showing up wherever I am. I was hoping to throw them off," Marty said.

"With the hat?"

"It's a good disguise," he protested.

"Yeah, really effective," Mel said. "Why don't you just tell your daughters to back off?"

"I have, but they're convinced I'm knitting with only one needle." He looked sad, which garnered him more sympathy from Mel than his usual feistiness did.

"Oh, Marty," she said. "What can I do?"

"Let's just try to keep everything on the down-low, yes?"

Mel nodded and he glanced at a slip of paper on the table. "Oh, I forgot to tell you, you got a call from a Cassie Leighton. She said it was urgent."

Mel took the slip from Marty's fingers. There was a return call number on the bottom. Cassie and Mel went back a few years. When Mel had opened up her bakery, Cassie was already established locally as the owner of A Likely Story, a small independent bookstore and indie press that had been around for over ten years.

Being two of the few female small business owners in Old Town had made for an insta-bond they had never tainted with jealousy or power struggles. Instead, they always had each other's backs at the monthly local business owners' meetings and never let the other get disregarded or abused.

At this moment, Mel knew she had two choices. She could go try and talk to Oz and calm him down or she could call Cassie back. Given that Officer Clark looked like she was going to handle the Oz situation whether he liked it or not, Mel decided to call back Cassie.

She circled the counter and picked up the business phone. Marty watched her for a moment but a surge of customers coming through the door distracted him, giving Mel some peace.

Cassie answered on the third ring. "A Likely Story, this is Cassie, how can I help you?"

The greeting came at Mel like gunfire. Cassie was upbeat and friendly, but today she sounded stressed.

"Cassie, it's Mel at Fairy Tale Cupcakes. I got a message that you called," she said.

"Yes! Mel, I'm in trouble and I need your help," Cassie cried.

Mel felt the hair on the back of her neck prickle and she glanced at her arm to see goose bumps pucker her skin. Weird.

"Sure, what is it?" she asked.

"I need you to cater a last-minute event for me," Cassie said. "I'm so sorry for the short notice, but I've got a book signing for Elise Penworthy tomorrow night. My original caterer can't make it, and I need someone who is amazing and talented and brilliant and, most especially, fast."

"Elise Penworthy?" Mel asked. "Isn't she the author who wrote a fictionalized — *not* — account of all of the shenanigans she witnessed during her years living in the snooty Scottsdale neighborhood called the Palms?"

"That's the one," Cassie said. "With the book of the same name that I published for her. The preorders alone are in the thousands, we have a sold-out ticketed event for five hundred people for tomorrow night, and the book's been optioned for a movie. Mel, I need you!"

"Five hundred cupcakes by tomorrow night? Cass, if it was any other week, we'd be all over it," Mel said. "But Angie and Tate are getting married next weekend and, well, there's been some —"

Angie appeared beside her, snagged the phone out of Mel's hand, and said, "We'll do it."

Mel jumped and stared at her friend. Angie's eyes were smudged by rings of watery mascara, her face was still pale, and the end of her nose red. Mel glanced over her shoulder and saw the brothers standing there. She glanced back at Angie. Mel could hear Cassie talking on the phone but couldn't make out the words.

"Yes, it's Angie," she said. "Thanks. No, we have plenty of time before the wedding. In fact, this is perfect because it will give me something to do."

Mel nodded. Now she understood. Angie wanted to bury herself in this last-minute job so that she didn't have to think about Blaise, or their driver, or anything else.

"All right," Angie said. "I'll let you work out the details with Mel. And, Cassie, can you save me a copy of the book? Thanks."

Angie handed her the phone and Mel asked, "Are you sure? This could be an all-nighter."

"Positive," Angie said. "I need this. Take the order and let's get to work."

FIVE

Champagne cupcakes. Five hundred of them. And per Elise Penworthy's specifications via Cassie, they needed to be absolute perfection. Sure, no pressure. Mel called Joe to let him know she wouldn't be home for dinner. Joe took the news well, arriving at the bakery kitchen with a stack of pizzas from Oregano's Pizza Bistro and their shared cat baby, Captain Jack.

The brothers took three of the pizzas and parked themselves at a table in the front part of the bakery, which was now closed for the evening. They dragged Tate and Angie with them as the brothers refused to let either of them out of their sights until their wedding. Also, they needed reinforcements because everyone knew if Tony was left alone with the pizzas, they would vanish in one inhale. The skinniest of the DeLaura brothers, Tony also had the biggest appetite.

"Where's the rest of the crew?" Joe asked Mel as he maneuvered her into her snug office with a pizza in one hand and Captain Jack in the other. Mel took Captain Jack and nuzzled him before letting him run around her office, which was really more of a glorified closet.

Joe sat in the only chair, her desk chair, and pulled her onto his lap. He reached over her to flip up the top of the pizza box and then handed her a slice — green olive and sausage, her favorite — before taking one for himself.

"How are you doing?" he asked.

"Still sad," she said. "It's like this ache in my chest that's relentless. I can't believe I'll never see Blaise smile or laugh again, and I didn't know him as well as Tate and Angie."

"I'm so sorry."

"That's mostly why we took the book-signing gig. Angie said she needed something else to think about."

Joe nodded. He swallowed and then asked, "Have you heard from Stan?"

"Not a word," she said. "He put a detail on everyone, including Oz, who is not enjoying Officer Hayley Clark, not even a little."

"Is she cute?" Joe asked.

Mel looked at him.

"I just meant if she was cute, it shouldn't be such a hardship," Joe said.

"She is cute," Mel said. "I think that makes it worse."

"Why?"

"His girlfriend, Lupe, has been away for a long time and the last time she was here . . ." Mel stopped talking. She didn't like to gossip about her employees.

"They didn't get along?" he guessed.

"It seemed tense."

"Do you think they broke up?"

She shrugged. Oz hadn't said anything, but whenever Mel asked him about Lupe, he got a weird look on his face.

"Poor Oz," Joe said. "It's hell realizing you love someone and can't be with them."

Mel leaned back to study his face. "It's even worse when you think they're out of your league."

"But it's magical when they finally become yours," he said. He hugged her and Mel dropped her head onto his shoulder, smiling when she felt him plant a kiss in her hair.

If someone had told her terminally awkward and pudgy twelve-year-old self that she would one day be engaged to Joe De-Laura, the man of her dreams, she would have looked them dead in the eye and said,

"Shut up!"

Instead, she turned and kissed his cheek and said, "It sure is."

They were quiet, watching Captain Jack attack scraps of paper, climb the shelves of the bookcase, and smack the fronds of the plant hanging in the corner of the room as if they had done something to offend him.

When Joe finished his third slice, he crumpled his napkin and tossed it onto the box. Mel finished her third as well, except she had to dump the crust. She just couldn't finish it.

A sharp rap sounded on her office door but before Mel could call out a greeting the door swung open. Her mother, Joyce Cooper, stuck her head in and her face lit up at the sight of them.

"Melanie," she said. "And dear Joe." Joe had been "dear Joe" to her mother from the moment they had started dating and remained so even during their brief breakup. Mel wasn't sure, but sometimes she suspected her mother loved Joe more than her.

"Hi, Mom," Mel said. She started to scoot off of Joe's lap, but her mother held up her hands in a stop gesture.

"Don't move on my account," she said. "I just came by because my friend Ginny said that she heard from Monica Wexel, who was talking to Abby Dresden at the art gallery, that you were making the cupcakes for Elise Penworthy's book signing tomorrow night at the Orange Blossom Resort, but I said that couldn't possibly be true because you would have told me, because you know that I know most of the people who were written about in that book, and surely, you'd want me to know.

"I mean, Elise Penworthy is said to have dragged her ex-husband and his hot young wife through the proverbial wringer in that book, of which I would love to get a copy. Not only that, but she goes on to destroy everyone in her neighborhood who took her husband's side in the divorce, which because of his wealth and influence was just about everyone."

"Uh." Mel stalled. She wasn't sure what to say and she was a bit worried that her mother had run out of oxygen and was about to pass out. She didn't. Pity.

"Mel just got the job a few hours ago," Joe said. "In fact, I'm sure she was about to tell me that she was going to call you after her dinner break and share the news."

"Really?" Joyce clasped her hands in front of her chest and gave him an *Aw* look.

Truly, if Joyce's eyeballs could shoot hearts out of them like an emoji, Mel was pretty sure Joe would be covered right now. While she was thrilled that her mother liked Joe, she couldn't help but notice that her mother was so besotted she didn't really hear what Joe said sometimes. As in, he told her he was sure Mel was about to tell him she was going to call her mother, not that she actually was going to call her.

What a conniver! She hadn't been about to do any such thing. Then again, it did keep her mother from thinking she was out of the loop. Joyce hated that.

"I'm sure it was one of the top fifty things I was about to do," Mel said. "Maybe even top twenty-five."

Joyce frowned at her.

"I'm kidding," Mel said. "I would have called you. Promise."

She hopped off of Joe's lap and circled the desk and hugged her mom. The blue-green hazel eyes so like her own had faded over the years and were now more blue than green. Mel thought about all her mother had been through, losing her husband, managing two children who were barely adults on her own, and it was small wonder the worry line in between her eyebrows was so deep. It looked deeper today.

"You heard about Blaise, didn't you?" Mel asked.

"Are you all right?" Joyce asked. It was unspoken acknowledgment that she was really here for that reason but didn't want to say it.

"I will be," Mel said.

"And Angie and Tate?" Joyce asked. "It had to be an awful shock to lose their friend."

"It was," Mel said. "Tate went with Uncle Stan to tell Blaise's mother. He didn't go into it with me, but I gathered from Angie it was one of the hardest things he'd ever done."

Joyce nodded. "Are they here? I'd like to say hello."

"You mean check on them?" Mel asked.

"Yes, but with more subtlety than that," Joyce admitted.

Mel smiled. "You're such a good mom."

To her surprise, Joyce blushed.

"They're in the kitchen with the brothers," Joe said. "I'll walk you in so they don't think you're a robber and try to tackle you or pelt you with cupcakes."

"Thank you, dear Joe," Joyce said.

Mel and Joe exchanged a look and she gave him a small shake of her head. Because Joyce was a worrier, Mel did not want anyone to tell her that Stan suspected someone was out to sabotage Tate and Angie's wedding by killing off their vendors. Joyce would worry herself sick about it, so just like Joe's and Tate's parents, she was to be kept ignorant of the possibility.

Mel scooped up Captain Jack and snuggled him close. His soft white fur soothed her and when she looked at him with his black patch of fur over one eye, she couldn't help but smile. He batted her nose and she put him down so he could continue his shenanigans. The boy did have a pirate's soul.

Back in the kitchen, Mel scrubbed up with the detail of a surgeon before continuing the baking. For the tops of the champagne cupcakes, she had gathered a variety of decorations. She wanted champagne buttercream on top with different sized balls to make it look like the frosting was actually bubbles. If her idea proved out, it was going to be incredibly festive-looking and even the high-maintenance Elise Penworthy would approve.

She glanced at the table in front of her. She did a quick mental calculation. Using their industrial cupcake pans, which baked thirty-six cakes in a batch, they were almost halfway there with a little more than two hundred of the champagne-flavored cakes done. She glanced at the clock. It was almost nine.

No worries. They could do this. Still, she began moving a little faster as she started the next batch. It was going to be a long night.

Angie stood behind the table and yawned. Not a petite, bride-to-be yawn — oh, no, this was a jaw-cracking-bear-going-down-for-hibernation yawn. Mel was pretty sure she saw the filling in Angie's back molar.

"Drink your coffee," she said.

She pushed a large paper cup in Angie's direction. Feeling as wrecked as Angie, Mel had already done caffeine recon at the resort and managed to talk the managing chef in the kitchen into hooking her up with some supersized java.

"You're a goddess," Angie said.

They had finished the last of the champagne cupcakes in the wee hours of the morning. The results were pretty amazing, although she wouldn't say it was worth the lack of sleep.

The conference room in the Orange Blossom Resort on the north end of Old Town Scottsdale was big and posh. The Mission-style lighting was a nod to Frank Lloyd Wright with stained-glass panes of rectangles in varying earth tones. The room was large and rectangular with rough stone walls and thick wooden beams running across the ceiling.

Mel and Angie were manning the cupcake towers — there were five — at the back of the room next to the bar. While they arranged the towers, the resort staff scrambled to set up the upholstered chairs. A raised platform at the far end of the room had two comfy armchairs with a table in between them. This was where Cassie would interview Elise.

Mel had heard the event had been sold out for weeks. The price of admission paid for a signed book, a cupcake, and a seat at the talk. Given that most of the crowd was local, Mel had brought plenty of brochures advertising the bakery.

"So, let me get this straight. This chick writes a fictionalized tell-all about her neighborhood, sells it to a small local press, and now it's being optioned for a movie?" Ray asked.

Ray was the brother on duty for the evening. For the past half hour, he'd been slouched against the wall behind them, reading Elise's book.

"Yup," Angie said. "Did you get to the part about the wife-swapping parties yet?"

"No, I just finished the bit about the

doctor's wife and her affair with the delivery guy," he said. He fanned himself with the book. "Steamy stuff. You sure Tate is okay with you reading this?"

Angie blinked at her brother and then scowled. "Yes, he even lets me watch R-rated stuff on TV."

"Hey, now," Ray said. "There's no need to get snarky."

Angie rolled her eyes and Mel maneuvered herself between Angie and the cupcake table on the off chance Angie decided to lob a cupcake at her brother's head.

"Where is Tate, anyway?" Ray asked. "I didn't think he'd let you out of his sight."

"He had a meeting with our attorney who vets all of the franchise applications," Angie said. "He couldn't get out of it, but he'll be here before the talk is over."

Ray nodded. He glanced down at the book and then back up to scan the room.

"Go ahead and read," Mel said. "They haven't opened the doors yet."

"Thanks." Ray flashed her a smile and then stuck his nose right back in the book.

"I never pictured Ray as a reader," Mel said. "Is it the beautiful prose or the salacious tidbits?"

"Tidbits, for sure," Angie said. "The last book Ray read cover to cover was Captain

Underpants to our niece and nephew."

Mel nodded. She could see that. She chugged her coffee, hoping to fight off the urge to crawl under the table and take a nap. She hoped that Elise was an entertaining speaker, because right now she and Angie were running on fumes.

She checked the time on her phone for the third time in as many minutes, when the doors to her right were opened and a crowd started to shuffle in. Cassie had instructed Mel and Angie to hold off on passing out the cupcakes until after Elise had given her talk, that way the people waiting for their book to be signed would have something to do.

At the time this had seemed like a great idea, but all Mel could think now was that if they gave out the cupcakes ahead of time, they could get the heck out of here.

The crowd surged in, hurrying towards the seats in the front. A few people looked longingly at the cupcakes, but several resort staff stood in front of the table directing people to their chairs and explaining that the cupcakes were for later.

As soon as the door opened, Ray put the book facedown and came to stand in between Mel and Angie. In their matching Fairy Tale Cupcakes pink aprons with the bakery's retro logo on the front, Mel knew they represented the bakery well. With Ray standing between them with his thick gold chain tangled in the chest hair that sprouted out of the collar of the skintight black V-neck T-shirt he wore under his leather jacket, well, he was definitely giving a mixed signal.

One woman, with her bleached blond hair swept up in a cloud on her head, her skin a shade of copper not found in nature, and her girls pushed up and out leading her way like two beacons, paused to take Ray in. She eyed him like he was a cupcake and then batted her false eyelashes at him while biting her lower lip. Ray was halfway over the table before Angie cuffed some sense into him with a quick slap upside the head.

"Get ahold of yourself," she snapped.

The woman frowned at Angie and then at Ray before she spun on the heel of one stiletto and moved up the middle aisle to a seat close to the front.

"Sorry," Ray said. He ran a hand over his face, which had become red and sweaty. "It's just been a while."

Angie held up a hand and closed her eyes. "Things a little sister does not need to hear."

Ray shook himself from head to toe, like a dog shaking water off its coat, and said, "I'm good. I got this."

The three of them stood smiling at the incoming crowd. Well, Mel and Angie smiled while Ray maintained his resting bitch face. Mel was pretty sure that alone kept people from coming any closer.

Once the crowd settled, Cassie appeared on the platform. She did a quick mic check.

"Good evening, everyone," she said. She paused to smile at the crowd. "Can everyone hear me?"

Mel and Angie, being at the back of the room, gave her a thumbs-up. The sound was a go.

"Great," she said.

She surveyed the room, trying to acknowledge everyone with her bright blue gaze. Her tousled brown hair was cut in a pixie style that accentuated her heart-shaped face. Cassie was somewhere in her forties, although Mel wasn't sure if it was on the younger or older end. She was funny and vivacious and whip-smart, so Mel knew that this interview with Elise would be entertaining on Cassie's end for sure.

"I want to thank you all for coming tonight," Cassie said. "Before I bring out our guest author, I want to thank the Orange Blossom Resort for letting us meet here. There are just too many of you to cram into

80

my little shop. Also, I want to thank Mel and Angie from Fairy Tale Cupcakes for providing the refreshments. If you haven't had one of their amazing cupcakes, you are in for a treat."

Mel and Angie waved when most of the crowd turned to glance at the cupcake towers behind them.

"She didn't mention me," Ray said. He sounded grumpy.

"Why would she?" Angie asked. "You didn't do anything."

"I'm here, aren't I?" Ray said. "Standing right here."

Angie shook her head and Mel concealed her laugh with a delicate cough. What Ray lacked in fashion sense, he more than made up for in self-esteem.

"And now, I'd like to bring out our guest author tonight," Cassie said. "Please welcome Elise Penworthy."

The crowd applauded, a few more enthusiastically than others, and Mel wondered how many of them knew Elise from before she was published. How many of these people could really call her a friend or neighbor or even an acquaintance? Was the crowd mostly known to her or was it people who just wanted to pretend they knew her before she was famous?

Mel squinted to get a good look at Elise as she strode through a side door into the room. It was quite the grand entrance. She was dressed in pricey designer clothes — white slacks and blouse with a beige cardigan that flattered her middle-aged girth, topped by a long white-and-brown silk scarf looped around her neck with one end trailing behind her almost down to the floor.

Perfectly manicured and coiffed, Elise had bloodred fingernails and her hair was styled in a choppy shoulder-length bob that had been hit so hard with copper and platinum highlights that it dazzled almost as much as the diamonds at her ears and wrists under the overhead lights.

She had the face of a woman who had once been a looker, but wrinkles marred her forehead and the corners of her eyes, jowls pulled at the once delicate face, and her teeth, while blindingly bright, were a bit out of alignment, with one incisor protruding on one side of her mouth, giving her smile a sarcastic twist.

She paused as she made her way through the room to clasp people's hands or give them an air kiss and a gentle hug. If this crowd adoration was honey, Elise was lapping it up.

She blew the room a kiss and climbed the

three short steps up to the platform, where she enfolded Cassie in a hug. To Mel, it was the first one that seemed genuine. The two women took their seats, Cassie handed Elise a mic of her own, and the crowd settled in to listen.

"Tell us, Elise," Cassie said. "What inspired your novel *The Palms*?"

"Well." Elise drew the word out, moving her gaze over the crowd as she let the anticipation weave its way around the audience, tightening about them until the tension had them in a stranglehold, barely breathing as they waited for her disclosure. "I was inspired by my hus—"

"Liar!"

Six

The shout came from the middle of the crowd. Elise drew back as if she'd been slapped. She scanned the crowd and her eyes narrowed as she found the source of the disruption.

"You husband-stealing slut!" Elise jumped up from her seat. She clutched the mic in her hands as if it were a club that she intended to use to bludgeon someone. "How dare you show your face here!"

"How dare I?" The accuser stood. She ripped the wide-brimmed hat off of her head and her long blond hair fell in fat curls down her back. "That's a laugh. How dare you write these horrible disgusting lies?"

Collectively, the crowd turned from Elise to the angry woman and back. It was a volley of accusations and insults and no one wanted to miss a single serve.

"I'm guessing that woman is the one Elise's husband left her for," Angie said out of the corner of her mouth so that only Mel could hear.

"I'd say that's a safe bet," Mel said.

Cassie stepped forward as if she thought she might need to restrain Elise from doing a stage dive to get to the other woman.

"Ladies, this is not the appropriate forum for this discussion," Cassie said. The words were right, but her voice lacked the authority to subdue the two angry women.

"This is my book signing. If you don't want to hear what I have to say, I suggest you leave, Mallory." Elise said the name with venomous relish.

"Wow, she really hates her," Ray observed.

"I will not leave." Mallory stomped her foot.

She looked to be about the same age as Mel and Angie, but she was definitely the sort of woman who was used to being pampered. Her hair and skin looked like they'd just been polished at a spa, her clothes were haute couture, but there was no air of having a job or responsibilities or of being accountable or work-weary coming off of her.

Elise writing about her unfavorably was probably the worst thing that had ever happened to Mallory, and the most infuriating part of the whole thing was likely the fact that there was nothing she could do about it. The anxiety on her face was almost comical.

"Sweetie, you have two choices. You can kick up a fuss and I'll have security escort you out of the building or you can sit there and listen to my book talk like a grown-up," Elise said.

Mallory pushed her way out of her row so that she stood in the middle of the central aisle. She wore a pink micro minidress that hugged her curves and ended about an inch below her bottom. Beige platform sandals added a half foot to each of her legs, making her taller than average. She glared at Elise, tipped up her chin, and planted her hands on her hips in a defiant stance.

"Make me."

Angie made a gurgling sound in her throat as if she couldn't believe what she was hearing.

Elise waved a hand at the security men, stationed by the main doors. Mel hadn't noticed them before but now she wondered if they had anticipated some trouble since Elise's book was known for being a thinly veiled portrayal of all the dish found in the Palms neighborhood, including her ex-husband's affair with a much younger woman, aka Mallory.

"You wouldn't dare!" Mallory cried.

"Oh, wouldn't I?" Elise asked. The smile she turned on Mallory was pure malice. "After you ruined my marriage, stole my life, and made me a pariah in my own neighborhood, why wouldn't I?"

She nodded and the security team surged forward. Mallory let out a squeal and broke into a run headed right for the cupcake towers. The look in her eye was one of pure spite and Mel knew exactly what she was thinking. She was going to destroy the cupcakes to get revenge on Elise.

"Oh, hell no," Angie cried.

She turned to bolt around the tables while Mel stood paralyzed as she watched hours of work swing in the balance of one woman's cupcake-icidal rage.

Mallory was three yards out with the security team hot on her high heels when a tackle came from the side and she was sent crashing to the floor by a blur in a black leather jacket.

Mel rose up on her tiptoes to peer over the table. Sure enough, Ray had taken the woman out but had gallantly spun his body so that she landed on top of him.

"Nice one, Bro!" Angie leaned over her brother and lifted up his hand to give it a solid high five.

"Ugh," Ray grunted.

Mallory used her elbows to his midsection to push her way to her feet. She was disheveled and wobbly and the security guards grabbed her by the arms before she could get away.

Elise had left the platform and was striding down the middle aisle, looking like she was taking a victory lap. It was very clear who was on whose turf now, and she seemed to be relishing it.

She leaned close, putting her heavily made-up face right in Mallory's fresh one and said, "Escort her from the premises."

"Mallory! Elise! What the hell is going on?" A man in a suit and tie charged into the room. His thinning gray hair was styled up in spikes as if to hide the pink skin of his balding skull, his middle-aged paunch hung out over his belt, and he was huffing and puffing as if running into the conference room from the front desk was more of a workout than he was used to.

"The ex?" Angie mouthed to Mel from across the table. Mel shrugged, but it seemed likely.

One of the security guards helped Ray to his feet. Ray brushed his clothes off, not that they needed it, and stepped back. He resumed his sentry position with his arms crossed over his chest and a forbidding look on his face.

"Your child bride crashed my book signing," Elise said. She gave Mallory a scathing glance. "Funny, I didn't think she was old enough to drive."

There were a few laughs from the crowd and a corner of Elise's mouth lifted. She was drawing strength from the people who had come to see her.

"Elise, that is beneath you," her ex-husband said.

"Really, Todd?" she asked. "The whole reason we're divorced is because *she* was beneath *you.*"

"Do something!" Mallory stomped her foot and glared at her husband.

"That's right," Elise goaded the couple. "The new Mrs. Cavendish wants you to contain the former one. Too bad you have absolutely no power over me. None. I'm Elise Penworthy now and I can do and say whatever I want, and I want to tell everyone exactly what a pitiful, middle-aged cliché you are."

Mallory growled and Todd's face turned bright red. Todd Cavendish made a valiant effort to wrestle back his dignity by casting a withering glance at Elise, but it was nullified by his thinning hair, potbelly, and the furious glare being directed at him by his new wife, who was easily less than half his age.

"I had no idea you were so classless," Todd said. He sniffed as if he felt he was above a sordid scene.

"Says the man who married a girl still wearing a school uniform every day," Elise snapped. "Was it the pigtails, the plaid skirt, or the knee socks that got your . . . um . . . attention? Really, we all want to know."

"I'm going to slap her so hard," Mallory howled. She shook off the security guard still holding her and took a step towards Elise.

"No, you're not," Todd said. He grabbed his young wife's arm and marched her towards the door.

Elise raised her hand in a wave and cried, "That's right, it's a school night. You really should be tucking her into bed. Toodles."

"This isn't over, Elise!" Todd yelled. "I will sue you for slander, libel, malicious intent —"

"Blah, blah, blah," Elise said. "If you don't mind, I have an event here." She waved her hand in the direction of the exit.

Todd dragged his wife through the door, slamming it behind him so hard it rattled in its frame.

"Well, that was delicious!" Elise turned to the crowd with a big grin. She was still standing in the middle of the aisle and she walked the length of the room, shaking hands and accepting congratulations. At the end of the rows, she paused to glance at the cupcake towers and then at Angie and Mel.

"Those are spectacular," she said. "Thank you for making them on such short notice."

Mel blinked. After Elise's attack on Mallory, she hadn't expected her to notice them or their cupcakes, much less show appreciation for their hard work.

"Thank you," she said.

Elise gave her a small nod and then glanced down at Mel's left hand, where Joe's ring sparkled. "You're getting married?"

"Eventually," Mel said. She gestured at Angie. "But her big day is in a week."

Elise turned to look at Angie. She opened her mouth to say something then paused. She pressed her lips together, and then, as if she just couldn't stop herself, she said, "You might want to run while you can. If you step back and look at it, marriage really isn't in the best interest of the woman."

Mel's gaze darted to Angie. This could go very wrong very quickly. To her surprise, Angie smiled at Elise and it was genuine.

"No offense, but judging by what you married, I don't think the problem is with marriage so much as groom selection," she said. "Don't you worry about me, I picked a perfectly ripe melon and I thumped a lot of them before I found him."

Elise stared at her for a beat and then tipped her head back and laughed. Mel felt herself sag in relief.

"Angie!" Ray shouted. He looked horrified. "Don't say that in front of me."

Elise glanced between them and Angie explained, "Brother."

"Ah," Elise said. She moved over to stand beside Ray and said, "And he's a nice defensive end, too."

She patted Ray's behind, and Mel almost choked on her own laughter when Ray went up on his toes and turned as red as a stalk of rhubarb. Elise winked at him. She glanced at the table again.

"I like you cupcake bakers," she said. She turned to go back to her seat, but then turned back and looked at Angie and said, "Good luck on your marriage. Word of advice? Never let him forget how lucky he is to have you."

"No worries there," Angie promised.

A look of understanding passed between them, and Mel felt oddly left out. She was getting married, too, after all. Didn't she warrant some special advice from the author? Clearly not. Huh. She shrugged it off as she settled in to listen to the rest of Elise's talk.

The audience was on the edge of its seat, eager to listen to Elise dish the dirt on her former friends and neighbors, even though she was careful not to use real names and she repeatedly insisted that it was all fiction, made up when she found herself dumped, divorced, and desperate.

No one believed her. The question-and-answer portion was mostly pleas for Elise to name names, but she dodged the requests with a wink and a shrug. When Cassie announced it was time for Elise to sign books, the horde turned its attention on the waiting cupcake towers.

Mel and Angie handed out cupcakes while Ray stood behind them glowering. More than one woman took a look at him and changed course to get in line to have her book signed instead of risk being tackled by the big, brawny, leather-clad bruiser.

"Ray," Mel hissed.

"What?" he asked.

"Take a walk," she said.

"What?"

"You heard me," she said. "You're scaring

the customers. Go scout the perimeter or something."

"I'm not supposed to take my eyes off of Angie," he said.

"So, keep your eyes on me from over there," Angie said. "Seriously, you're killing the cupcake-loving vibe."

"Fine," he agreed. "But I'm going to be right there." He pointed one stubby finger at the side of the room. He scanned the crowd and his voice boomed when he added, "Still in tackling range."

Angie rolled her eyes but the ladies looked collectively relieved to have Ray away from the table. Cupcake distribution swiftly picked up its pace after that.

A few cupcakes were left and Mel boxed them up for Cassie and Elise to enjoy after the event.

Cassie was standing beside Elise, opening the books to their title page for Elise to sign. The line was still pretty deep, but Mel wanted to say good-bye to Cassie before they left.

Ray was hauling the decorative towers they had used for their cupcakes to the van, refusing to let Mel or Angie set one foot outside of the resort without security.

"Cassie, we're going to head out," Mel said. "But I thought you'd like to keep the leftover cupcakes."

Cassie glanced up from the pile of books she was managing. She gave Mel a big smile and gestured to a resort staff person who'd been helping with the line to take over opening the books for the customers.

"Thank you so much," Cassie said, and she took the cupcakes. "Elise and I will enjoy these back at my townhouse with some champagne when we toast the success of this event."

Mel glanced at the line that wound down the wall. There was no doubt, Elise was well on her way to being a bestselling author.

"Enjoy them," Mel said. "And if you ever need us to fill in again —"

"Don't you worry," Cassie said. "After this you're back to being my go-to bakery. Such a tragedy about Brianna at the Cake Stop." Cassie lowered her voice. "She wasn't my first pick but Elise wanted her because anyone who lives in the Palms orders their cakes from her."

Mel tipped her head. She knew Brianna, only in passing, but she knew her. She'd always thought she was a nice hardworking baker, even though her cake had always seemed a bit dry.

"What happened to Brianna?" she asked. "Why did she have to cancel?"

"She didn't cancel," Elise said. "You didn't hear? I thought for sure it would have been murmured through the bakery network. Brianna was found dead in her kitchen. Apparently, there was a gas leak from her oven. Can you imagine?"

"No," Mel said. She felt queasy. "I can't."

"Elise, can I have just one more picture?" A photographer stepped in front of the next person in line and held his camera up.

Mel glanced at Angie to see if this was making her think of Blaise. Judging by the sad look on her face, it was.

"I'm telling you," Cassie said, "I am so relieved by the turnout tonight. Everything was going to heck in a handbasket this week and I was sure we were doomed. But thanks to you and James" — she paused to point to the photographer — "we managed to pull it out."

Mel felt her heart thump hard in her chest. What were the odds? She had to ask.

"Is James filling in for someone?" she asked.

"Yes, we originally had Blaise Ione booked to take the event photos. He and Elise go way back," Cassie said. "He took her author pictures and the cover photo on the book, you know."

"I didn't." Mel's voice was breathy, and

not in a good way, but rather in the way that happens right before a fainting spell.

Mel reached out and grabbed Cassie's arm to steady herself. This was too weird to be a coincidence. Way too weird. She turned to see if Angie had heard, but Angie was watching Elise talk to the next woman in line.

"Hello, dear, would you like the book personalized or just a signature?" Elise asked.

The woman in line grinned at Elise and said, "Oh, Elise, it's so good to see you. You can just sign it to me."

Elise tipped her head to the side. It was clear she had absolutely no idea who the woman was. She didn't even try to pretend.

"And your name would be?" she asked, with her pen poised over the page.

The woman, tiny and fragile-looking, with her slight build and glasses that looked too heavy for her face, stared at Elise with such a look of hurt that Mel felt sorry for her. Clearly, meeting Elise meant much more to the woman than it did to Elise.

"I'm Janie Fulton," she said. "I lived three houses down from you on Crestwood Drive for twenty years."

Elise gaped at her. Mel got the feeling she still didn't know who Janie was, but she decided to bluff.

"Janie, darling, it's so good to see you," Elise cried. "You look really . . . well."

"Thank you," Janie gushed. "I've been keeping an eye on everyone for you, and I know everything that's happening in the neighborhood, so I can help with the next book."

"Aren't you a dear?" Elise asked. She looked a bit stiff. "But this book has only just come out, and I have to get through this publicity tour first and then, of course, they're already talking movie."

"Of course. I know you're so busy," Janie said. "But maybe we could get together for old times' sake sometime."

Elise finished writing in the book and closed it, handing it to Janie. "Sure, doll, thanks for coming."

It was a stone-cold dismissal as Elise looked past Janie at the next person in line. Janie's shoulders slumped. She opened the book and glanced at the personalization. Mel wouldn't have thought it possible, but Janie looked even more defeated.

"She spelled my name wrong," Janie said to Cassie, who was standing beside Elise. "She wrote a *y* instead of an *ie.*"

"Oh, no," Cassie said. "I'm sure she'd be happy to make it right."

She gestured for Janie to wait, when Elise erupted out of her seat and snapped, "You!"

Seeing the look that was directed at the woman behind her, Janie yelped and moved out of Elise's line of sight lest she be turned to stone.

"Me," the woman behind Janie returned. She put one hand on her hip and tossed her perfectly highlighted hair.

Elise and the woman commenced their stare-down and the entire room stood frozen, watching. Were they about to rip each other's hair out or exchange nasty insults? Mel did a quick scan to see if there were any sharp implements in the vicinity besides Elise's pen. Nope, they were good.

"Eeee!" the two women squealed at the same time, and then Elise was leaning over the table to hug the other woman close.

Mel sagged in relief and she noted that Cassie and Angie did the same.

"I can't believe you're here, Shanna!"

"Only for you, dearest," Shanna returned. "Now sign my book to me, and make it naughty."

Elise bit the end of her pen and resumed her seat. She signed the book, talking all the while. "We simply have to get together while I have time. What are you doing after this?"

"Actually, I have plans," Shanna said. "My

whole life has been in utter turmoil."

"Really?" Elise asked. "Why?"

"Because, darling, after my husband read about my torrid affair in an advance copy of your wicked little book, I couldn't hide it anymore, now could I?"

Elise glanced up at her with a look of shock. Her face, which just moments before had a healthy rose glow, drained of color, leaving her sickly looking.

"But I never meant —"

"Sure you did," Shanna said. "Admit it. You wanted to ruin me so you weren't alone in your misery. Well, you caused Carl to throw me out, so well done."

SEVEN

If looks could kill, Elise would be bleeding out where she sat. The entire room went still, looking to see what happened next.

"What's the matter, darling?" Shanna asked. "You look positively ill."

"I just . . . I never . . . I'm so sorry," Elise said.

Mel got the feeling the words were not ones she used very often, as it appeared she had to choke them out.

Shanna gave her a wicked smile. "Don't be. All of his psychotic outrage at his impending humiliation caused Carl to stroke out before he changed his will and I inherited billions! You set me free, my dear, and I am ever grateful."

Elise's eyes went wide and she clapped her hands. "That's wonderful. I mean, um, I'm sorry for your loss?"

"Don't be. It was no loss. He was a bully who thought I was an accessory to be seen and never heard. I am not grieving, not even a little," Shanna said. "I'm leaving next week for a six-month cruise around the world. You simply have to meet up with me when you finish this pesky book business."

"Spanish Riviera?"

"Absolutely."

Elise signed the book and the women exchanged an air kiss. Shanna took her book and sauntered away, looking every bit the privileged billionaire that she was.

Angie turned a bug-eyed look at Mel, who shrugged. This was not her world. Inheriting billions off the corpse of a dead husband who was apoplectic that he'd be publicly shamed? She would never be able to relate. She was kind of glad about that.

"Hey!" Ray appeared beside Angie. He was frowning and he pulled them both away from the table by the elbow. "So, I was just outside talking to the driver."

"Why?" Angie asked.

"I thought he might be available to fill in for you on your big day since your limo —"

Angie's lower lip wobbled. Mel tucked her hand behind Ray's elbow and pinched his arm right through the leather.

"Ouch!" He tugged his elbow away. Mel gave him her scariest face and jerked her head at Angie. "Yeah, okay, don't talk about

102

dead guys, I got it."

Angie looked like she was getting ready to wail. Ray, sensing disaster, started talking really fast.

"So, check this out," he said. "The driver here is a last-minute replacement for a guy who was found dead, who happens to be the same guy you and Tate hired."

"Meaning?" Angie asked. She looked confused.

"Oh my god, seriously?" Mel asked.

Both Ray and Angie looked at her in question.

"I just found out that Brianna, the original caterer, was found dead in her kitchen," she said.

"Well, that's taking the rule of three to a dark new level," Ray said.

"No, you're missing the point," Mel said.

"Me, too," Angie said. "Why the excitement?"

"Because the photographer, caterer, and driver for Elise's event were all murdered," Mel gasped. "You had the same driver and the photographer in common but the caterer was just Elise's. Don't you see? You and Tate aren't the targets of these murders. Elise is," Mel said.

As one, all three of them turned to look at Elise. Sensing their scrutiny, she paused in signing a book and asked, "What? Is there a spider on me?"

"No, but you have to get out of here," Mel said. "Your life is at stake."

Elise blinked. Almost in slow motion, she handed the book to the man who was waiting and then she threw back her head and laughed.

"I don't know who you are, cupcake baker," she said, "but your sense of comic timing is fantastic."

She turned to the next person in line, still chuckling. Mel turned to Cassie. "I'm not kidding," she said. "She has to get out of here."

"Mel, you're acting crazy," Cassie said. "What's gotten into you?"

"Three murders," Mel said. "Didn't you find it the least bit odd that the photographer, the caterer, and the driver you hired for tonight's event were all killed this week?"

"I thought it was just a series of unfortunate events, like Mercury was in retrograde or something," Cassie said. "Why would you think it has anything to do with Elise?"

"Because there are no coincidences," Angie said. She had pulled herself together and was looking as serious as a heart attack. "Three deaths and the only thing they had in common was this book signing."

"We need to call Uncle Stan," Mel said. "He'll want to know about this and the signing will have to be shut down."

"What?" Cassie cried.

"I'm sorry," Mel said. "It's the only way to keep Elise safe."

"But the books and the customers and my sales," Cassie said.

"They'll get their books," Mel said. "But is Elise's life worth the risk if there is a killer out there?"

Cassie took a few seconds longer than Mel would have thought necessary to shake her head.

"All right, fine," she said. "I'll tell Elise we need to pack it up."

She moved to stand beside Elise and they exchanged a tense whispered conversation. Elise looked surprised and then angry. Finally, she shook her head and put up her hand, indicating that she wouldn't listen to any more, and turned back to the next person in line, clearly dismissing Cassie.

"She's refusing to leave," Cassie said. "What do we do?"

They all watched Elise for a moment. She had the glow of being in the limelight shining out of every pore. She was positively radioactive, and it was certain, she wasn't going to go quietly.

" 'Dyin' ain't much of a living, boy,' " Mel said.

"*The Outlaw Josey Wales,*" Angie identified the movie quote. "I'll call for backup."

"What do you want me to do?" Ray asked.

"Stand right here and do not let Elise out of your sight," Mel said. "If anyone makes a false move, have security haul them out of here."

"I'll call Tate and the brothers," Angie said.

"I'll call Stan," Mel said.

They moved to the side of the room and placed their calls. Mel kept one eye on the line while she waited for Stan to pick up. His phone rolled over to voicemail and she frowned. Never, ever, had Stan not picked up when she called.

She glanced at Angie. "How goes it?"

"I told Tate to get here as fast as he could and now I'm on hold with Tony," she said. "He's setting up a conference call with all of the brothers, including Joe."

"Good," Mel said. "Uncle Stan didn't answer."

Angie gave her a worried look. "Maybe he's in the bathroom."

Mel nodded. "I'll try again."

This time when it rolled over to voicemail she left a message. She frowned at her phone, wondering what was up with Uncle Stan. Panic thrummed through her. Maybe he'd had a heart attack — no, more likely an ulcer given the amount of antacid tablets he chewed. She debated calling her mother, but she didn't want to send Joyce into a panic for nothing. Stan had been her shoulder to lean on ever since Mel's father had died.

She listened to Angie tell her brothers what was happening. There was a little bit of yelling — not a surprise — coming from her phone, and she held it away from her ear.

Mel's phone vibrated in her hand and she checked the display to see Joe's number.

"Hi, Joe," she answered. "Aren't you supposed to be on the other line with Angie?"

"Once the yelling started, I decided my time would be better spent checking in with you," he said. "Is it true? Did they have the same vendors?"

"All but the caterer," Mel said. "Oz is making Tate and Angie's cupcake tower."

"Weird," Joe said. "Did you talk to Uncle Stan?"

"I tried but he's not answering," she said.

"That's odd. Has he ever not answered a call from you?"

"No, not even when I accidentally pocket-dialed him while making out with a boyfriend," she said.

Joe laughed. "I bet that was a moment. Wait. Now I'm picturing you making out with someone else. Argh, I think I'm jealous."

"You're cute," Mel said. "That was years ago. Uncle Stan showed up where we were parked and blasted us through the window with his Maglite. Mortifying for a woman in her twenties. The guy never called me again. Shocker."

"I think I'm gonna kiss Stan on the mouth the next time I see him," Joe said. "Listen, I just finished feeding Captain Jack and now I'm driving over. I'll swing by the station house on my way and see if anyone has seen Stan. Would that help?"

Mel let out a breath she hadn't realized she'd been holding. "Yes, actually, that would be great. If I hear from him, I'll call you."

"See you in a twenty minutes," Joe said. "And, cupcake, you may want to wait outside of the book signing. You know, like out of the building and a block away."

"You know I can't do that," Mel said. "Elise could be in danger."

"Which is exactly why you should leave," he said. He let out a frustrated sigh.

"There's no way to talk you out of this, is there?"

" 'Fraid not," she said. "We've got the hotel security on high alert and Ray is here. We'll be okay."

"Be better than okay, be careful."

"I promise."

"I'll be there as fast as I can."

The call ended and she glanced up to see Angie holding her phone away from her ear. The sound of male voices in mid-squabble was pouring out of her phone.

Angie put her mouth near her phone and said, "Okay, I've got to go now. See you later. Bye." Then she ended the call.

"Are they on their way?" Mel asked.

"No idea," Angie said. "Probably not since we're no longer targets. It may take them all night to fight it out since Joe left the conversation."

"He's on his way here and he's going to check in with Stan on his way."

"Good." Angie moved so that she and Mel were standing back-to-back and able to survey the entire room. "I'm not sure what to do other than watch."

"Me, either," Mel said. "I wish Elise would leave. I've got a bad feeling about this."

"I do, too," Angie said.

Her voice sounded weird, and Mel turned to study her friend's face. With her long dark hair pulled back in a ponytail and no makeup on her face, Angie looked more like a twenty-something than a thirty-something. The frown lines across her forehead indicated something was bothering her, and Mel suspected that she knew what it was.

"It's okay to be relieved," she said.

"I'm not," Angie protested. "I mean, I am, but not the way you think. It's not that I'm relieved that Tate and I aren't the targets, it's more that I'm relieved that it wasn't because of us that Blaise was killed. Ugh, I'm a horrible person."

"No, you're not. You're just a friend who is heartbroken. Of course you're relieved that it has nothing to do with you. That's perfectly natural. What did Tate say about it?"

"I didn't tell him what we learned. I want to share the news in person. I think he's going to need a hug when he hears it."

"You're probably right," Mel said. "I know he's been struggling."

They stood quietly while Elise signed, Ray loomed in front of them like a human shield, and Cassie monitored the line. Mel noted that Cassie wasn't letting people loiter or engage Elise in conversation. Instead, she kept the people moving and in no time they were down to the last few customers.

Mel watched the last two middle-aged women with a beady eye. If either one of them was a psychopath, she was going to bring her down. They weren't and they both left the room without a bit of resistance. Cassie signaled to the hotel workers to close the doors and when they did, Mel saw her sag in relief.

"That was terrific," Cassie said to Elise. "An amazing turnout. With the movie deal kicking up interest, I think this book is going to be on the bestsellers' list for a long time to come."

Elise gave her a grumpy look. "That's great, but you didn't let me bask. Not even a little. You practically chased my fans right out of the room."

"That is for your own safety," Cassie said. "I know you don't want to believe it, but I do think Mel and Angie are right. It's weird that three of the people hired to work your event are dead."

"Please," Elise said. She waved her hand at Cassie. "No one is more upset than Mallory at the book's publication and clearly she just came here to make a scene and yell at me. If anyone was going to murder me or those around me to get even with me, it would be her. Scottsdale is part of a major metropolitan area — murders happen."

Mel exchanged a look with Angie. Elise seemed awfully cavalier about the deaths of three people all by rather grisly means. Her narcissism really was breathtaking.

"Elise, you have to take this more seriously," Cassie chided her. "Your life could be in danger."

"Pish," Elise said. "I'm going to the bar to celebrate my fame and fortune. Join me?"

"I really don't think that's a good idea," Cassie said.

"No one asked you to think, did they?" Elise asked. She tossed the end of her scarf over her shoulder and strode out of the room. "Come on, first round is on me."

"What do I do?" Cassie asked Mel.

"We have to stay with her," Mel said. "If someone is out to get her, they won't do it with an audience. This may be their best chance."

Ray pushed off the wall and said, "Well, since you two are safe, I'm tapping out." He pointed at Mel and Angie. "You two I'll take a bullet for, but no one else." He headed for the door and the ladies fell in behind him.

"Aw, come on, Ray," Angie said. "After this long night of surveillance, you could probably use a beer. You've earned it. My treat."

Ray made a face like he was considering it. "Since you put it that way. Lead on."

Angie looped her arm through her brother's and led him down the ornate hallway towards the wood-paneled bar tucked into a room beside the main entrance. Mel and Cassie fell in behind them with Mel trying to glance around Ray's broad shoulders to get a glimpse of Elise. She must have hightailed it to the lounge for a cocktail, because there was no sign of her in the lobby.

The bar was quiet, with only a few businessmen sitting at a center table watching a basketball game on the large-screen television. A pitcher of beer was in front of them, and several plates of bar food. They were clearly in for the long haul.

"Where did she go?" Cassie asked. "She said she was going to get a drink, right?"

"I don't see her," Mel said. "That's weird. We were right behind her."

Angie and Ray went to the bar, leaving Mel and Cassie to look for Elise. Mel saw a woman in the hotel uniform of a pair of navy slacks and white dress shirt walking by and she called out to her.

"Excuse me," she said. "Did you see a

113

woman come in here, middle-aged, dressed all in white with a beige sweater and a long brown-and-white scarf? She just did a book signing?"

"No, sorry," the woman said. She barely slowed her walk, and Mel just caught the name Laura on her nametag before she fled the room.

"That was abrupt," Cassie said.

"And not helpful," Mel agreed. She joined Angie and Ray at the bar.

"Good evening, pretty ladies," the bartender greeted Mel, Angie, and Cassie. "What can I get you?"

"A beer," Ray answered. "And none of that fancy microbrew stuff. I want a real man's beer."

The bartender ignored him and his scowl, and Mel took the opportunity to question him.

"Did you see a middle-aged woman come in, dressed in white with a beige sweater and a scarf?" she asked.

The bartender shook his head. He had a thick head of hair, which he wore in a knot on his head. His beard was trimmed close and his mustache was long and curled up on the ends. The white dress shirt he wore looked a few sizes too small as it molded to his muscular frame, looking on the verge of tearing right down the middle.

"I haven't seen anyone come in except for those guys and you all evening," he said. He pointed to the table of men watching the game. "You can see why I was so happy to see three pretty ladies arrive."

"They're all taken," Ray said with a glower. "Now how about my beer?"

The bartender scowled at Ray. "I'm just making conversation, don't have a fit."

"Oh, I'll have a fit if I want," Ray argued.

The bartender turned away to pour Ray's beer, but Mel put a hand on his arm, holding him in place, and said, "Sorry, but is there another bar in the resort or is this it?"

"This is it," he said. "But there is seating outside. If you're looking for someone, she might have gone out there."

He pointed at two glass doors on the opposite side of the room before grabbing a glass and pouring Ray's beer. Mel turned and glanced at Cassie. "I'll bet that's where she is," she said. "I'll check out there and you can check the booths in here."

"I'll come with you," Angie said.

"No, you stay and watch the door in case she comes in," Mel said. "I don't want to lose her again."

"Be careful," Angie said. "Ray, go with her."

Ray had just lifted his pint glass to his lips. He glanced between them and put his glass down. "Fine."

"Call me if you see her," Mel said to Cassie.

Mel crossed the room and pushed through the heavy glass doors. It was cooler outside and she took a deep breath of the night air. The immaculate lawn of the golf course beyond the patio smelled damp and fresh with a recent watering.

Cushy loungers filled the patio and there was a fire pit off to the side with a couple sitting beside it, enjoying the quiet.

Mel approached the couple and asked if they'd seen Elise, using the same description she'd given the bartender and the hotel staff person. The couple shook their heads.

"Sorry," the woman said. "We've been the only ones out here for the past hour."

"Thank you," Mel said. She turned and headed back inside. Maybe Elise had gone to the bathroom or perhaps she'd run into someone she knew.

She was halfway to the doors when she heard a scream. Mel jumped and glanced at Ray, checking to see if he'd heard it, too. His eyes went wide and as one they hurried to the doors.

Mel yanked the door open and stepped

inside. Angie had hopped off of her stool and was hurrying towards the back of the bar. Mel followed. As she turned the corner, she saw Cassie standing beside a booth on the opposite side of the room. A brown-and-white scarf was just visible, hanging off of the bench seat.

"Mel, it's Elise," Cassie cried. "I think . . . oh my god . . . I think she's dead!"

EIGHT

Mel ran, noting in her peripheral vision that Angie and Ray did, too. She got there first and one look into the booth and she knew Cassie was right to freak out. Elise was slumped forward onto the table, her face pressed against the wood, her eyes closed. The fancy pen she had been using to sign books was lodged right in her back.

Mel dove into the booth, thinking that maybe she had a chance to save her. How long had Elise been ahead of them? Five minutes? Ten? How long did it take to stab someone? Not that long.

She unwrapped the scarf from around Elise's neck, she checked her pulse, she patted her cheek, trying to bring her back. Angie climbed into the booth on the other side. She put her hand in front of Elise's mouth and nose, feeling for breath.

"I can't tell if she's breathing," Angie cried. "No inhale or exhale, nothing."

"Move aside, move over," Ray ordered. "And call 9-1-1. We need to get her horizontal so that she doesn't come to and have a fainting spell."

He lifted Mel up and put her outside the booth. Then he carefully lifted Elise up into his arms and walked over to an empty pool table nearby.

Angie fumbled with her phone making the call while Mel and Cassie followed Ray, trying to be of help.

"Her wound needs to be above her heart, so she has to be on her side," Ray said. Mel arranged Elise's feet while Cassie adjusted her arms.

"Good," Ray said. He moved the lamp hanging over the pool table so he could see Elise's back. He hissed out a breath at the sight of the blood. Mel thought he looked a little woozy, but he shook it off. "Come on, author lady, don't die on me. Not today."

"The pen! She was stabbed with her own pen?" Cassie cried. "Should we remove it?"

"No," Ray said. "Right now it's staunching the blood flow from the wound. Someone get me a clean towel. We need to put pressure around it."

Cassie rushed off towards the bar. Mel watched in fascination as Ray went to work, checking Elise's airway, her breathing, and her circulation.

"I think she fainted," Ray said. "Not a big surprise, and she's likely gone into shock."

Mel could hear Angie telling the emergency dispatcher the name of the resort and where they were. She stayed on the line while the dispatcher asked her questions.

"How did you learn to do all this?" Mel asked.

"I used to be a lifeguard at the public pool," Ray said. "We had to take a lot of first aid."

"What the hell is going on here?" a shrill female voice demanded.

Mel turned around to see Detective Tara Martinez standing there, looking furious at the scene in front of her.

"What are you doing here?" Mel asked.

"Stan sent me," Tara said. "He's on his way. What the hell happened here?"

"This is Elise Penworthy," Cassie said. She handed Ray a clean towel. "Someone tried to kill her, and he's trying to save her."

Ray took the cloth and pressed it around the pen in Elise's back. Then he patted her cheek, trying to bring her around. Tara bent over the table next to Ray and glared at him.

"DeLaura, what do you think you're doing? You can't just manhandle a person —"

A gasp, a cough, an enormous sucking

sound came out of Elise's mouth and Ray grabbed her shoulder to keep her from moving. As if he'd fished Elise out of the ocean, she began to suck in air. The color didn't return to her face and her mouth twisted in pain, but she was definitely alive.

"I'll be damned," Ray said. "That stuff on the Internet really does work."

"Sweet chili dogs," Tara said. "The Internet? Are you insane?"

"Hey, I saved her, didn't I?"

"Cassie," Elise croaked. "Cassie."

"Yes, I'm here." Cassie knelt down to be level with Elise. She took her friend's hand and asked, "Are you all right? Do you remember anything? Who did this to you?"

Elise's eyes shone with a fierce light as she stared at the bookseller. "You did!"

Cassie's eyes went wide. "What? How could you think — Elise!"

Elise's eyes rolled back into her head and her body sagged.

Ray moved forward and checked her pulse and her breathing. "It's all right. I think she just passed out again, probably from the pain."

"Hey, over here!" Angie jumped up and down and waved her arms. "The ambulance guys are here!"

"Thank god," Ray said. "I don't think I

can do this again."

The emergency medical technicians took over for Ray and the group backed off. Tara moved so that she was standing beside Cassie. Mel knew that wasn't a coincidence. Cassie, however, was so riveted on her friend's condition that she didn't notice.

They stood huddled in a group, watching as the medical professionals took over Elise's care. They checked her vitals, and left the pen right where it was. She was hooked up to several machines, and then they were lifting her onto a stretcher. Once they were on their way, Cassie snapped out of her vigil.

"Wait! I'm coming with you," she said.

"I don't think so," Tara said. "I've got some questions for you Ms. —"

"Leighton. I'm Cassie Leighton, I own the bookstore A Likely Story," she said.

"So, you're the one who set up this signing?" Tara asked.

"Yes, I also run the indie press that published her book, but I didn't hurt her," Cassie said. "I swear."

"Then why did she say you did?" Tara asked. Her voice was not combative but not kind, either.

"I don't know. I don't understand it. I would never. I'm her friend, her best friend, heck, her only friend."

Tara didn't look like she believed her. She glanced around the room. "No one leaves until I say so."

"But my patient," Ray protested. "I brought her back from the light. I really need to stay with her."

"No," Tara said. "I'll make sure she has an officer with her at all times. The rest of you sit." No one moved, and she looked like she'd happily lock them all up. Her face contorted into what Mel suspected was her scary detective face and she barked, "Now!"

They all sat except for Ray, who seemed to think that Tara's scary detective face was her way of flirting with him.

"It's okay, babe," he said. "I get it. You don't have to feel bad about yourself."

"What are you talking about?" Tara frowned.

"You and your feel—" Ray began but Angie interrupted.

"Oh, no, Ray, don't do it," Angie said. He ignored her.

As the EMTs wheeled Elise out of the room, Tara went to follow them and Ray fell into step beside her. The look Tara gave him should have shriveled him up on the spot, but Ray kept on going.

"Look," he said. "Don't judge yourself too

hard on this thing between us. I know you can't help it. In fact, why don't we just go grab some dinner and we can talk about your feelings and stuff?"

"Feelings? Stuff?" Tara squawked. "The only feeling I have for you is one of mild repugnance."

"That's a good thing, right?"

"Are you seriously hitting on me, De-Laura? *Now?*"

"Merely offering to assist you through your confusion."

"I am not confused!"

"No? Then why are you holding your Taser in your hand when I know you were about to call your partner?" he asked.

Tara glanced down at her hand and blushed. "I . . . that's . . . because if you don't back up, I'm going to hit you with fifty thousand volts at twenty-five watts."

"Sounds kinky," Ray said. Then he gave her a slow wink.

"I swear, one more word and I'll lock you up —"

"Detective Martinez, what's going on here?" Uncle Stan stepped into the room with Joe and two uniformed officers right behind him.

Joe moved beside Mel and gave her hand a quick squeeze. The warmth of his fingers around hers made her realize how icy cold her hand was. She didn't know if it was shock or hunger causing her system to short out. She suspected it was both.

"We have a stab victim," Tara said. "And she's already identified her attacker."

"Wait!" Cassie cried. "No!"

Tara ignored her and looked at the big, burly officer beside Joe. She said, "Jackson, I want you to ride with the victim, a Ms. Elise Penworthy, to the hospital and stay with her at all times. If there is any change in her condition, contact me immediately."

"Yes, ma'am." Jackson turned and hurried after Elise.

"But I want to go with her," Cassie protested. "She's going to be terrified if she wakes up by herself."

"Given that she identified you as the person who assaulted her," Tara said, "I think she'd be more frightened if you went with her."

"But I didn't do it," Cassie protested. "The pen that was used is still in her back. Get it fingerprinted. It'll prove it wasn't me."

Stan glanced between Cassie and Tara as if assessing his partner's read on the situation before he asked, "She was stabbed with a pen?"

"The same one she signed her books with," Cassie said. "It was her personalized pen. She had it specially made for her signing." Cassie burst into great big noisy sobs and Mel put her arm around her shoulders in an attempt to soothe her. Tara looked as if she considered Cassie a big faker, while Stan had a more considered look on his face. He was still open-minded.

"Hey, I saved a life," Ray said.

All eyes turned to him.

"How? By getting out of the way?" Stan asked as he met Mel's gaze. She gave him a slight shake of her head, letting him know she didn't believe Cassie had stabbed Elise.

"Funny, really funny. I'll have you know I brought her back from the jaws of death," Ray said.

Joe raised his eyebrows and Mel met his questioning glance with a nod.

"He did," she said. "Ray was amazing. He knew just what to do. He likely saved Elise's life."

"Right, and to get back to what really matters, we have our suspect right here," Tara said. She frowned at Mel, who still had an arm around Cassie. "Ms. Leighton."

Uncle Stan glanced at Cassie. His expression was intimidating, but Mel knew it was also the grimace that happened when his heartburn was kicking up. Cassie Leighton didn't know this and when she met his gaze, she promptly burst into tears again.

"I didn't do it," she protested. "I would never."

Mel patted the bookseller's back in a show of solidarity. "She didn't do it. I know she didn't."

"Here we go," Tara scoffed. She turned her glare on Uncle Stan. "Why is she even here?"

Mel felt her jaw clench. "Because I'm a witness."

Tara stared her down. "How do you figure? Did you see the person who shoved the pen in the vic's back? Or did you see someone following her, looking like they were about to shank her? No, you didn't, did you?"

Mel sucked in a breath and drew herself up to her full height. She gave Cassie one last quick squeeze and stepped forward so that she loomed over the shorter woman. If Tara was intimidated it didn't show.

"Now, Mel," Uncle Stan said. His voice was cajoling, as if he really thought he could talk her out of being super irritated with this woman.

"Don't," she said to him. Then she turned back to Tara. "I happen to have been at the book signing where we saw both her ex-husband and his new wife make a scene, as well as one of her old friends from the neighborhood. The book Elise wrote has brought out a lot of animosity, meaning there are plenty of people who might have wanted to stab her and most of them were at her signing tonight."

"Except she already told us who did, so there really isn't much point in searching for someone else when we have the primary suspect right here," Tara said.

"The point would be to get to the truth," Mel said.

"So bored." Tara stretched her mouth wide in a fake yawn and patted her lips with one hand.

Mel took another step towards her, not really sure of what she planned to do, but it was rendered null and void as Joe slipped an arm around her waist and pulled her back out of striking range.

"It sounds like you all have a lot of information to share," Joe said. "Right, Stan?"

Stan was popping an antacid tablet and nodded. "Yeah, let's divide up the interviews. Martinez, you take Ray and Angie, and I'll take Ms. Leighton and Mel."

"What?" Tara fumed. "Why do I get stuck with Dumb and Dumber?"

"What'd you call me?" Angie snapped.

"Relax, Sis," Ray said. "She's just trying to look like she's not interested in this." Ray made a sweeping gesture at his own body and Angie rolled her eyes.

"Okay, so she got half of it right," Angie said.

"Harsh, Ange, real harsh," Ray said.

Mel took a moment to turn her back on the group and fire off a quick text. If this situation was going the way she feared, Cassie was going to need professional help of the lawyerly kind, and not from the side of the courtroom Joe sat on.

"Angie! Mel!" Tate appeared in the doorway to the bar. "I got here as fast as I could. Are you all right? What happened?"

He dashed across the room and grabbed Angie in a hug that lifted her right off of her feet. Then he kissed her. It might have gone on longer, but Ray grabbed Tate's collar in his fist and lifted him up until he was forced to drop Angie.

"Save it for the honeymoon, Harper," Ray said.

"Right," Tate said. He held up his hands in surrender and Ray dropped him back on the ground. Tate glanced from Angie to Mel. "You're both okay?"

"We're fine," Angie said. She took Tate's

hand in hers. "And it turns out, Blaise's murder had nothing to do with us. Somehow, it's all connected to Elise Penworthy and her book *The Palms*."

"What? I don't understand," he said.

"The caterer, the photographer, and the driver hired to work Elise's book signing were all murdered," Mel said. "And someone just tried to kill Elise. You two just happened to have the same photographer and driver. It really was just a coincidence."

"That's horrible. Those poor people," Tate said. He looked upset, as if he couldn't process so much bad news all at once. "And yet, I'm so relieved we had nothing to do with it. Ugh, I'm a horrible person."

He looked at Angie and she nodded and said, "No, I feel the same way. I didn't want to be responsible for Blaise's death, either."

They hugged and the group moved away from them to give them a minute to talk.

Uncle Stan gestured for Mel and Cassie to come with him and he led them towards a booth in the corner. Mel was grateful to have Joe there as her fiancé, but not so much as a county prosecutor.

"Will this be a conflict of interest for you?" she asked. "Shouldn't you probably leave so that the case doesn't get tainted?"

"I'll recuse myself from the case should

there be one," he said.

"Oh, good, then you won't be mad that I texted for backup," she said. "I don't think Cassie should answer any of Uncle Stan's questions."

"Why not? Do you think she had something to do with the murders or with the attack on the author?"

"No, not at all. I'm just not certain she can account for her whereabouts the whole time. It was crazy busy with all of the people and the books and such. So, I figure it won't hurt for her to have proper representation."

"Mel . . ." Joe said. "Tell me you didn't. Not him."

"All right, I won't tell you," she said.

"Melanie Cooper, my favorite cupcake baker," a voice boomed from the doorway to the bar.

"Oh, for cripe's sake," Uncle Stan muttered. "Who called that guy?"

"Sorry, Uncle Stan," Mel said. "It had to be done."

"You know, if you weren't my favorite niece I'd disown you right now," he said.

"I'm your only niece."

"Pity."

Steve Wolfmeier, a local defense attorney, strolled across the bar towards them. In his shiny suit and shinier shoes, he looked like someone who could slide through a tar pit and not get a bit of black ooze stuck on him. In other words, he was the perfect attorney for a person in a jam, which Cassie was.

"Hi, Steve," Mel said. She waved him over.

He stopped in front of her and Joe. The two men glared at each other. Steve studied Mel and Joe with a frown.

"I heard he put a ring on it," he said.

Mel held up her hand. The diamond Joe had given her a few months before sparkled.

"I could have gotten you one three times that size," he said.

Mel felt Joe bristle beside her.

"You know what they say, it's quality not quantity," she said.

"I'd give you both," Steve said.

"That's it," Joe said. "How about we chat outside?"

Mel quickly looped her hand through Joe's arm and reined him in. "Not really the time for that. Steve, this is Cassie Leighton, owner of the bookstore A Likely Story. Her author was just assaulted and, well, I'm going to let her explain what happened."

"Cassie — can I call you Cassie?" Steve held out his hand.

"Sure," she said. She looked a little dazzled by the aura of don't-worry-I-got-this Steve had going on. It was one of the many reasons he was the best.

"Cooper, I'm going to confer with my client," he said.

Stan threw up his hands as if he had reached the end of his patience. "Sure, go ahead. Why don't you take her out for ice cream while I just sit here and think up new and different ways to ticket you in your shiny BMW?"

"Please, BMWs are for peasants," Steve said. "I drive a Porsche."

"Oh, you must be very good at what you do," Cassie said.

"I'm the best."

"And yet, you still don't have the girl," Joe said.

He looped an arm around Mel and pulled her close. She knew she should go all liberated woman on him and protest but her inner girly-girl was giddy at Joe's possessive streak. Such was the inner battle of the modern woman.

NINE

"Okay, that's enough. I'm choking on the testosterone in the air. Take your client to that booth and talk," Stan said. "You have fifteen minutes and not one second longer."

"They don't call me 'Steve Fifteen Minutes Wolfmeier' for nothing," Steve quipped.

Joe snorted.

"Wait, that came out wrong," Steve said.

Joe doubled up, laughing. Steve looked like he wanted to punch him, so Stan gave him a hearty shove to the back towards the nearby booth and then turned back to Joe. With his back to Steve, Stan's grin about split his face.

"I'm sorry," he said. "I just need a minute."

Mel frowned at the pair of them.

"Really, you two?" she asked. "Three people have been killed and another stabbed and you're getting your yucks by mocking a defense attorney, who is at least helping his client."

Both men looked duly chastened.

"Sorry, cupcake," Joe said.

"Yeah, sorry," Stan said. "Very unprofessional of me. It won't happen again."

"For at least fifteen minutes," Joe said. Stan snorted.

Mel elbowed Joe hard in the side and he made an *oomph!* noise.

"Sorry," he said. He clutched his side and gave Uncle Stan a look.

"You don't need to do that to me," Uncle Stan said to Mel. He raised his hands in the air. "Message received."

"Good," Mel said.

Uncle Stan gestured for her to take a seat at a nearby table and asked, "While we're waiting, how about you tell me everything that happened here tonight?"

Mel recounted everything she could remember. She tried to be as specific as she could about Todd, Elise's ex; and his second wife, Mallory; and about the woman, Shanna, who had appeared to be a friend, but maybe it had just been an act. In the retelling, it occurred to her that the most likely candidates were the ex and his new wife. Certainly, they had been the angriest, but would Mallory have made such a scene and brought so much attention to herself if she was planning to murder Elise later?

Equally puzzling was why Mallory, or whoever went after Elise, had felt compelled to kill the people associated with the book signing. What did the driver, the caterer, and the photographer have to do with her anger about her appearance in the book? It didn't make any sense. Unless Elise had been right when she said the murders were all coincidence. Mel was betting she didn't believe that anymore.

"Enough!" Detective Martinez shouted.

Mel, Joe, and Uncle Stan turned to see what the commotion was. Tara was standing beside the table where Ray, Angie, and Tate sat and she looked flushed and flustered. Ray was smiling at her as if enjoying her obvious upset.

"Detective Cooper," Tara called across the bar. "A little backup here."

"What is Ray up to now?" Joe asked.

"No idea, but you stay here and keep an eye on that situation," Uncle Stan said. He gestured at Steve and Cassie. "I don't trust him not to break her out of here if he thinks it's warranted."

"It isn't," Mel said. "She's innocent."

"I would agree with you except for one thing," Uncle Stan said. "When you were recounting the timeline for us, you admitted that she was on her own, searching the booths while you were checking outside."

"So?" Mel protested. "There was a bar full of people —"

"There were four guys near the bar, drinking beer, watching a game," Stan said. "I already got that intel from the security personnel when I arrived."

Mel snapped her fingers. "That's it. A place like this, they have to have a security camera system. I'll bet the bar is under surveillance and we'll be able to see Elise's attacker."

"No, we won't," Stan said. He ran a hand over his eyes.

"Why not?" Mel persisted. "It's a good idea." She glanced at Joe. "Isn't it?"

He scanned the bar. When he turned back to look at her, it was with regret. "There are no security cameras in here."

"What? Why not?" she asked.

"Because hotel bars are notorious places for people to hook up on the sly and no hotel wants to invade its guests' privacy by providing the damaging footage that swings their divorce towards a poor financial outcome," Joe said, exchanging a look of frustration with Uncle Stan.

"Meaning they're protecting the cheaters," Mel said.

"Yep," Joe agreed.

"Damn," Mel said.

"Indeed," Uncle Stan said. He rose from his seat. "I'm going to join my partner. You keep an eye on Wolfmeier and his client. I know you don't like it, Mel, but unless she has an alibi, I'm going to have to bring her in."

"You're right," she said. "I don't like it."

"Consider this, then," Uncle Stan said. "Someone went to great lengths to kill off the people working on Elise Penworthy's book signing. Don't you think it might be likely that her bookseller is in their sights, too?"

Mel gasped. She hadn't thought of that.

"Before you get your back up about me bringing her in, remember that jail might be the safest place for her."

Stan didn't bring Cassie in. Mel wasn't sure if it was because she had argued so hard on Cassie's behalf or because Steve would use any false step against the police to get his client off. Either way, Stan and Tara did not bring Cassie in but instead went to the hospital to check on Elise and make sure that she was kept isolated and under watch.

On the chance that Cassie was a target,

Officer Hayley Clark was redirected from watching over Oz to shadowing Cassie. Because Officer Clark was already at the bakery, the group decided to stop by the bakery for some restorative cupcakes while delivering Officer Clark her new assignment.

Mel wanted to check on Oz. She'd felt bad sticking him with the bakery all evening while he was trying to gear up to make Angie and Tate's wedding cupcakes. He was an amazing chef but he was still pretty young, barely out of culinary school, and she knew he'd been putting a lot of pressure on himself to make Angie and Tate's cupcake tower perfect.

The bakery was closed but Oz, Marty, and Officer Clark were sitting in the kitchen when Mel, Joe, and Cassie entered through the back door. Oz had an amazing aqua-colored fondant rolled out in front of him on the worktable and he was shaping delicate leaves out of it for use on the wedding cupcakes.

Officer Clark jumped up from her seat and checked the door behind them. She was clearly looking to see if they'd been followed. Mel felt like telling her that they were fine but she suspected the intense young woman would check the alley anyway.

Marty took one look at their faces and disappeared into the walk-in cooler, while Oz dropped the knife he'd been using on the fondant and went to brew a pot of coffee.

While Mel and the others took seats at the table, the back door unlocked and Tate, Angie, and Ray came in. Officer Clark went to close and lock the door, but was stopped by a foot being wedged inside.

"Hold up," the person on the other side said. "It's Tony and Al. We're here to check on Angie."

Officer Clark glanced back at Angie. She came forward and peered out the window. She turned to the officer and said, "It's my brothers. They're okay."

"Big family you have," Officer Clark said. She sounded put out. "I'm going to walk the perimeter of the building. Lock the door after me. I'll knock four times when I need you to let me back in."

She ducked out, closing the door quietly behind her. Oz watched her from his spot by the coffeepot. He shook his head and Mel caught his eye when she rose from her seat and locked the door.

"Problem?" she asked.

"She's just a bit high-strung," he said. "Now that she's off my case, it's all good."

"How is the author Pennywise?" Marty

asked as he came back with a tray loaded down with a variety of cupcakes.

"Penworthy, Elise Penworthy. Last we heard she was stable," Mel said. Cassie's face looked pinched at this description and Mel patted her arm. "She's going to be all right."

"Does she have any family?" Oz asked. "Is there anyone who would want to be there for her?"

"Just me," Cassie said. "After her divorce she was pretty much banished from the community, which is why she wrote the tell-all fictionalized account of the neighborhood. She has no family, and as far as I know, I'm her only friend, but the police made it very clear that I shouldn't be there since . . . I . . . I'm . . ."

"You're a suspect," Marty said.

"Yeah." Cassie's shoulders slumped.

"It's all right," Mel said. She gave everyone a pointed look. "Elise is in excellent care. If there is any news, Uncle Stan will call us immediately."

Cassie swallowed, visibly pushing down the sobs that were threatening. "You're right. I know you're right. I just feel so helpless."

"Wait," Marty said. "Maybe it's because I'm older than dirt, and I spend a lot of time thinking about what will happen when I die, but I have to ask. If this Elise has no family, who is going to get the rights to her book, the royalties and all of that, if she dies?"

"Um . . . well, me," Cassie said.

Mel turned from Marty to Cassie as if in slow motion. She could not have just said that, could she? On what crazy planet did a bookstore owner get the rights to an author's book?

Her thoughts must have shown on her face because Cassie nodded and said, "It's weird, I know."

"You think?" Angie asked. "Because I'm guessing if Uncle Stan knew this, you would be sitting in a different place entirely right now."

"I told Steve, and he said it wasn't a problem," Cassie said, rejecting the suggestion.

Joe frowned. "That was rather confident of him. I have to tell you, from a prosecutor's perspective that gives you motive, and you already had means and opportunity."

"Cassie, he's right," Mel said.

"But it makes no sense," Cassie protested. "Why would I harm the very person I was helping to be successful? And the vendors? Why would I hurt the people I hired to work the book signing? They were people I relied upon and did business with for years. How can you believe that of me?"

"I'm not saying I believe it," Mel said. "I'm saying" — she paused to gesture to Joe — "others might see it as a reason for you to commit murder."

Cassie looked at Joe with wide eyes. He studied her for a moment and then shook his head. "No, you're right. It makes no sense. If you wanted ownership of the book, why kill the others when you could just murder the author?"

"Exactly!" Cassie said.

"Unless it was to cover up the murder of the author by throwing suspicion onto someone else," Marty said.

All eyes went back to Cassie and she dropped her head into her hands.

"This is a nightmare."

Mel took a cinnamon cupcake and put it in front of her, knowing it was Cassie's favorite flavor. Cassie made no move to eat it.

The rest of the group, comfort eaters like Mel, needed no encouragement. Everyone reached for their cupcake of choice and began to peel off the wrappers while Oz poured coffee for the lot of them.

Cassie picked up her coffee and cradled it

in her hands as if to warm them. Mel suspected she was still in a bit of shock from the events of the night.

"You know we can't get involved in this," Marty said. Everyone looked at him and he rolled his eyes. "Okay, *I* can't get involved. If the daughters find out, they'll go ballistic and try to have me put in a home."

"No one is putting you in a home," Angie said. She looked like she could spit fire at the mere suggestion. "They'll have to go through all of us to do it."

"No offense, but I don't think they really consider a bunch of cupcake bakers an obstacle," Marty said.

"We've been underestimated before," Mel observed.

"But we always win," Tate said. He patted Marty on the shoulder and that seemed to settle the matter.

"One thing I don't understand," Oz said. "Why were the other vendors killed? What did they have in common besides the book signing? I mean it just seems . . ."

"Excessive?" Joe offered.

"Yeah," Oz said. He bobbed his head and his bangs swung back and forth in front of his eyes.

Joe looked at Cassie and asked, "What do you think? Did they have anything in common besides the signing?"

"Not that I know of," Cassie said. She put down her coffee cup and picked at her cupcake. "I've used them all before for different events but I've also used others. They all work in the area, but other than that, I don't see how they're connected."

"Were any of them in the book?" Tony asked.

Joe gave his younger brother an impressed look.

"Not really a big brain leap there," Tony said. "The book has been pretty controversial ever since word leaked out that Penworthy was writing it."

"It's true," Cassie said. "She started getting threatening phone calls and e-mails before she'd even accepted her movie deal. It is a very thinly veiled fictional account of that exclusive neighborhood. Elise barely disguised the people that she wrote about."

"What do you mean?" Mel asked.

"Hair plugs," Cassie said.

Marty clapped a hand on his bald head. "Really? And here I thought I was rocking the no hair thing."

"You are. I wasn't talking about you," Cassie assured him. She looked at Mel and Angie, and asked, "If I say 'hair plugs,' who did you see tonight that brings that image to mind?"

"Oh, totally, Elise's ex, Todd Cavendish," Angie said. "It was a sad scraggly mess up there."

"Exactly," Cassie said. "Well, in the book, she actually refers to him as 'Hair Plugs' and you can bet everyone who lived in the Palms knew who she was talking about, especially since she referenced the woman he left his wife for as 'Child Bride,' which was what Elise always called Mallory."

"Nicknames like that could apply to a variety of people," Al said. "How does anyone know exactly who she's talking about?"

"She didn't cloak the scandals very well, either," Cassie said. "Chapter three is devoted to the failed banker who has a women's shoe fetish, a borderline personality disorder, and a gold incisor."

"Rick Jakelisk, a total nut job," Tony said. Everyone looked at him. "What? His daughter was in my class in high school, and she was one messed-up dudette with daddy issues. Now I know why."

"See?" Cassie said. "And you didn't even read the book, did you?"

Tony shook his head. "But I know most of the people who live in the Palms since they went to the same high school that we did. In fact, I'd be willing to bet our entire family knows most of the people mentioned in the book through school."

"Hit us with another one," Al said, as if it was a game.

"All right." Cassie thought about it for a moment and gave them all a considering look. "Baby Talk and the Unibrow had a thing for wife swapping until they tried it at a backyard barbecue with their new neighbors, who were a very religious couple, who put their house up for sale the day after the 'incident.'"

"No way! The Swansons were into wife swapping?" Al choked on his cupcake. "I dated their daughter Anastasia. For the record, she did not have her dad's unibrow nor did she baby-talk like her mom."

"I don't remember her," Tony said.

"That's because I broke up with her after our second date because her mom tried to corner me in the bathroom. I thought it was just my imagination, but I still didn't want to go over there ever again. OMG, I feel so violated."

Angie gave her brother a hug. "That is creepy. I'm glad I didn't know about her; I'd have drop-kicked that woman."

"Thanks, Ange." Al rested his head on his sister's shoulder.

"I think I still want to drop-kick them,"

Joe said.

"You can see why Elise's book has blown the doors off the neighborhood," Cassie said. "Reputations have been shredded, families maligned, friendships destroyed. It's been bad, and Elise is loving every vengeful bit of it."

"That could make for a whole lot of enemies," Joe said. "I think I'm going to call Stan. We might want to have more than one officer watching over Elise."

He rose from his seat and took his phone into Mel's office. Four knocks sounded on the back door, and Oz hurried across the room to open the door for Officer Clark.

"What are you doing, Ruiz?" she snapped. She glared up at him. "I could have been the killer."

"You knocked four times," Oz said. "Wasn't that the signal?"

"The killer could have knocked four times," she said. She tossed her hair back.

"But it wasn't the killer, it was you," he argued. His voice was annoyed and Mel got the feeling he would have preferred it if it were the killer.

"You have to be more careful," Officer Clark berated him. "Just because you aren't considered to be high-risk anymore, doesn't mean there's no risk."

She was winding up to continue her lecture on safety. Oz turned around and walked away. Officer Clark followed behind him, looking like a stray puppy who had attached itself to a person.

"I mean, what if the killer just happened to use four knocks and you opened the door, and they came in here and blew everyone away? How would you feel then?"

"Dead," Oz said.

Al and Tony both turned away as if they couldn't contain their laughter but didn't want to offend Officer Clark by losing it in front of her. Marty just shook his head and Mel wasn't sure if he was more boggled by Officer Clark or Oz.

"You're intentionally missing my — Oh!"

Her words were abruptly cut off as Oz held up a cupcake in front of her. It was one of their Pucker Up ones, a lemon cake with a tart lemon buttercream frosting.

"Have a cupcake," he said.

She glanced up at him. "Thank you."

The smile she sent his way was a stunner and Mel glanced at Angie to see if she was getting this. Angie looked back at her with her eyebrows raised as well.

"Okay, then, I have work to do," Oz said. He reached around Tate and scooped up the parchment paper with his fondant, which had begun to dry out, and then he pushed through the swinging doors into the front of the bakery.

Mel gave Officer Clark a side eye and noticed she was watching the door where Oz had disappeared with a speculative gleam in her eye. Huh.

Now that they knew their sister wasn't a target, Tony and Al left, taking Marty with them. Tate and Angie followed shortly after. Mel knew that they were still processing the fact that their friend was gone, but she suspected their grief was less complicated now that they knew Blaise's death had nothing to do with them.

Joe and Mel were ready to go, too. Mel said good night to Oz and told him not to stay up too late. Since he had moved into the apartment above the bakery, he'd taken to doing the midnight baking that Mel used to do. In fact, it was getting so that she relied upon him to start the baking day without her. She wondered if maybe it was time to give him a raise.

He locked the door after them and Joe and Mel walked Cassie to Officer Clark's squad car. Clark opened the back door for her, but Cassie waved her off.

"I'm not sitting in the back," she said. "I'll have nightmares."

"It's pretty cramped up front with my computer taking up half the seat," Clark said.

"I don't care, Officer Clark," Cassie said. "I refuse to look like a criminal when I arrive home."

Mel had a feeling her brush with jail had been too close for comfort. She couldn't really blame her.

"All right," Clark said. She opened the front passenger door. "And since we're going to be spending so much time together, Ms. Leighton, you might as well call me Hayley."

"And you can call me Cassie, thank you," Cassie said. Then she turned to Mel. "And thank you for all of your help tonight." She gave Mel a quick hug and turned to get into the car. Before she sat down, however, she whipped around and looked at Mel in alarm. "Oh, no, Peanut! Who's going to take care of Peanut?"

"Peanut?" Mel asked.

"Elise's dog," Cassie said. "We have to go get her. The poor thing will need food and water and a walk. Besides, what if the person who assaulted Elise goes to her place? Peanut could be in danger!"

TEN

"When she said 'we,' how did that turn into you and me taking care of the dog?" Joe asked as he followed Hayley's squad car to the townhouse Elise had been renting for the month.

Mel shrugged. "Cassie is allergic."

"Do we even know what kind of dog it is? It could be one of those tiny little yappers or a massive beast that leaves poop the size of watermelons in the backyard."

Mel cringed. She had no idea what to expect. She just knew that she wasn't going to leave a dog shut in a townhouse when they had no idea when Elise would be discharged from the hospital.

"Hayley called Uncle Stan and he said it was okay so long as we didn't touch anything but the dog," Mel said. "He's going to try and meet us there."

"He's not going to meet us there," Joe said. "Because he's single and lives alone and he would be the most logical choice to take the dog. He won't risk it."

Mel had a sneaky suspicion Joe was right. "Maybe we could get my mom to take it."

"I'm not doing that to Joyce," Joe said. He gave a small smile. "I don't want her 'dear Joe' to turn into 'damn it, Joe.'"

Mel laughed. "Honestly, I'm just hoping that the dog is cat-friendly. I don't want to traumatize Captain Jack. He's had enough upheaval in his little life, being abandoned as a kitten and all. The last thing he needs is a dog making his life a misery."

"Agreed," Joe said. "Captain Jack has right of refusal on the dog."

They parked next to Hayley's squad car and followed Cassie towards the entrance to the townhouse. There was one main entrance to the luxury building, which led to a bank of elevators. Because of the late hour there wasn't a person in sight. Cassie led the way, using a keycode to access the elevator.

As if sensing everyone's questioning gaze, Cassie said, "She gave me the code to her townhouse so I could water the plants while she was on the book tour."

"And I'm sure she'll verify that if it's needed," Hayley said as they filed into the elevator. She crossed her arms over her chest and studied Cassie with a speculative glance.

Having been on the end of a few suspicious gazes in her time, Mel felt for the bookseller. It was not the best seat in the house, for sure.

"Yes, of course," Cassie said.

She led the way out of the elevator into a narrow hallway on the seventh floor. The luxury apartments were built with a flair for mid-century modern and were mostly glass, metal, and lots of sharp angles, with starburst light fixtures as a nod to the atomic age.

"Peanut can be timid, so we should go in quietly so as not to cause her any stress," Cassie said.

She unlocked the door and made her voice soft when she called out, "Hey, Peanut, it's Aunt Cassie. Are you okay, baby girl?"

There was no answering bark. She reached inside the door and flipped on the light switch. She staggered back in horror and pressed her hand to her chest.

"Oh my god, the place has been ransacked! It must have been the killer. Ack, what if he harmed the dog? I can't bear it!"

Hayley pushed past Cassie with her hand on her gun. Mel peered around the two women to see what sort of carnage had occurred. Joe grabbed her hand in his and did the same.

A feather floated towards them and Hayley batted it out of the air. The sound of nails scrabbling on wood sounded and Mel glanced into the room to see a chubby black dog with a pushed-in nose and pointy ears come careening around the sofa right at them. At the last second the dog turned, going back the way it came, and sent a spray of feathers up into the air in its wake.

Joe pushed past Hayley and reached down on the floor. He picked up the very empty, very limp cloth of what was formerly a throw pillow.

"I'm not sure the place was ransacked so much as dog-sacked," he said.

Peanut came galloping past them again with her tongue hanging out of her mouth. She looked ridiculously happy. Then her back legs gave out and she did a big skid into the feathers like a pro ballplayer sliding into home base.

Mel laughed. The look of surprised delight on the dog's face was hilarious.

"Peanut," Cassie said. Her voice was full of admonishment, but it didn't slow the dog down one bit. The feathers the puppy had kicked up fell like snow, and Cassie sneezed.

"I'm going to wait outside," she said.

Hayley glanced from her to the dog and nodded. "Wait right in the doorway."

Cassie's response was a triple sneeze. Mel and Joe exchanged a look.

"You go that way," Joe said. He pointed to the left. "And I'll go the other. Let's try and catch her in the middle."

"Don't touch anything but the dog," Hayley said. "I'm going to check the rest of the apartment."

She shuffled through the knee-deep feathers into the kitchen and then turned down the hallway to check the back rooms.

"Hey, Peanut," Mel said. She hunkered low and tiptoed around the couch. "Whatcha doin'?"

"Making a mess," Joe answered. He, too, was crouched with his arms out, as if getting ready to tackle the dog.

Feathers stuck to Mel's clothes and drifted up towards her face. Peanut was on the other side of the couch, where the feathers were deeper. She had her butt in the air and was wagging her stumpy tail as if this was the greatest game ever.

Mel had to bite her lip to keep from laughing. In a cuteness competition, this dog would win hands down.

"It's okay, Peanut, we're not going to hurt you," Mel said.

"That's right, puppy, we're the good guys," Joe said.

Peanut's head moved back and forth as she studied them. Mel got the feeling she was looking for the weak link. Sure enough, just when they were within grabbing range she sprang to her feet and bolted right between Mel's legs, almost knocking her down as she went.

"Peanut, wait!" Mel cried.

She spun to chase her if the dog headed to the door, but Peanut was not about to give up her pile of feathers. Instead, she galloped around the back of the couch and plowed into them face-first, skidding across the throw rug and landing with her backside on Joe's foot. Even Joe was charmed as he let out a belly laugh that made Peanut quiver with doggy joy from her snout to her feet.

"She's insane," Joe said to Mel.

"Happy, at any rate," Mel said. She bent down to scoop Peanut up, but the dog wriggled out of her grasp and did two more loops around the couch, kicking up feathers, before she skidded to a stop between Mel's feet. Not to be thwarted again, Mel bent over and snatched her up before she could get to her feet.

"Gotcha!" she cried. She felt as if she'd

just won a hog-wrestling match. The wriggling bundle in her arms didn't seem to mind being held, and with a snort of approval, a little pink tongue licked Mel's chin.

"What the hell happened here?" Stan's voice barked from the door.

Mel crossed over to the doorway. She held up the dog and said, "Peanut, meet Uncle Stan."

The dog and the man studied each other as a feather drifted down and landed on Stan's head. Mel heard Joe chuckle behind her as Stan glowered at the lot of them.

Mel ducked her head to keep from laughing out loud.

"The apartment is clear," Hayley said. "No sign of anyone having been back there. I think our looter kept it to just the one pillow."

"Good grief, it looks like the scene of a massacre," Stan said.

Mel held the dog close. Peanut tried to lick her face again, but Mel was catching on and dodged her.

"We'll need to get her food, leash, bowls, and a bed if she has one," Joe said. "We are more of a cat house than a dog house at the moment."

"I'll gather her stuff," Mel said. She thrust Peanut into Joe's arms and then went into the kitchen. She had to open three cupboards before she found the garbage bags, but once she did she began to load the dog's food bag from the pantry as well as her bowls from the floor. Cassie went and grabbed the dog bed from the other side of the room, sneezing as she held it out at arm's length. Mel stuffed that into the big bag as well.

Stan cased the apartment, looking for anything that might give him a clue as to who had stabbed Elise and potentially killed the vendors associated with her book signing. Mel watched him confer with Hayley. They both looked pretty grim.

As she passed the kitchen counter, Mel saw a box of books. She glanced inside and noted that it was Elise's author copies of *The Palms.* It had a snazzy pink-and-aqua cover, a nod to the heyday when the Palms was built. The mid-century modern development was built in the late fifties and early sixties and still had many of the prominent features of the time.

Mel snagged a copy and dropped it into her bag. She'd return it. She just wanted to give it a quick read and see if there was anything in it that might provide a clue as to who had the biggest grudge against Elise.

Mel and Joe drove home with Peanut in

Mel's lap, her head sticking out the passenger-side window while Mel held on to her leash. Joe glanced over at them every now and then and shook his head as if he couldn't figure out exactly how this had happened.

"There is one thing I can't let go of," he said. He turned his car into their neighborhood and wound down the quiet street towards home.

"What's that?"

"Cassie getting everything if anything should happen to Elise," he said. "That's just weird."

"Cassie explained it. She is Elise's best friend. Plus, Elise didn't have anyone else."

"Not even her dog?" Joe asked. He studied Peanut for a moment. "She wouldn't have been the first crazy rich lady to leave her fortune to her dog."

"Well, she's not dead, so it doesn't really matter who she would have left everything to. Besides, Cassie didn't do it," Mel said for what must have been the hundredth time.

"I know you believe that," Joe said.

He turned into the driveway of the ranch house they shared in the Arcadia neighborhood. With Joe's parents around the corner and Mel's mother nearby, it felt as if they were coming home not just because they lived together, but because so many of their significant lifetime memories had happened in this neighborhood.

"It's more than believing," she said. "I know it."

"How?" Joe asked.

This was one of the many reasons she loved him. He didn't ask to be argumentative. He genuinely wanted to know how she could be so sure that Cassie was innocent.

"Because of the multiple murders. Think about it this way: As Elise's main bookseller, how would the deaths of the people Cassie hired to work Elise's book signing benefit her?" Mel asked. "It makes no sense. She uses those vendors all the time. If she murdered them, how would she get her events catered or photographed, etcetera? She'd be harming her own business."

"I'll give you that," Joe said. "I can't figure why she'd do that unless she had something greater to gain. If she got all of Elise's money, she might have decided that retirement was in order. So who cared if she murdered off everyone involved in the release of the book, and used them to distract the police from herself?"

"No, Cassie loves her shop. She'd never leave it voluntarily," Mel insisted. "It has to be someone else, like Hair Plugs Todd or Child Bride Mallory."

"Statistically speaking, it usually is someone involved with the victim," Joe said. "Which I'm sure Stan and Tara are looking into first."

He parked in the garage and they climbed out of the car and entered the house through the laundry room. Mel carried Peanut into the house, hoping that she could facilitate the first meeting between Captain Jack and the dog. Joe gathered Peanut's things and followed her.

"Okay, sweetie, this is your new home," Mel said.

"*Temporary* home," Joe corrected her. "You did see what she did to that pillow, right?"

"I'm sure she was just acting out because she was left alone all day."

"Or she likes shredding things," Joe said. "I think I'll go hide all of my shoes."

Mel set Peanut on the floor. She sat down and looked up at Mel as if waiting for something. Her tongue was hanging out and she was snort-breathing after the excitement of the car ride.

"Are you hungry?" Mel asked.

The dog blinked at her. She took it as a yes.

"Let's go set your bowls up in the kitchen," Mel said.

Peanut trotted along beside her as if she knew *kitchen* meant food. Mel rounded the corner and Peanut put on a sudden burst of speed. She didn't stop until she slammed her face into Captain Jack's bowl of dry cat food.

"Oh, hold up there, that's not going to be —"

A hiss sounded from above and Mel glanced up to see Captain Jack sitting on the counter. His tail was swishing and the dark patch of fur over his eye looked particularly pirate-like. Mel snatched the bowl of food from Peanut and put it on the counter beside Captain Jack.

She stroked Jack's fur and he arched his back. Mel had a feeling he was still irritated, but not willing to give up the pets.

"Now, Jack," Mel said, "you're going to have a roommate for a —"

Ruf ruf ruf. Peanut barked, having just realized a cat was perched above her like a vulture.

"I see it's going well," Joe said over the barking as he returned to the room. He hurried over to Peanut's bag of stuff and started to dish her food.

She kept barking and Captain Jack returned the greeting with a hiss.

Joe put the food down beside Peanut and she glanced at it and then the cat, all the while still barking. Obviously torn between antagonizing the cat and eating, Peanut let loose a flurry of barks and then turned her attention to her food.

Captain Jack remained perched above her with his tail swishing, but he wasn't hissing anymore. Mel continued to pet him.

"It's okay, buddy," she said. "We're just helping the canine out until her person gets better."

Jack rose on his hind feet and used his full body weight to rub his head into her hand. Mel picked him up and snuggled him for a bit until he was his usual purring feline self.

"Maybe this will work out," Joe said. He glanced from the dog to the cat and shrugged.

Peanut finished her food and turned to lap up some water. She let loose a big belch and sat down. As if she'd forgotten there was a cat in the house, she blinked up at Jack in Mel's arms and then started barking again.

Startled, Captain Jack leapt out of Mel's arms and landed on the counter with a reproachful hiss. He turned his back to them and strode the length of the counter.

Peanut followed him from the ground, still barking.

Jack hopped from the counter to the back of the couch to the back of a chair and then bolted down the hall to go hide in the bedroom. Peanut scrambled to follow, barking all the way.

Mel and Joe exchanged a look and Mel asked, "Dog or cat?"

"Cat," Joe said. "At least I know he likes me."

"Fine," Mel said.

Together they followed the ruckus into their bedroom. Captain Jack was up on the bed while Peanut circled the bed, barking at the cat like she'd treed a lion.

Mel reached down and scooped up Peanut. "I think she just wants to meet him."

"Meet him or eat him?" Joe asked. He was scratching Captain Jack behind the ears, soothing his ruffled fur.

"Meet, I'm pretty sure," Mel said. "Should I put her on the bed?"

"Could be a bloodbath. We don't want her to do to Jack what she did to that couch cushion."

"Good point," Mel said.

She sat on the bed and held Peanut in her lap. Ecstatic to be up on the bed, Peanut stopped barking and sat, panting with her tongue hanging out.

"I think she just wants to be a part of the pack," Mel said.

Captain Jack gave Peanut a disgusted look. She may have wanted in but Jack clearly wasn't there yet. When Peanut rolled out of Mel's arms and onto the bed with her belly in the air, Jack turned his back on her and hopped off the bed, trotting out of the room with a swish of his tail.

Peanut then turned her gaze on Mel. She looked so desperate to please that Mel couldn't resist giving her a belly rub.

"It's okay, Peanut," she said. "He'll come around, you'll see."

ELEVEN

Mel snuggled deep into her bed with Peanut sacked out between her and Joe's feet. Joe had passed out while reading through a deposition and Mel noted the even sound of his breathing, indicating he was fast asleep.

Reassured that her bedside lamp wouldn't disturb him, Mel finished a recipe text to Oz and then plugged in her cell phone and opened the copy of *The Palms* that she'd snagged from Elise's apartment. The book began with a scene from a backyard barbecue when Elise was new to the neighborhood. Everything was very suburban until the host of the party, a person Elise referred to as Beer Gut, circulated through the party collecting everyone's house keys.

Of course, everyone threw their keys in thinking it was to keep people from driving drunk. It wasn't. Instead, at the end of the party the wives were to fish a set of keys out of the bowl and that was the man they were to go home with. Elise had been shocked.

Mel was right there with her. She tried to picture a party where that happened and Joe's reaction. She glanced at her man. While she'd been reading, Peanut had wedged herself in beside Joe, who was still dead asleep and hadn't noticed. Now they both had their heads on Joe's pillow and were snoring softly. It was ridiculously adorable.

It didn't take Mel much imagination to know that Joe would lose his cool at a party like the one Elise described. Not only that, they wouldn't be returning to any of the neighborhood parties anytime soon or ever.

Elise's husband, or rather her alter-ego/protagonist Ellen's husband, known only as Hair Plugs, had a different reaction. He wanted her to go along with the party game. He felt that it would help them network with their neighbors and get to know people. Elise . . . er . . . Ellen was unhappy with his reaction. She felt he should protect her and get her out of there, not think about his career. Mel was with her on that one.

Hair Plugs put the pressure on, however, and Ellen soon found herself going home with a man who wasn't her husband, a man she called Turtle. Mel could not put the book down. She felt like she was watching a slow-motion train wreck and yet she couldn't look away or stop reading.

Ellen's night was awful. She couldn't go through with sleeping with the man so she got him roaring drunk and snuck out when he passed out. She walked home by herself as the sun rose, wondering what had happened to her husband and what would happen to their marriage now that they lived here in this neighborhood called the Palms.

Mel was riveted. She only closed the book when it landed on her face with a splat when she started to doze out of sheer exhaustion. From the opening chapter Elise penned a story about the seedy underbelly of the wealthy suburb and its sleazy inhabitants. Mel wondered if Elise would have written the book if her husband hadn't divorced her so he could marry Mallory, known as the Child Bride in the book, who it turned out was on the prowl for husband number two.

As the novel told it, Hair Plugs was so determined to have his new wife accepted by his peers that he had done everything he could to make certain Ellen was rejected by all of her former friends. In the divorce, he tried to have it written into their agreement that Ellen would move away and leave the neighborhood to him and his new wife.

Added to the crushing blow of being forced to give up her home and her friends, it was an especially wrenching maneuver because "Ellen" couldn't have children and the new wife wanted to start a family right away.

In the morning, Mel wasn't surprised she'd spent a fitful night with disturbing dreams about Elise, Hair Plugs, and pens that spurted blood instead of ink. The one thing she couldn't figure out from the beginning was why Ellen stayed married to Hair Plugs, or rather Elise to Todd. Surely she could have left him at some point in their marriage when everything started to go horribly wrong.

She woke up to Captain Jack batting her nose. She reached out from under her covers and rubbed his head. He purred and then began to walk on her, up and down from her shoulders to her knees and back, which was his way of insisting that she wake up and feed him. Right now.

"All right, all right," she said. She pushed the covers off and glanced at Joe. Peanut was still wedged up against him, sharing his pillow and snoring softly just like Joe. She had also managed to maneuver herself under the covers.

As if sensing her gaze upon him, Joe opened one eye, and said, "She snores."

"Uh-huh."

"She's under the covers."

"Yup."

"She can't stay."

"For now or forever?"

"For now," he said. "I wasn't aware forever was on the table."

He moved to get up, being careful not to jostle the dog. What a fibber! He was totally smitten with Peanut.

"It's all right if you wake her," Mel said. "She probably needs to go out."

"Oh, well, she's had a rough night," he said. He tucked the covers in around her. "I figure she could use the rest."

Mel shook her head at him. " 'He went for her like she's made outta ham.' "

"*Best in Show*?" Joe asked.

"Look at you, getting the movie quote right," she said. "I'm so glad the bakery crew has been such a good influence on you."

Joe rolled his eyes but it was with a smile.

Captain Jack, clearly unhappy that he wasn't the center of attention, gave a howl. The noise snapped Peanut awake and she bolted up, getting tangled in the covers as she tried to make a leap for the cat.

Jack hissed and hightailed it out of the bedroom. Peanut launched herself off the bed to give chase.

"And they're off," Mel said as she hurried after them.

Mel let Peanut out into their fenced backyard and fed Captain Jack, who seemed much happier with his food bowls up on the counter. When Peanut came in, she was so distracted by her food, she forgot all about the cat.

Mel brewed a pot of coffee and took up the book where she'd left off the night before. She was fully engrossed when Joe entered the kitchen. He had to say her name three times to get her attention and then he pointed his thumb at Captain Jack.

"He's not coming around, is he?" Joe asked.

"What makes you think that?" she asked.

They watched as Captain Jack swatted yesterday's mail off the counter onto Peanut, where she was licking her empty bowl as if more food might appear if she licked deeply enough.

"A hunch," he said. He glanced at the book. "Good reading?"

"Horrifying," she said. "It's got it all — sex, power, the rich behaving badly — and Elise barely concealed people's identities. I can see why there was outrage. If not for the dirty deeds then for some of the nicknames. Can you imagine being known as Foot Stink or Oozing Sores?"

"Those are bad, but enough to try and murder her?"

Mel didn't like to admit it, but she *could* see someone being angry enough to kill Elise for this book. It wasn't just the insulting names she had for everyone, it was also the secrets, the bad behavior, the cheating, the lying, and who really hated whom and what they did to show it.

It was like a how-to manual on cruel and outrageous behavior that she couldn't stop reading. When Joe kissed her good-bye to leave for work, she glanced up and looked at him, really looked at him. Then she dropped the book and hugged him.

Joe hugged her back and then pulled back to look at her. "What's up?"

"Just insanely glad that I chose you," she said. "You're a good man, Joe DeLaura."

He kissed her and then smiled. "Not to be argumentative, but I'm pretty sure I chose you."

Mel grinned at him. She'd had him in her sights since she was twelve and he was sixteen. There was no way he'd pined as long as she had and he knew it. Nice of him to pretend, however, and it was just one more reason why she loved him.

"What's the plan with the fur people?" he asked.

"I'm going to take Peanut with me to work and beg Oz to let me keep her in his apartment," she said. "I just don't think she should be alone, and Captain Jack could probably use a break from her."

"That'll get us through today," Joe said. "I'll ask my brother Dom if he has any baby gates we could borrow. We can use them to barricade the dog in the living room tomorrow and keep her from destroying the whole house."

"See?" Mel asked. "It's all coming together."

Joe gave her a dubious look but he didn't argue. He kissed her one more time, rubbed Captain Jack's ears, and patted Peanut on the head. Mel watched him go, admiring the cut of his suit and the prosecutorial way he carried himself.

When the door shut behind him, she glanced at the pets and said, "I'm going to marry him."

Captain Jack gave her a bored look as if this was old news, but Peanut barked as if in approval. Of course, the girl got it.

■ ■ ■ ■

Mel had to go to the bakery no matter how much she wanted to stay home and work her way through a pot of coffee and Elise's book. When she arrived, she found Angie already in the kitchen with Oz. They were standing by the worktable, looking at several cupcakes. Angie had her arm around Oz's waist, and she was leaning against him.

"Everything okay?" Mel asked.

"It's perfect," Angie sobbed. "Look!"

Mel approached the table and felt her eyes go wide. On the table was a small tier of cupcakes done in Angie's wedding colors of aqua and pewter. Each cupcake was an explosion of delicate white blooms with aqua leaves tucked in and small pewter-colored accents. They were intricate and lovely and Mel marveled at the detail Oz had wrought in the fondant and the frosting.

"Oz, these are by far your finest work," she said. She grinned at him and saw a flush color his cheeks.

"They're only practice," he said. He waved his hand as if he didn't think much of them. "I just wanted Angie's approval before I start working on the final product."

175

"You have it," Angie said. She let go of him and clutched her hands in front of her. "Oz, it just means the world to me that you're making my cupcake tower."

"Don't mention it," he said. He looked as if he really meant that.

Peanut, who had strolled in beside Mel, was clearly desperate for attention. She sat on her haunches and barked at Oz.

He glanced down at the dog as if eager to have the attention off of him. "And who do we have here?"

"Her name is Peanut and I was wondering if she could hang out in your place for the day since she and Captain Jack could use a little time apart," Mel said.

"You and Joe got a dog?" Oz asked.

"Sort of," Mel said. "She belongs to Elise Penworthy, so we're fostering her until Elise gets out of the hospital and can care for her again."

"That's cool," Oz said. "I'll take her up and get her settled."

Mel handed him a bag of dog stuff. "Have I offered you a raise lately?"

"No," he said. "And I'm definitely due." He jerked a thumb at the front of the bakery and said, "Go look and see what I had to put up with today. I'll bet you double my salary."

Mel gave him an alarmed look and headed towards the swinging door that led into the bakery. Angie fell in behind her and together they eased the door open and peered out front.

They scanned the bakery, looking for what might have upset Oz. Mel glanced at the counter, where Marty was supposed to be working. There was no Marty, just some guy with jet-black hair and Clark Kent glasses.

Mel narrowed her eyes. The Clark Kent wannabe had bushy gray eyebrows.

"Marty," she said. "What are you doing?"

"Aw, man, how'd you know it was me?" he asked.

"The stooped shoulders, droopy pants, and gray chin stubble gave it away," Angie said.

Marty reached up and pulled off his wig and glasses. "I don't understand. This disguise always worked for Superman."

"You are not Superman," Mel said.

"Yeah, you're more like Heartburn Man or High-Fiber Diet Man," Angie said.

Marty lowered a bushy eyebrow at her. "Now, was that nice?"

"No," Angie said. She hung her head. "I'm sorry. I just don't see why you feel the need to be in disguise. Tell those thugs your daughters hired to go to h—"

"Are they still following you?" Mel asked. "How does Olivia feel about that?"

"I don't know. She threw me out," he said.

"What?" Mel asked. "But I thought . . ." She didn't know what she thought, so she stopped talking.

She didn't want to make Marty feel worse by rejoicing in his breakup. Still, Mel had always hoped he'd find someone a little more stable than Olivia. Then again, without Olivia to intimidate his daughters, they might pack Marty up and drag him back to the Midwest with them. Mel hated that. Marty, like Oz, was family.

"It's okay," Marty said. "I'm bunking with Oz."

Mel and Angie exchanged a look. Oz hadn't mentioned Marty moving in with him, but then maybe he had enough on his plate being in charge of the wedding cupcakes and all.

The front doors opened and a mom with two kids came in. Marty went to wait on them while Mel and Angie backed up until they were in the kitchen once again. Angie's phone chimed and she took it out of her apron pocket. She glanced at the display and frowned. "Wedding stuff. I have to take this," she said.

Mel nodded. She glanced down at her

handbag and noticed Elise's book sticking out of the top of it. Maybe she could do a little reading before diving into the baking for the day.

She entered her office and closed the door. She put her cell phone on her desk and then put her purse away and sat in her chair with her feet up on the desk. Elise's writing was a bit overdone, but Mel could overlook the overblown turn of phrase for the sheer circus-like atmosphere of the neighborhood of the Palms. It was like an old black-and-white forties movie where the heroine in a peignoir threw a martini shaker at the back of the man who was betraying her with the neighbor.

Mel devoured the juicy novelized version of Elise's life, learning among other sordid details that Mallory Cavendish, aka the Child Bride, had apparently been the new wife of the pervy elderly neighbor Elise called the "Fossil." When Fossil died, Hair Plugs rushed in to console the young widow, and the next thing Ellen knew, she was kicked to the curb for a younger model who wanted to have children, something that Hair Plugs decided at the age of fifty-five that he desperately needed.

Engrossed in the book, Mel didn't hear her phone chiming until there was a pause and then it started again. She wrenched her gaze from the book and looked at her phone. She was trying to imagine a day where Joe announced to her that he really wanted a family, and could she just move aside for the young woman he had found who was going to do that for him? Gah, she was so outraged on Elise's behalf, she marveled that Elise hadn't gutted Todd like a fish.

It wasn't that he had fallen in love with someone else — that happened, and graceful and considerate uncouplings were possible. No, it was that he wanted her to leave with nothing. No money, no friends, no security. She was to just pack a bag and leave their home, her home of twenty years, and go start over in some old-lady condo that he refused to give her enough money to buy. He felt she was overdue to get a job. Yeah, because women in their mid-fifties with no job skills were in such high demand in the job market. Mel was seething on Elise's behalf.

She looked at her phone and tried to focus on the number. The display read Cassie's name. She frowned and picked it up. She hadn't expected to hear from Cassie so early.

"Hey, Cassie, oh my god, I'm reading the

book," Mel said. "I can't believe Elise didn't —"

"Mel!" Cassie interrupted. Her voice was shrill and Mel stopped talking immediately. Something was very, very wrong. "Oh, Mel, Elise is dead."

TWELVE

"What?" Mel cried. "How? When?"

"This morning, early, from complications." Cassie's voice was quiet, as if she could hardly push enough air through her grief to form the words.

"Where are you?" Mel asked. "Are you all right?"

"No," Cassie said. "Mel, they've arrested me for her murder."

"But that's crazy!" Mel said. "Are you at the station? Does Steve know?"

"Yes, he's on his way," Cassie said. "Mel, I wanted to call you and tell you I was arrested because I don't want you to believe I killed Elise. No matter what they say, you know me. Please don't believe this about me."

"I don't, Cassie," Mel said. "I know you didn't do it. I believe that. I really do. Listen, Tate and Angie's wedding is this weekend and I have no time, but I'll do everything I can to talk to Joe about the charges against you and see if I can convince him to drop them."

"He won't," Cassie said.

"You don't know that," Mel protested.

"My fingerprints were on the pen they pulled out of Elise's back," Cassie said.

"Oh, no."

"Because of that and the fact that I stand to inherit everything, they think there's enough proof and motive that it was me." Cassie's voice broke and she started to cry. "This is a nightmare."

"Don't give up, Cassie," Mel said. "Steve is the best and I'll do what I can, too. How about the bookstore? Is it okay, can your people manage without you?"

"Yes, it's all set," Cassie said. "Thank goodness I hired a couple of retired librarians to run the show. I know they'll stand by me until the bitter end."

"I will, too," Mel promised. "Try not to worry."

"Thanks, Mel," Cassie said. "I just can't believe she's gone. I just can't."

She ended the call and Mel lowered her phone and stared at it. How could Uncle Stan have arrested Cassie? She knew he wouldn't talk to her about it over the phone. She was going to have to go down to the station to confront him in person. She could only hope he was alone and that Tara wasn't there to run interference.

She dropped the book on her desk and grabbed her bag. Angie was pacing around the kitchen on her phone when Mel came into the room. Mel gestured that she was going out and Angie raised one finger for Mel to wait.

"Can you hold on?" Angie asked the person on the other end of her call. Then she glanced at Mel and asked, "What gives?"

Mel blew out a breath. "Elise passed away and they've arrested Cassie for her murder. I'm going to talk to Stan."

Angie's jaw dropped. She lifted up her phone and said, "I have to go. I'll call you back."

"No!" Mel shook her head. "Your wedding. You have stuff to do."

"No, I don't," Angie said. "Everything is a go. That was my cousin Denise insisting that I not put her at the same table with our other cousin Mindy. Of course, I already have them at the same table and I am not changing it!"

Mel studied her. "Looking to get away?"

"Please." Angie put her hands together in a pleading gesture.

"Is Oz back?"

"He's working out front with Marty," Angie said.

"Excellent," Mel said. "This shouldn't take long, but I'll let them know where we're going just in case."

Once Marty and Oz were up to speed, Mel and Angie took Mel's Mini Cooper over to the police station, which was only three blocks away.

Mel scored a parking spot on the street and they hustled into the station. Officer Lopez, who was on desk duty, glanced up and then frowned.

"No cupcakes?" he asked.

"No time, Lopez," Mel said. She blew past him, down the hall, where she knew Uncle Stan's office was. She rounded the corner at top speed and slammed into a solid wall of man muscle. She would have landed on her butt except the solid wall reached out and grabbed her.

"Mel!" Manny Martinez lifted her up and hugged her close. He set her back on her feet and then held his arms wide for Angie.

"And the bride," he said. He hugged Angie and she hugged him back with a big grin.

"You're here!" Angie said. She glanced around him and asked, "Where are Holly and Sidney?"

"Still in Vegas," he said. "They're flying

down the day before the wedding. I took a few extra days off so I could join Tate's bachelor party and visit my family."

"Oh, yeah, that's tonight," Angie said. A look of concern flashed over her face and Manny shook his head at her.

"Ange, I'm a detective with the Las Vegas PD, Joe's a prosecutor, and all of your brothers are going to be there," he said. "What mischief could we possibly get up to?"

She gave him a flat stare and then laughed.

"You're right." Angie hugged him again. "I've always liked you, did you know that?"

Manny grinned at her and Mel was pleased to see the camaraderie between them. For a while, Angie had been less than thrilled with Manny's interest in Mel, not surprising since Joe was Angie's brother. It went without saying that Angie was and always would be Team Joe.

Manny was tall and built and had a killer grin. There had been a time when Mel and Joe were on a break that she'd thought about giving Manny a chance, for about a nanosecond, but Joe had won out. Which was just as well since Manny had found true love with the owner of the first Fairy Tale Cupcakes franchise, a former Vegas show-girl named Holly Hartzmark and her daughter, Sidney. Mel couldn't be happier for him.

"It's great to see you, Manny," she said.

"But?"

"No but," she said. "I just need to talk to Uncle Stan."

"About the arrest he just made?" Manny asked.

"How do you know about this?" she asked.

"Please, the whole station is buzzing about it," he said. "They were taking bets on how long it would take you to get here, although Lopez said he thought you'd bring cupcakes, so I think he's disqualified. Plus, I used to be Stan's partner, so he clued me in."

"You are not working this case," Mel said.

Manny raised his hands in the air. "In an advisory capacity at most."

"Cassie Leighton did not murder Elise Penworthy," Mel said.

"You don't know that," a voice said from behind Mel.

She spun around to see her uncle Stan standing there. He looked as if he hadn't slept, and she felt bad that this case had blown up on him. The media presence alone was making this investigation a misery. He certainly didn't need Mel showing up and causing a fuss, but if she didn't, who would look out for Cassie?

"I do know it," Mel said. "The pen could have been taken from the signing. Cassie was in charge of the pen and the books, so of course her fingerprints were on it."

"There's more to it than that, Mel," Stan said. "And I'm not going to discuss it with you, so don't ask."

Mel raised her hands in the air. "There is no way Cassie would have murdered a photographer, a driver, and a caterer. None. She had nothing to gain by doing that. I am telling you, someone set her up as a last-minute fall guy and my money is on Hair Plugs."

Uncle Stan glared at her. "You've been reading the book."

"Yes, and it reads like a who's who of people who wanted to murder Elise Penworthy."

"Mel, you have Angie's wedding to focus on," Stan said. "Why don't you take care of that and let me run my investigation my own way."

It was a curt dismissal and Mel wanted to argue, but Uncle Stan's eyebrows had knotted themselves together in a severe frown, so she knew arguing with him about this would be pointless.

"Fine," she said.

Manny cringed and Mel knew he was

thinking that when a woman says *fine,* she is anything but. Uncle Stan did not seem to care until Mel looked him right in the eye and said, "I guess I'll just have to ask Joyce what she thinks about all of this."

Uncle Stan's eyes went wide. "You wouldn't."

"Watch me," Mel said. She turned and spun on her heel. She nodded at Manny as she swept from the station, leaving Angie following in her wake.

"Bye, Uncle Stan. Later, Manny," Angie called. "See you both at the rehearsal dinner, right? Tell Holly to call me!"

Mel stepped outside and sucked in a breath. Angie paused beside her and studied her face.

"That was a bluff, right?" she asked. "You're not really going to talk to your mom, are you?"

"Oh, yes, I am," Mel said. "Just as soon as I get today's baking done."

"So, Mom, have you read *The Palms*?" Mel asked.

"That overwritten, bloviated novel of suburban intrigue?" Joyce asked. "Every word."

Mel laughed. She was sitting at the counter at her mother's kitchen. There was a tub of snickerdoodle cookies open in front of them and Joyce had just poured Mel a hot cup of coffee.

"She wasn't very subtle with her descriptions of people, was she?" Joyce asked. "No wonder someone tried to kill her."

Mel was about to take a bite out of her cookie, then she put it down. "They did more than try, Mom."

Joyce met her gaze over the edge of her mug. "What happened?"

"Elise passed away early this morning," Mel said. "They believe it was complications from her stabbing, but they haven't confirmed it yet."

"Oh, dear." Joyce bit her lip and looked regretful. "I feel awful for trashing her writing just now."

"No need," Mel said. "The writing is not good but the subject matter is compelling. I was up all night reading."

"Did you get to the part about the man she nicknamed Baby Doll?"

"The one who enjoyed wearing kitten heels and baby doll outfits?" Mel asked. "Oh, yeah, she really enjoyed skewering him."

"He's a real estate agent," Joyce said. "I play Bunco with his wife. I don't know how I'm going to look her in the face."

"I wouldn't mention the whole baby doll thing," Mel said. "And don't wear kitten heels."

"As if I would," Joyce said. She picked up a cookie and broke it into halves, then quarters.

Mel watched her as she stuffed one quarter of the cookie in her mouth and then another. "What are you doing? Portion control?"

Joyce broke another cookie in half. "No, I'm just anxious. I always play with my food when I'm anxious."

It was true. Many a family dinner had been spent watching Joyce move her mashed potatoes around her plate like they were prized building materials and her fork was a backhoe.

"What's bothering you?" Mel asked.

"Nothing's bothering me, exactly," Joyce said. Then without taking a breath she added, "Oh, all right, if you're going to badger it out of me, the truth is I'm seeing someone."

Mel choked on her cookie. Little crumbs landed in her windpipe and she coughed and swallowed and sucked air, but still they were stuck. Her eyes began to water and Joyce reached around behind her and slapped her hard on the back. It didn't help.

Before it turned into full-on assault, Mel held up her hand to ward off her mother while lifting her coffee mug with the other and taking a healthy swig.

"Okay, I'm good now," Mel said. "Um, Mom, do you remember the last time you decided to try dating?"

"Yes, dear, he was murdered on our first date," Joyce said. "Kind of hard to forget, but I think I'm ready to try again."

"Really?"

"Yes."

It was a firm yes with no wiggle room. Mel didn't know what to say. On the one hand, it was nice for her mom to find someone. On the other hand, what if she hated him? Not that it was her place to have any opinions about who her mother dated. If Joyce was happy, then Mel was happy. Really, she was.

"Does Charlie know?"

"Yes, your brother called last night and we had a long talk about it."

"So, he knew before me?"

"Please do not make this a thing."

"It's not a thing," Mel protested. "It's just that as your daughter, I thought I would get preferential treatment when it came time to divulge the details of your love life."

"There are no details," Joyce said. "I've

told you all I'm telling you for now."

"Seriously?" Mel asked. "No name? Address? Snapchat snap?"

"What's that?"

"Never mind," Mel said. "How am I supposed to have Uncle Stan run a background check with no name?"

"Your Uncle Stan does not need to run a background check," Joyce said. She finished off her cookie quarters by stuffing both of them in her mouth. Very suspicious.

"Oh my god, Uncle Stan already knows, doesn't he?" Mel asked. "You told him before me, too."

"You have Angie's wedding," Joyce said. "And now you have all of this murdery drama with Cassie getting arrested. I didn't want to add to your burdens."

Mel stared at her mother. Something wasn't right. Her mother was being very cagey, as if she was ashamed of her new beau or something.

"He's not one of the people in the book, is he?" Mel asked. She could only imagine how Uncle Stan would handle that.

"No, heavens no," Joyce said.

Mel felt her internal daughter alarm system ratchet down from Defcon one back to a solid three.

"So, when do I get to meet him?" she asked.

"When the time is right," Joyce said. "It's all pretty new."

"You're not going to do anything crazy like elope, are you?" Joyce looked at her with one eyebrow raised and Mel ducked her head and said, "Oh, yeah, *I* tried that. It didn't take."

"We're just dating," Joyce said. She tucked her silver-streaked blond hair behind her ear and Mel noted that her mom was still a very pretty woman.

"Well, whoever he is, he's a lucky man, and if he doesn't treat you right, just let me know, and I'll sic the boys on him," Mel said.

Joyce reached across the counter and squeezed Mel's hand in hers. "Thanks, honey. Now, do you want me to ask around and see if there is any local gossip on who might have been angry enough to stab Elise over her book?"

"No," Mel said. "I mean, if you hear a juicy tidbit at the hairdresser or Bunco, report back in, but don't go fishing. Whoever killed Elise was willing to stab anyone associated with her signing and I don't want you to make yourself a target."

"All right," Joyce agreed. "I'll be careful, I

promise."

Mel left her mother's house with a plastic tub of meatloaf, potatoes au gratin, and a bag of salad. Dinner for her and dear Joe. Mel marveled that she could never visit her mother without leaving with a full dinner. It was as if her mother forgot she had been to culinary school and actually knew how to cook. Of course, Mel had specialized in sweet instead of savory, but still.

She zipped back to the bakery. She wanted to help Cassie, but she was beginning to freak out that the wedding was just days away and her mom was dating someone. Who was he? How had she met him? Should she ask Uncle Stan to run a background on the guy?

She arrived at the bakery to find Angie sitting at the worktable in the kitchen. She had her clipboard with her and was sitting there staring at it as if she expected it to bite her.

"What's wrong?" Mel asked. "You look freaked out."

"I am, because nothing is wrong," Angie said. "As awful as it is, we found a new photographer who seems nice, and everything is right on schedule with no hiccups, boo-boos, or errors. That's weird, right?"

"No, I'd say that's a relief," Mel said.

"Besides, you've already had enough to deal with considering Blaise's death. I know how hard that's been on you and Tate."

"Yeah," Angie said. Her expression was strained. "Tate and I are going to his service tonight. I feel so awful. Here we are getting married and his poor mother . . . ugh."

"I can't even imagine how devastated she is," Mel said. "Joe and I were planning to go, too. Did Tate say whether they have any suspects?"

"No. He called a while ago and said the police have no one in custody except for Cassie, but I just don't see her murdering Elise, Blaise, the driver, or the caterer," Angie said. "I don't understand what the police are thinking. Do you think they know something we don't?"

"Maybe," Mel said. "Uncle Stan is playing it pretty close to the vest, but I'll bet Steve is going to prove Cassie had an alibi for those other murders and then the case against her will unravel."

"Unless they think someone else killed Cassie's vendors and that the murders are unrelated," Angie said.

"But that makes no sense," Mel said. "They all have to be connected somehow."

"I agree, but how?" Angie asked.

"What do the caterer, the driver, and

Blaise have in common?" Mel asked.

"They were working Elise's book signing?" Angie said.

"Why?"

Angie made a face. "Because Cassie hired them, obviously."

"Why?"

"Mel, I love you like a sister but if you ask me why one more time," Angie warned.

"Just hear me out," Mel said. "We know Blaise's business was centered in the area, just like the driver and the caterer."

"Meaning what?"

"If they were all the preferred businesses of the Palms neighborhood, then it stands to reason that the person who killed them was someone who used their services who felt betrayed by them," Mel said.

"You're thinking Elise got some of her information from these businesses and used what she learned in the book?" Angie nodded. "That makes sense."

"A photographer would have access to all sorts of behind-the-scenes information," Mel said. "What if Blaise had been hired to do some skeevy boudoir shoot?"

Angie made a face and said, "Or a driver? Who knows what happened in the backseat of his car while he was schlepping these rich people around town?"

"And Brianna the caterer," Mel said. "We've walked into some weird situations of our own when delivering cupcakes to a party."

"Do you think Stan is considering this?" Angie asked.

"I'm going to call him and find out," Mel said. "But I'm betting they'll find that whoever killed all of the vendors is someone who used all of them and believes that the vendors gave Elise information about them to use in her book."

"There's only one problem with this theory," Angie said. "Blaise wasn't the sort to gossip. I just can't see him talking to Elise about another client."

Mel nodded. Blaise was a good guy, but that didn't mean he hadn't accidentally told Elise something and it got back to his client.

"Maybe he didn't, but the murderer believes he did," Mel said.

"That I could see," Angie said. "Especially if this person is operating from a place of rage. Why let Cassie take the fall for it, though, unless they have a beef with her, too?"

"Well, she is publishing the book, so it's perfect revenge for that," Mel said. "The murderer is probably thrilled that she's been arrested and questioned, and if she gets convicted, well, that will work out well for the real murderer, won't it?"

"You sound pretty sure of this," Angie said.

"I have to be," Mel said. "The alternative is that Cassie is the murderer, and that is unacceptable."

THIRTEEN

The bakery and last-minute wedding details took all of Mel's time over the next few days. She checked in with Cassie daily, but Cassie, who had been let out on bail because it could not be proven she was a flight risk, was keeping a low profile. She hadn't gone to work, letting her staff run the bookstore. She hadn't even gone home because Steve, her attorney, felt it best that she stay out of the media spotlight.

Instead, she holed up in a townhouse in a gated community that Steve's law firm kept for just this purpose. When Mel called Steve to thank him for looking out for Cassie, he told her that with Cassie's fingerprints on the murder weapon and the fact that she would inherit the rights to Elise's book, the case was going to be a battle.

"But it's a battle you think you can win, right?" Mel asked.

"I'm going to try," he said.

Mel was standing in the bakery kitchen, putting the final touches on a batch of marble swirl cupcakes — both the cake and the frosting were swirled vanilla and chocolate. They were the special of the day and she was late getting them out front. Marty had already barked at her twice about it.

"You know, I have a theory," she said.

"Oh, this should be good." Steve did not even try to mask his sarcasm.

"Don't be a hater, it is good," Mel insisted. "I've been reading the book and —"

"Then you know Elise didn't use anyone's real name," he said. "Making it difficult to prove who she was vilifying."

"Yes, but she did use all of their distinguishing characteristics," Mel said. "Hair Plugs —"

"Ugh, he was the worst," Steve said.

"You're reading the book?"

"My client published it and it's critical to her case," he said. "Of course I read it."

"Past tense? Read it? That fast? Oh my god, you read it before she was your client," she said.

"What? No, I didn't," he protested.

"Oh, come on," Mel said. "Admit it. The Palms is most of your client base, it's only natural that you should read it. Oh, no, you're not in it, are you?"

"Oh, hell no!" Steve said. "I'd never let that happen. I may be an ambulance-chasing dirtbag, but I'm not trashy novel worthy, not yet."

Mel laughed. "So, how many of your clients were in there?"

"Several," he said.

"Any of them worth considering for murder?" she asked. "And if so, would that prove to be a conflict of interest for you?"

"No, my clients are the type to ruin you financially, not with a pen to the back," he said.

"But you'd let Uncle Stan know if you thought there might be someone he should take a closer look at, right?" she asked.

Steve was silent for several seconds. Mel could tell he was carefully debating his answer.

"Possibly," he said.

"Not a ringing endorsement of your trustworthiness," she said.

"Client confidentiality," he said. "It's a thing."

"Whatever. I think the moral imperative here is that you don't let an innocent woman go to jail for a crime she didn't commit."

"Mmm." It was the most noncommittal grunt Mel had ever heard.

"Is there any way I can see her?" she asked.

"No," Steve said. "If you have information or questions, I'd prefer you go through me. I don't want to risk having any reporters find her."

"That makes sense," she said. "How is she holding up, for reals? Don't give me the press answer."

"She's . . . scared," he said. "She's built that business up from nothing and now she stands to lose it all. She's definitely scared and a little angry."

Mel couldn't help but notice an admiring note in Steve's voice that she'd never heard before.

"You like her," she said.

"And I'm hanging up now," Steve said.

"Oh my god, you *really* like her," she said.

"How do you figure that?" he asked. "What could I possibly have said that played into your whatever it is that's going on in your head?"

"Does she know?"

Thump. Thump. Thump.

"Did you hear that noise?" he asked. "That was me, banging my head on my desk."

"Well, that's an extreme reaction," she said. She was trying very hard not to laugh.

"A simple, 'Why, yes, Mel, I do like her very much' would have sufficed."

"You're out of control," he said. "Just because you're all engaged to DeLaura and everyone around you is getting married does not mean the rest of the planet is pairing off, too."

"If you say so," Mel said. "But I'm telling you, your tone of voice gave it away."

"Ugh," he groaned. "So maybe I like her a little. I mean, I'm a defense attorney; most of my clients are guilty as hell and it's all I can do to get them a reduced sentence. In my line of work, it's rare to have a client that you just know is innocent."

"Oh, you know it, huh?" Mel asked.

"Okay, I'm officially hanging up now," he said. "Anything you want me to pass along to Cassie?"

"Tell her not to worry, and use your big-time lawyer voice to make it sound sincere," Mel said.

"Will do," he said. "So, tell me the truth. Did you have even one twinge of 'Oh, hey, I should really have given Steve a chance' during this embarrassing conversation?"

Mel laughed. "I'm sorry, no. You know I've always belonged to Joe."

"And the hits keep coming," he said. But he didn't sound upset, more resigned. "Hey,

Mel, I'm happy for you."

"Thanks," she said. "I'm happy, too."

Steve ended the call and Mel glanced down at the sparkly diamond on her finger. She'd been so consumed with Tate and Angie's wedding that she hadn't given much thought to her own wedding to Joe. Maybe it was time to get moving on that.

"Mel, there you are!" The back door to the bakery slammed open and there stood Ray.

"Are you looking for me or your favorite Chocolate Peanut Butter Cupcake?" Mel asked.

"You, but if you have a cupcake to throw at me, I won't say no," he said. Ray strode into the bakery in his usual black leather jacket and jeans.

Mel marveled at how he looked like he really belonged on the Jersey shore and yet he had spent most of his life in Scottsdale, Arizona, a town known more for golf than good-fellas.

Mel moved to the cooler and plated two of Ray's favorites. There was still coffee in the pot that was hot, so she poured him a cup of coffee, too.

"All right," she said. She put the cupcakes in front of him at the table. "What do you have to tell me?"

"I heard from a very reliable source that there is video of Elise Penworthy's ex threatening her right before the book came out," he said.

"Seriously?" Mel asked. "That would be huge. Who has the video?"

"That's the problem," Ray said. He paused to take a bite out of one of the cupcakes. He was still chewing as he explained, "Word is the second wife has it and she's holding it over husband dearest as leverage in their marriage."

"Huh, so the Child Bride is no fool," Mel said. "I bet he'd do anything to keep that video from surfacing."

"I'm thinking you need to have a chat with wife number two," Ray said.

"Oh, sure, how am I supposed to make that happen?"

Ray polished off the last of the cupcake and took a sip of coffee. "My same source told me she's taking tennis lessons at her country club." He paused to look at his phone. "In a half hour."

Mel narrowed her eyes at him. "Why are you telling me this and not Uncle Stan or Detective Martinez?"

"Do you really think either of them is going to listen to me?" he asked.

"No," she said.

Ray held his hands wide in a gesture that indicated there was her answer.

"My source also said that she suspects there is something going on between Child Bride and her tennis pro."

Mel's eyebrows rose. "That's some source you have."

Ray gave her a grin. "It's the tennis pro's wife."

"Okay, hold up," Mel said. "How do you know the tennis pro's wife?"

"We went to school together," he said. "She's a nice girl. She also asked me to get the money shot on her husband and the Child Bride so she can file for divorce and take him to the cleaners. Full disclosure, the money shot is worth five hundred smackers."

"Oh my god, so you have a whole other agenda going?"

Ray shrugged. "I can't get into the club, but you can."

"How do you figure?" Mel asked.

"You look the part," Ray said.

"Meaning what?"

"You're all tall and blond," Ray said. "Total country club material, plus I had my friend put you on the roster. You'll be able to scoot right in and ask questions."

"You're crazy," Mel said. "The rehearsal

for the wedding is in three hours. How am I supposed to get to the country club and then back to the church in time?"

"I'll drive you," he said.

Mel glanced down at her hot pink apron over her jeans and white T-shirt. "Not really dr—"

Ray held up a garment bag that had a lady's tennis outfit in it.

"You've really thought of everything, haven't you?" she asked.

"Oh, yeah?" a shout sounded from the kitchen's swinging door. "Well, you snore!"

Marty burst into the kitchen looking pink in the face and irritated.

"Problem?" Mel asked.

"Oz is the worst roommate ever," Marty said. "And I say that as someone who lived with Olivia Puckett, the most anal-retentive roommate ever!"

"It is a studio apartment; maybe you need to find someplace else to live until you've sorted things out with your daughters and decided what's happening with Olivia," Mel said.

"You can bunk with me for a small fee," Ray said.

Marty glared at him. "No."

"Marty, that's rude," Mel said.

"Sorry. No, thank you," Marty said. "I'll

figure it out. Maybe I'll sleep in the van tonight."

"No, we talked about this," Mel said. "No more sleeping in the van for anyone. If your daughters caught you doing that, you know they'd haul you back home in a heartbeat."

Marty pointed a bony finger at the bag. "What's that?"

"Mel's outfit," Ray said. He thrust it at Mel. "Speaking of which, we need to get going."

"Where are you going?" Marty asked. "The wedding rehearsal is in three hours."

"The Palms Country Club," Ray said. "We've got a lead on who might have killed Elise. Mel is going undercover to see what she can find out. She'll be back in plenty of time."

Marty glanced between them and started to take off his apron. "The Palms? Hang on, I'm coming with you."

"You?" Ray asked. "How are you going to fit in at a country club with a tennis pro?"

"Are you kidding? I can ace being a tennis player. All I have to do is know when to jam the drop-shot lingo at them. Besides, if I make a call indicating I'm looking to be a member and they run my financials, they'll be all over themselves to let me in. It'll give me a chance to snoop around and see if I can learn anything of interest."

"Oh, yeah, that's right," Ray said. "You're loaded. If you change your mind about needing a place to sleep, my fee just went up."

"Why do I get the feeling that this is a bad idea — so, so bad?" Mel asked.

Ray thrust the bag at her. "Go."

The Palms Country Club sat in the heart of the neighborhood. It was built in the fifties to cater to the wealthy and it had never changed. Mel chose to drive her car, and she turned onto the palm tree–lined drive into the country club, stopping at the gatehouse.

A man in uniform — a goldenrod-colored polo shirt with a palm tree logo embroidered on the upper left, and navy pants — leaned into her car window. He took in her tennis outfit, and Marty in his Bermuda shorts and golf shirt beside her. He glanced between them, obviously trying to figure out if they were related or if Marty was her sugar daddy. Mel had to bite her lip to keep from laughing.

"Good afternoon, may I help you?"

Ray was under a blanket on the backseat of her car and Mel hoped the guard didn't see the lump he formed. She decided to turn her charm meter up to that of super cheerleader wattage.

"Hi, I'm a guest," Mel said. She did big gestures while she talked, hoping to keep the guard's eyes on her. "I'm Melanie Cooper, and I brought my friend Martin Zelaznik with me, as he's considering membership."

"How do," Marty said. He leaned forward so the guard could get a better look at him. The guard studied him for a minute and then wrote Marty's name down on the clipboard.

"I'm going to call ahead and let someone in membership know you're coming," he said. "Just a moment."

He ducked back into his booth.

"Is he gone?" Ray asked. "Ow, ow, ow, my back is seizing up."

"Hush," Marty said. He faked a coughing fit on the off chance the guard heard Ray.

"Here you go, Ms. Cooper." The guard came back with a paper parking slip for her to hang on her rearview mirror. "Guest parking is just to the south of the entrance. Enjoy your day."

"Thank you," she said. She sped away from the station and through the open gates. "Okay, we're clear. You can get up now."

Ray burst out from under the blanket like a whale breaching the ocean's surface. He sucked in a great gulp of air as if he'd been suffocating.

"Settle down," Marty snapped. "Sheesh, you're all red in the face and sweaty looking."

"I don't like small dark spaces," Ray said.

"You were under a blanket," Marty retorted. "Relax."

"Both of you, pipe down," Mel said. "I need to get to the tennis court in two minutes."

She parked and they hurried from the car. Mel's outfit was about two sizes too big and she wasn't sure if she was mad at Ray for thinking she was bigger than she was or not. As it was, her skirt was being held up by a row of safety pins. Ray carried her tennis racket for her. He told her if anyone asked who he was she was to tell them he was her bodyguard.

As soon as they stepped through the front doors, a woman in a plum-colored suit tailored to fit her every curve greeted them.

"Mr. Zelaznik, what a pleasure to meet you," she said. "I'm Courtney Reyes. Our membership committee chairperson just called and said I was to give you a full tour of the club. If you're ready?"

Marty looked at the beautiful woman and then at Ray and Mel. His eyebrows were high on his forehead. "See ya, kids."

He walked away without looking back.

"How does that ugly buzzard have all the luck?" Ray asked.

"Tennis," Mel said. She snapped her fingers in front of his face. "Focus, Ray."

"Yeah, yeah, got it," he said. He took Mel's elbow and hustled her through the building, passing a restaurant, a lounge, a gym, and a conference room before pushing through another door that led outside. They followed the oleander-lined walkway, which led to a series of tennis courts.

Mel could hear the repeated *pah* of tennis balls being hit and she felt her hands sweat. Probably, she should have mentioned the only time she'd ever played tennis was in gym in high school, and during that unfortunate season she had only managed to hit the ball over the net once, lobbing it right into her gym teacher's crotch. The nickname "dead shot" had followed her around for the rest of that school year.

"Now, listen," Ray said. "My friend re-arranged Anton's schedule so that his lesson with Mallory Cavendish includes him coaching her to play against a woman who is looking to join the club and be coached by him as well. He's expecting you to be a player of some skill as Mallory is a serious player and is training to play in the club tournament."

Mel stopped walking. "I don't know if I can do this."

"What?" Ray goggled at her. "Of course you can. Need I remind you we took on a crazed killer just a few months ago?"

"Yeah, that's not the argument that's going to work here," she said.

"Listen, you want to know if the Child Bride is the killer and I need a shot of the tennis pro being inappropriate with her," he said. "Mel, I have five hundred bones at stake here. Now, get moving."

"Fine, but if we get into trouble, we're telling Joe it was all your idea," she said.

They began to walk by the courts. Mel watched tan women in cute skirts with matching tops and visors hustle around the court as they whacked all of their life rage out on the little yellow-green balls. She didn't want to be presumptuous, but there appeared to be a lot of anger management happening out there.

"There they are," Ray said. He handed Mel her racket and took out his phone. He opened the camera app and then held the phone up to his ear as if taking a call. "I'm ready. Let's go."

"So, let me get this straight," Mel said. "I'm supposed to get her to admit she has video of her husband threatening Elise while you catch her in a clinch with her coach."

"Yeah, so if she doesn't admit to having the video, try to get her to confess to fooling around with her ball boy."

Mel rolled her eyes. "This is so stupid."

Ray opened the gate to the court, which slammed shut after them with a bang, making Mel jump. She had the panicked thought that Mallory might remember her from the book signing, but even if she did, Mel had just been working it and during Child Bride's altercation with Elise, Mel had been back at her table.

Mallory looked like a model in her sexy hot pink halter top and tennis skirt with the slit up one thigh. Mel glanced down at her polo shirt and pleats and felt like she was in a Catholic schoolgirl uniform. She frowned at Ray.

He waved at the coach and then gestured that he was on a call. The pro looked at him in his leather jacket with a frown and Mel figured she'd better jump in and distract him before he realized they were just a big sham, the canned ham of shams in fact.

"Hi, I'm Melanie," she said. "I'm here for

a lesson."

Mallory frowned at her and glanced at Ray. "Who's that?"

"My . . . dog walker," she said. There was no way she could say "bodyguard" with a straight face. She saw Ray's eyebrows meet in the middle of his forehead in consternation. Served him right for sticking her in this hideous outfit and for getting the size wrong.

"Dog walker?" Mallory asked. "Where's your dog?"

"He's having his weekly therapy session," Mel said. "He has issues, so Raymond came with me today."

"Oh," Mallory said. It was clear she had no idea what to make of Mel or Ray. She gestured to the tennis pro beside her. "This is Anton Argosi, our coach."

"I see on my schedule that you are a talented tennis player, looking to join the club. You are pleased to join us today," Anton said.

Mel blinked. His slash of white teeth was so spectacularly perfect that she was temporarily blinded. Add in his perfect physique, thick head of dark curls, and Italian accent and Mel was halfway to smitten herself.

She glanced at Mallory, who looked utterly entranced by the pro. Yeah, if there

216

wasn't something going on between them Mel would swallow her tennis racket.

"May you go across the court," Anton said. He gestured for Mel to take the other side.

Mel didn't really see how she was going to question Mallory from over there. She glanced at Ray and he made a shooing motion with his hands for her to go.

Mel twirled, grabbing the waist of her skirt as she went to keep it from falling down. She moved into position and stood hunched over with her racket across her body, trying to do her best Serena Williams pose. Given that she barely knew how to swing a racket, it felt forced. She rocked from foot to foot, shifting her weight, trying to look ready.

"You return the ball, yes?" Anton yelled.

Mel nodded. Sure, if a small miracle was involved.

Anton took Mallory to the base line. He stood behind her and demonstrated with lots of hands-on instruction how she should toss the ball into the air and then hit it. One ball whizzed by Mel on the right. Another ball whizzed by her on the left. When the third one came at her dead center, she yelped and hit the ground, putting her racket over her head.

There was a snort of laughter from the

sidelines and Mel glanced over to see Ray with a fist at his mouth, as if he could force himself to swallow the laughter that was trying to roar up out of him. She wanted to hit him with her racket.

"Miss, are you all right?" Anton jogged towards the net, leaping over it as if it were no higher than the curb. He knelt beside her and Mel felt her face get hot under his concerned gaze. This was mortifying.

She pushed off the ground and Anton gently hooked her under the arms and pulled her to her feet. Mel was a tall girl but Anton topped her by a couple inches.

"*Bella,* oh, you have . . . here." Anton reached up and with a gentle hand he brushed away some dirt from Mel's cheek.

His touch was gentle, the lightest brush of skin on skin. His warm brown eyes met hers and his smile was kind. Mel found herself smiling back at him.

"Thank you," she said. Her voice came out raspy and breathless and she had to clear her throat.

"Hey, hey, hey." Ray stomped across the court. "Hands off, buddy."

Anton dropped his hand and glanced at Ray, who looked like he wanted to snap Anton like a pretzel. Yeah, good luck with that. Anton was lithe but he was all muscle

218

and Mel had a feeling he could take Ray out and not even break a sweat.

The *pah* of a tennis ball being hit brought their attention back to Mallory. She had assumed her serve position and launched a tennis ball at them. Ray grabbed Mel and yanked her out of the way, while Anton reached up and snatched the ball out of the air.

He started to speak in rapid-fire Italian. He did not sound pleased. Ray and Mel began to back up as Mallory tossed her long blond curls and pouted as if pleased to have his full attention again even if he was yelling at her.

"Oh, this is good," Ray said. He fumbled with his phone, trying to turn on the camera and be subtle about it.

"I haven't gotten a chance to ask her any questions about the video," Mel protested in a harsh whisper.

"Who cares?" Ray hissed. "I've got five hundred riding on a passionate clinch. If this goes my way, *bah dah boom.*"

"Really?" Mel asked. Then she glanced at Anton and Mallory. Anton took Mallory's racket and tossed it aside, then he pulled her up close and tight.

Mallory stuck out her chin in a taunting manner and Anton put his hand in her hair and held her head still as he lowered his lips to —

"Hey! How's the lesson going?" Marty yelled through the chain-link fence that surrounded the court. "Did you know they have a steam room here? And the golf course is sweet. I am seriously considering membership."

Mallory and Anton broke apart.

"Damn it!" Ray said. He swiveled his head in Marty's direction. "Old man, you are killing me."

FOURTEEN

"Me?" Marty puffed out his chicken chest. "What did I do? And who are you calling old?"

Courtney was standing beside him, smiling at him, which only made Marty puff out his chest even more. Mel glanced at the three of them. She grabbed Ray's hand and looked at his phone. They were out of time. She needed to get her information and she needed it now.

She glanced down at the ball by her feet. The odds of making the shot she needed to were slim but better than nothing.

She scooped up the ball and jogged to the center of the court.

"Hey!" she cried. "Let's try that again."

She tossed the ball up into the air and smacked it with the racket. She had her eyes shut, so it was definitely flying on a wing and a prayer. She heard the *pah* of the hit and then the ball hit something hard and there was a cry of pain and then a stream of furious Italian in a very high-pitched voice.

She opened her eyes to see Anton cradling his privates. Well, all right, she was two for two.

"Oh, I'm so sorry!" she cried.

She glanced at Ray and Marty, who were both covering their lower regions and cringing as if in sympathy pain. Courtney's eyes were huge and she spun on her high heels and hurried from the court yelling, "I'll go get some ice. Don't move, Anton."

Mel walked over to Ray and Marty and said, "Stay here."

Then she dashed around the net and joined Mallory, who was helping Anton to go and sit down.

"I am so sorry," she said. "Really so very sorry. I never meant to hit your man." She directed her words to Mallory, who looked startled but didn't deny the relationship. Interesting.

They helped Anton lie down on one of the benches. His whimpering had lessened somewhat but Mel knew if she was going to get any information out of Mallory now was her time.

"I hope I didn't do any permanent damage," she said. "Are you two planning a family?"

"I . . . What?" Mallory looked at her as if she was cracked.

Mel made her most innocent face in return and said, "Oh, I just assumed because of how you are together that you're married. He's clearly mad about you."

Anton moaned and Mel felt a twinge of guilt. In her defense she'd had her eyes shut and the location of the hit really hadn't been intentional, she'd just hoped to hit him somewhere.

"We are . . . in love," Mallory said. She smoothed Anton's hair back from his forehead in a loving gesture that Mel thought was sincere. "But there are issues with us being together."

She looked up at Mel and her face crumpled. "In fact, it is highly likely that I will soon go to jail for a crime I didn't commit."

"What?" Mel put her hand over her heart in what was only half-feigned surprise. She hadn't realized Uncle Stan was this close to making an arrest, and she hadn't known Mallory was their first pick since they'd really seemed fixated on Cassie. To get Mallory to say more, she appealed to her vanity. "But you're a beautiful woman. What crime could you have committed?"

"I know," Mallory said. Clearly she was bewildered at how anyone could believe that a woman who looked like she did could be accused of a crime.

Yeah, as if beautiful women and men weren't capable of dirty deeds. Mel kept her face earnest but it was a struggle.

"My husband's ex-wife was murdered and the police seem to think I'm responsible," she said.

"His ex-wife?" Mel gestured to Anton. "How awful."

"She was awful," Mallory said. "And no, not Anton's wife. His wife is, well, she is another issue."

"So, you're not married?" Mel gestured between them. She tried to make her expression sympathetic even though on the inside she was shaking her head. How did these two knuckleheads think this was going to play out for them?

"No, but you were right about how we feel for each other," Mallory said. She stroked Anton's hair again and he moaned. "We are madly in love."

Mel really hoped Ray was getting this on his phone.

"But your husband's ex-wife was murdered and you're a suspect?" she asked. "Do you have an alibi?"

Mallory let loose a wail that shook Anton and he let loose a powerful stream of Italian that Mel was pretty sure was not happy words.

"No, because I was with him," Mallory cried. "I can't say anything or his wife will have him tossed out of the country."

"Too bad you can't prove your husband did it," Mel said. "Then you'd be free and you could go with him."

"I have video of my husband threatening Elise," Mallory said. "But he said he has the same thing about me."

"Did you threaten her?" Mel asked.

"Just once, but she totally deserved it," Mallory said. She tossed her hair. "She called me 'Child Bride' one too many times. Ugh, I hated her."

"Ice pack!" Courtney cried as she jogged on her high heels in little mincing steps towards them. "I have an ice pack!"

As Courtney bent over and put the ice pack on Anton with a familiarity that seemed more than that of coworkers, he took a moment to ogle her chest where her plum-colored jacket gaped, then he grabbed her hand and gave it a squeeze.

"Grazie, bella," he said.

Mel looked at Mallory, whose eyes narrowed at the gesture.

"Yeah, you might want to let the police

know about your alibi," Mel said. "I'm just sayin'."

When Mallory spun around and pushed Courtney away from Anton, Mel took it as her moment to escape. She jogged back over to Ray and Marty and said, "Let's go. I think it's about to get ugly around here."

They ran from the tennis courts, through the country club, and out into the parking lot.

"That was nice work back there," Ray said. "You got her wailing loud enough that I got video of her admitting they are having an affair, which is even better than a money shot."

"You're welcome," Mel said. She tossed him her keys. "You drive; I need to change."

"In front of us?" Ray looked scandalized.

"No, behind you," Mel said. "I have to put on my outfit and stuff for the rehearsal dinner. Don't be such a weirdo."

"I do not think Joe would be okay with this," Ray said. He stiffly climbed into the driver's seat.

Marty shrugged. "You seen one pair of —"

"Ah!" Ray interrupted.

"Stockings," Marty said. "I was going to say stockings, you pervert."

Ray zipped out of the parking lot, making

Mel's attempt to get dressed more challenging than it needed to be.

"Slow down there, Andretti," she said when he took a curve that almost put the Mini Cooper up on two wheels.

Mel slid across the backseat while she wrestled with the clothes she had tossed into a bag as they rushed out of the bakery. She changed out of her polo shirt and into her pretty floral blouse. She kicked off her shoes and grabbed her heels.

Ray took another corner hard and she slid the other way. Mel used the door handle to pull herself upright. Then she reached into the bag for her miniskirt. All she felt was the bottom of the bag. Oh, no!

"No, no, no, no, no," Mel moaned as she checked the bag. Empty. She rifled around the backseat, hoping her skirt had fallen out somewhere. Nope. Damn it!

"What's the problem?" Marty asked.

"My skirt," she said. "I must have forgotten to put it in the bag. Now I have to wear this oversized pleated wonder to Tate and Angie's rehearsal. Oh my god!"

"Relax," Ray said as he turned into the parking lot of the church. "No one is going to notice."

He parked in the lot. Joe was standing on the curb outside, waiting for them. No one else was in sight.

Mel glanced at her phone. They were fifteen minutes late. Angie was probably having a cow.

Joe opened the door for her and Mel climbed out. He tipped his head to the side and studied her.

"Going for the Catholic schoolgirl look?" he asked.

"Don't ask," she said.

"Mel, there you are, come on!" Judi Franko, Angie's cousin, was standing in the open doorway to the church, waving for them to hurry up.

Marty and Ray joined them, and Joe looked at Marty's outfit and then back at Mel. "Why do I get the feeling there is a story here?"

"Story?" she asked. "No story. More like a tale, a brief one, not even an anecdote, really."

"Uh-huh," he said.

Judi, clearly done waiting for them, dashed forward and grabbed Mel by the hand and said, "Maid of honor, focus!" She then took in Mel's overly large pleated skirt and one eyebrow quirked up above the frame of her glasses. "What sort of outfit is that? Is it trending? Are my girls going to want to wear that? Because I'm not sold on it."

"It's more what you'd call a fashion malfunction," Mel said. She glared behind her. "Isn't that right, Ray?"

"How is this my fault?" he asked.

"Mel, there you are." Uncle Stan was waiting just inside the church. He had his arms crossed over his chest and his expression did not have his usual happy-to-see-her glow.

"You look mad," she said.

"I'm not mad," he said. "More like irritated. Annoyed. Put out."

"What did I do?" she asked.

"Why don't you tell me, Sharapova?" he asked.

"Oh, you heard," she said.

"Only because the undercover we had watching Mallory Cavendish happened to catch the whole thing on camera. Mel, you're the niece of the lead investigator and you're engaged to a county prosecutor. The defense will have a field day with this."

"Oh."

"I sense some familial issues happening here," Judi said as she glanced between them. "I feel for you, I do, but we have a wedding rehearsal happening right here, right now. So. Move. It."

With that, Judi dragged Mel into the antechamber, shutting the door in Uncle

Stan's face.

"Talk later, Uncle Stan," Mel yelled through the door.

"Men. Sheesh, do they not get it? This is a wedding!" Judi raised her hands in the air as if asking the divine for patience, and then she spun on her heel and went back the way she came, calling over her shoulder, "Angie, I'll have your dad knock on the door when we're ready."

Mel turned around to see Angie standing with the other bridesmaids. She had two sisters-in-law and three nieces and then there was Mel. One of the nieces, Kaylee, a junior bridesmaid, looked Mel over from head to toe.

"That's some savage fashion you have going on there," she said. Then she took a picture that Mel was pretty sure was going to be all over Snapchat in a matter of minutes. Just what she wanted, to be shredded by fifteen-year-olds. It was like nothing had changed since she was fifteen.

"Hey." Angie broke free from the crowd, looking impossibly lovely in a red chemise dress that flared at mid-thigh. "What happened?"

"Noth—"

Angie raised her hand in a stop gesture. "Please, you know I'll get it out of you one way or another and they're going to come get us in a second."

Mel blew out a breath. "Okay, Ray, Marty, and I went to talk to Mallory Cavendish at her country club because there was a rumor that she was having an affair with her tennis pro and Ray was offered five hundred bucks for a picture by the tennis pro's wife."

"What?" Angie blinked. Then she shook her head. "That's Ray for you, always working an angle."

"Well, turns out they are having an affair," Mel said. "In fact, Mallory was with Anton — that's his name — at the time of the murder, but Anton's wife — aka the woman Ray is working for — threatened to toss Anton out of the country if he cheated on her, so Mallory can't come forward."

"Wow, it's like a telenovela," Angie said. "But in English."

"Half Italian," Mel corrected her. "Anton is quite the master of the romance language. It gets better. Mallory has video of her husband threatening Elise but she's afraid to come forward with it because he apparently has video of her doing the same, so they're at a stalemate."

"Oh, man." Angie stomped her foot. "I was here prepping the church all afternoon. I missed all of the good stuff."

"Not all of it," Mel said. "Uncle Stan is here and he is not happy with me. Apparently, Mallory was under surveillance and my association with the lead investigator and a county prosecutor would not be viewed in a favorable light."

"Oh."

"That's what I said," Mel sighed.

"Chin up," Angie said. "Look at it this way: Now that they know Mallory has an alibi, they can pursue other leads. Really, if you think about it, you did them a big favor by weeding her out."

"Genius!" Mel said. "I'm totally using that argument with Uncle Stan."

"Angie, love, are you ready?" Angie's father, Dom DeLaura Senior, peeked around the door. He looked intimidated by all of the females in the room.

Judi bustled around him, clapping her hands, completely unintimidated. "Okay, girls, showtime!"

The women all hustled to the door. Mary, Angie's sister-in-law, handed her a colorful bouquet made out of ribbons. Angie looked down at it and then up at Mel.

Her brown eyes glowed and she said, "Wow, I'm actually getting married."

Mel hugged her tight and then hurried after the other women. They lined up by height, with Mel being last because she was the tallest, but also because she was maid of honor.

She peered down the long aisle into the pretty church, with the afternoon light shining through the tall stained-glass windows at the end of the room making the front of the church glow in a rainbow of color.

The weight of it suddenly hit Mel. The importance of the role she was to play as her two best friends pledged their lives together. She watched as the girls started to walk down the aisle in single file. She glanced ahead and saw Joe standing next to Tate.

Judi was right. This was the most important thing happening in their lives right now and she couldn't be running all over town, trying to figure out who murdered Elise Penworthy when Angie and Tate needed her.

As she took her first step down the aisle, she vowed that until her two best friends took off for their honeymoon, this wedding was her number one priority. She would see them achieve their happy ever after if it was the last thing she did.

FIFTEEN

"Oh my god, I'm starving," Angie said as she and Mel slipped into the ladies' room at the Arizona Biltmore to primp before dinner.

Thankfully, Mel had been able to pop into one of the resort clothing shops and buy a pretty skirt that would get her through dinner and not make her look like she was fleeing parochial school.

"So, what's next on the investigation?" Angie asked.

Mel shook her head. "Nothing," she said. "I am tapping out."

"But what about Cassie?" Angie protested. "She needs you."

"She has Steve," Mel said. "She'll be okay. Plus, we've scratched one person off of the suspect list."

"Not to get hung up on a technicality, but does that actually help her?" Angie asked. "Or does it just make her look guiltier?"

"And we're done with this conversation," Mel said. "You are getting married tomorrow and that's what you should be thinking about."

"If I think about it I get nervous," Angie said. "It's much better for my mental health to contemplate murder."

There was a sound of flushing and one of the stalls opened. Mel and Angie exchanged a look as Tate's mother came out.

"Hi . . . er . . ." Angie stalled out as Mrs. Harper went to wash her hands.

"Oh, Angie," Mrs. Harper said. "Don't you think it's time you started to call me Mom?"

"Absolutely, Mrs. . . . er . . . Mom?" Angie said.

Mel turned away to hide her smile.

Mrs. Harper washed her hands and took a fresh white towel out of the basket on the counter. As she dried her hands, she said, "I know exactly what you mean about the wedding jitters. I was a nervous wreck when Mr. Harper and I got married. I don't remember a thing."

"Really?" Angie asked. A frown line formed between her eyebrows.

"I know, isn't it ridiculous?" Mrs. Harper asked. "You spend a fortune on a day that you don't remember a thing about. Promise me you'll pause during your big day and take a few moments to notice things. Like your flowers, the music, the sound of people laughing and talking, and the first sight of Tate when you walk down the aisle. Pictures are nice but you want to try and remember the feelings."

She squeezed Angie's hand as she passed them on the way to the door. "Oh, and, Mel, I really liked the skirt you had on at the rehearsal. Very fashion forward of you."

The door closed after her and Mel looked at Angie. "And there goes the politest woman who ever lived."

"I know. Fashion forward — only Emily Harper could come up with something nice to say about that skirt. You looked like you were missing your saddle shoes and pet poodle."

Mel laughed. "It felt as awkward as it looked. Come on, Tate's going to get antsy if we don't go out there. He'll think you pulled a runner."

Angie turned to look at Mel and her big brown eyes went even wider. "Mel, what would you do if I did?"

"Huh? What?"

Angie grabbed Mel's hands in hers and bit her lip. "If I decided I couldn't marry Tate; would you help me?"

"Oh, no, you're not getting cold feet, Ange," Mel said. "I mean it. You have loved him for years. How can you second-guess marrying him?"

Angie looked down at the floor. "I have to know. You're my maid of honor, would you help me? Would you help me run away?"

"No," Mel said. She didn't even think it over. She squeezed Angie's hands tightly in hers and said, "I would hog-tie you and throw you in a sack, then I would get Joe to do the same to Tate and then we would throw the two of you in a locked room until you figured it out. Because, Angie, you love him and he loves you and if ever there were two people who were made for each other it is you two."

Angie dropped Mel's hands and opened her arm wide and hugged Mel tight. "And that is why you are my maid of honor!"

Mel studied her friend through a narrowed gaze. "Was that a test? Because that would really be lousy."

"Not a test so much as a reassurance for me that if I freak out, you'll do what needs to be done," Angie said. She slipped her arm through Mel's and danced on her feet. "I'm going to marry Tate. This time tomorrow, I will be Mrs. Tate Harper."

Angie's exuberance was impossible to

ignore and Mel hugged her friend to her side. "Thank goodness!"

Together they left the ladies' room to join the party. Mel saw Joe talking to Uncle Stan and she made her way to them, knowing full well she was likely in for another lecture. The two of them had their heads together as if what they were discussing they did not want overheard. Mel's curiosity was fully engaged.

"Talking about the case?" she asked as she popped up between them.

"Mel!" Uncle Stan jumped and put his hand on his heart. "Quit sneaking around like that. In fact, quit sneaking around period."

"I didn't sneak," Mel said. "Ray asked me for a favor and I went because I thought it might help Cassie."

"It didn't." Uncle Stan frowned.

"I know, but at least now the police and the district attorney can take Mallory Cavendish off of their suspect list and focus on finding the real killer."

"You'd better tell her, and emphasize how she is to stay out of this investigation," Uncle Stan said to Joe. Stan looked grim and then he glanced across the room and saw Mel's mother, Joyce. His face softened and he gave them a brisk nod. "Excuse me."

238

Mel watched as he went to join Joyce. Since her father had passed, Uncle Stan had watched over Joyce, Mel, and Charlie in his stead. Mel had always been grateful to him for trying to help fill the dad-sized hole in her heart, but right now he was on her very last nerve with his bossiness.

Then again, if Joyce was seeing someone, maybe she needed Uncle Stan to step in since Joyce wasn't sharing with Mel. She should have asked Uncle Stan if Joyce had told him who she was seeing. She'd bet he'd already run a background check on the guy if she had. Hmm.

"You okay?" Joe asked.

Mel turned back to him and leaned into his side. "Yeah, I just feel as if things have been strained between me and Uncle Stan lately and I don't know how to fix it."

Joe was quiet for a second and then said, "The Elise Penworthy murder is a pretty high-profile case. He's got to be feeling the pressure, and having you associated with the case even peripherally is not going to make his job easier."

"I suppose, but what choice do I have? I can't abandon my friend. Still, it feels like something more than that is off," she said. She glanced back at Joe and found his warm brown gaze on her. "So, what did Uncle

Stan think you should tell me?"

Joe blew out a breath and put his hand on the back of his neck. He looked wary and regretful. This could not be good.

"The county prosecutor has decided to charge Cassie Leighton with the murder of Elise Penworthy."

"What?" Mel cried. Several heads snapped in their direction and she lowered her voice, although it was an effort. "That's preposterous."

"They feel that the evidence is strong and only going to get stronger," he said.

"Did you talk to her? Did you tell her that you know Cassie couldn't possibly have done this?"

"No, because I don't know that," Joe said.

Mel stepped away from him, looking outraged. "But you've met her several times. You've always liked Cassie."

"Yes, but that's before she was named as the prime suspect in an investigation for which my office is responsible. I can't just wave them away from the case because my fiancée is friends with the main person of interest."

"What did Steve have to say about this?" Mel asked.

"I have no idea," Joe said. "Because of my relationship with you and your relationship with Cassie, I'm recused, as it could be considered a conflict of interest."

Mel studied his face. He didn't say it but it was there in the firm set to his lips. He was disappointed to have been removed from one of the biggest cases to hit his office in months.

"I'm sorry," Mel said. "I never want you to have to choose between me or your career."

It was then that he hit her with his patent-worthy Joe DeLaura smile. With a dimple as an accent mark, his lips swooped up, showing off a slash of white teeth and making Mel's insides flutter. He'd been doing that to her since the very first day she set eyes upon him.

He cupped her face with one hand and lowered his mouth to hers in a swift, sweet kiss. "Cupcake, there was no choice. It's you, always you."

And just like that Mel was a big dopey pile of mush. She kissed him back and hugged him hard. She was going to marry this man.

"Now I'm going to ask you something that will likely make you mad, but I'm going to ask anyway," Joe said.

Mel stepped away from him so she could look him right in the eye. "Go ahead."

"Please stay away from this case," he said. "I know Cassie is your friend, but whoever killed Elise is likely the same person who killed *three* other people. That's big-time homicide — as in crazy, out of control, nut job — and I want you away from it."

"Is that your professional description of the murderer?" she asked.

"The county prosecutor is not fooling around," Joe said. "She wants whoever is responsible locked up, and if the state can prove it was one person, she's going to ask for the death penalty. You cannot get involved in this, Mel."

Mel narrowed her eyes. "Are you forbidding me?"

"Which part of my body should I cover if I say 'yes'?" he asked.

"The most vulnerable," she said.

Joe sighed. "You know I won't tell you what to do, but I'm asking you as your fiancé and the man who wants to spend his life with you, please stop investigating the case against Cassie. She has Steve in her corner and even though I hate to admit it, he's a hell of a defense attorney."

Mel stared at him. Refusing him anything went against her nature, but she also didn't want to lie to him.

"Joe, I just don't know if I can turn away

from someone who needs me," she said. "I can promise you I won't go looking for trouble, but if I find out something of interest, I'm going to follow up on it."

Joe frowned. It was clearly not the answer he'd been hoping for. Mel laced her fingers with his and swung his arms like they were kids on a playground.

"I promise I'll be very careful and not do anything dumb," she said.

He shook his head and she knew he was formulating his argument. This was the down side to being with an attorney — they were very good at arguing their case and they really liked having the last word.

"Hey, Joe, tell Paulie he's not allowed to wear white socks tomorrow," Tony yelled across the room. "I mean, come on, he's supposed to be representing the DeLauras."

Joe leaned close to Mel and whispered, "This conversation isn't over."

"Joe!" Paulie called. "Tell Tony I can wear whatever I want."

"You'd better go before they start communicating with their fists," Mel said.

"All right, we'll talk later. I don't know what the big deal is with white socks. Personally, I'm just relieved he's not wearing his Iron Man ones."

"Go. Before it gets ugly," she said.

"Fine." Joe kissed her forehead and gave her hand a quick squeeze.

Mel could feel that he wasn't happy leaving the conversation here. Like Stan, she could have told Joe what he wanted to hear, but she didn't want to lie to either of them and deep down she knew they both preferred the truth even if it gave Uncle Stan heartburn and caused Joe to worry.

Joe walked over to where his six brothers stood bickering. The middle of the seven, Joe had played the role of mediator for as long as Mel had known the DeLaura family. She studied the ridiculously handsome group of men in order of birth; Dom, Sal, Ray, Joe, Paulie, Tony, and Al. Dom, the oldest, was starting to go gray, his daughters were almost grown, and they were lovely as Angie's bridesmaids. Most of the other brothers were following his lead — married, or about to be, with kids in the mix — while just Ray, Tony, and Al were unattached.

They were a loud family. Everyone was always in everyone else's business. There were no secrets in the DeLaura house. It was one of the things she loved best about her future in-laws.

Mr. and Mrs. DeLaura watched their boys with obvious pride and then turned to accept the Harpers into the fold. Little did

Tate's parents know that when Tate married Angie, the DeLauras would then consider the Harpers family as well. That's how the DeLauras worked. The family was inclusive and ever expanding. There would be no split holidays between the DeLauras and the Harpers. Oh no, they would be shared, whether the uptight Mr. Harper liked it or not. Mel suspected not.

What an incredible gift it was. Mel realized she'd always been treated like one of the family by the DeLauras because she was Angie's best friend, but when she married Joe, it would be official. She grinned. She was going to belong to this family.

"What are you grinning about?" Joyce asked her as she moved to stand beside Mel.

"Just happy for Tate and Angie," she said. She didn't want to start talking about her marriage to Joe, because Joyce would start planning.

"They are a lovely couple," Joyce agreed.

They both turned to look at Angie and Tate. They were standing with Manny Martinez and his girlfriend, Holly Hartzmark, and her daughter, Sidney. It occurred to Mel that Tate and Angie would likely have kids soon. After all, the business was doing amazing and they were in their thirties.

"So, what do you think of the Biltmore?"

Joyce asked.

"Huh?" Mel turned back to her mother and met the blue-green hazel gaze so like her own.

"For your wedding to dear Joe?" Joyce asked. "You know, you really need to set a date. You're not getting any younger."

Mel smiled. She should have seen this coming. Joyce would never be at peace until Mel was married. Mel decided to make it easy for her mother for a change and accept the suggestion.

"I'll ask Joe what he thinks," Mel said.

"You will?"

"Yep."

"I . . . well . . . that's . . ."

"You okay, Mom?" Mel asked.

"Yes, it's just that you never listen to me," Joyce said. She gave Mel a look as if she was afraid Mel had contracted some rare tropical virus. "Are you feeling all right? You're not pregnant, are you?"

"Mom!" Mel wailed.

"Pregnant people act weird," Joyce said. "It's a fact."

Mel noticed heads were turning in their direction with wide eyes. Oh, man, if this crazy idea of her mother's got loose there'd be no corralling it.

"I am not pregnant," Mel said. She had to

say it loud enough so that Angie's cousins, who were clearly eavesdropping, could hear her.

"If you say so, honey." Joyce grinned at her as if she were in on a secret.

Mel slapped her forehead with her hand. "I need a drink."

"You really shouldn't in your condition," Joyce said.

"Oh. My. God." Mel turned on her heel and walked away from her mother to find a punch bowl to dive into or a crack in the wall in which to disappear.

She slammed right into Uncle Stan, who was approaching with two drinks in hand. Mel reached out and took one and downed it in one large swallow.

It was a Manhattan. It burnt like jet fuel. Her eyes watered. She sputtered and coughed.

"Mel!" Uncle Stan frowned. "That was for your mother."

"Yeah, well, she drove me to it," she said.

She gave him the empty glass and pushed past him and maneuvered her way over to Oz and Marty. They were chatting it up with a bunch of single cousins and an aunt who had flown in from New York for the festivities.

"What are you two doing?" Mel asked.

She threw an arm around each of their shoulders and hugged them hard. "Have I ever told you guys how much I love you?"

Marty swiveled his head in her direction and wrinkled his nose. "You smell like a cheap date; have you been drinking?"

"Not enough," Mel said.

Oz looked at her and shook his head as if he was seeing a side of her he could have lived without.

"It was one drink; relax, you judgmental jennies," Mel said. "Hey, do you think they're going to have karaoke? I could really bust out a ballad about now."

"What was in that one drink? Gasoline?" Marty looped his arm around Mel's back and gestured to Oz. "Come on, someone needs to carb up on some appetizers before she embarrasses herself."

With Oz and Marty trotting her after a waiter with a tray of crab puffs, Mel noted that the room was pretty full and dinner would likely start soon. Thank goodness, she was starving.

When Marty tapped the waiter's shoulder, he turned and held out the tray to them. Oz took the whole tray and when the waiter took a good look at the hulking man-boy with the lip rings and the bangs that covered his eyes, he clasped his hands together and backed away.

The three of them took the tray to the corner, where Marty handed Mel a napkin and said, "Eat."

Mel did not need to be told twice. After stuffing three of the delicate pastries into her face hole, Mel felt a bit better. Clearly the drink had been ill advised, but truly only her mother could drive her to drink that fast.

"So, how come you two are without the plus-ones?" she asked. She looked at Marty. "I thought you'd make up with Olivia in time to bring her to the wedding." He shrugged. She turned to Oz and asked, "And what about Lupe? Is she coming tomorrow?"

"She couldn't make it," he said. "She said to say 'hey.' "

"Oh." Mel frowned. The quick shot of alcohol was rapidly leaving her system as she sensed Oz's hurt. "Are you o—"

"Now, Oz and I have been thinking about Tate and Angie's wedding gift," Marty said.

Mel looked at him. He was standing just behind Oz and he was jerking his head towards Oz and bugging his eyes out, meaning something was wrong and Mel should tread carefully. She blinked twice to let him know she got it.

"I really think Oz making their wedding cupcakes is gift enough," Mel said. "Did you finish them?"

"This afternoon," Oz said. He looked like he'd wilt with relief. "All I have to do is get them set up tomorrow and we're good."

"I bet they're amazing," Mel said.

Oz's face blushed a little beneath the bangs, and Mel knew he was pleased. She couldn't resist, so she raised her hand and moved aside his hair so she could look him in the eye.

"I'm really proud of you, you know that, right?" she asked.

This time Oz turned bright red and he didn't have his hair to hide behind. To her surprise, instead of pulling away he tossed his head, moving his bangs to the side, and he grinned at her.

"Well, I did learn from the best," he said. He opened his arms wide and Mel hugged him.

"You know, us non-culinary types help out in the bakery, too," Marty said.

Mel and Oz looked at him and then opened their arms, pulling him in. Mel felt her heart swell.

"Group hug!" Angie's voice sounded from behind them and she and Tate appeared and muscled their way into the circle.

The five of them looped their arms about one another and Mel took a second to look at each of her people. They had been together through so much over the past two-plus years. She couldn't imagine her life without them, but tomorrow, two of them were going to get married and everything would change.

She was filled with a crazy sense of panic about the future and what that would be like. Would they all still get along, or would Angie and Tate start a family and no longer be a part of the day-to-day running of the bakery? Maybe they would decide they wanted their own franchise and they'd move to California or Maine? Mel felt her heart clutch. She wanted to be happy for them but inside she was freaking out. Completely freaking out.

Sixteen

She forced herself to breathe and remember this moment in time just like Tate's mother had told Angie to do. She didn't want to blink and have it all just fall away.

"Have I told you guys lately how much I love you?" Angie asked.

Marty, Oz, and Mel burst out laughing and Oz said, "Quick, get her a crab puff."

"No, I'm serious," Angie said. "I love you guys, all of you, and I just feel really, really lucky to have you in my life."

She ended with a sob, and tears coursed down her cheeks. Tate broke the group hug to gently wipe them off her face with his thumbs.

"You okay, honey?" he asked.

"It's just that everything's going to change," Angie said.

"Yes, it will, but I hope it'll be a good change," Tate said.

" 'Friendship isn't about being inseparable, but about being separated and knowing nothing will change,' " Oz said.

Mel and Angie looked at him. Angie's tears dried up as she tried to identify the movie quote. She looked at Mel and shrugged.

"*Ted,*" Tate identified the movie quote, and he and Oz shared some complicated handshake thingy that looked like they were trying to arm wrestle or fly; Mel wasn't sure.

"Dude movie. Whatever," Angie said. She laughed and the sad moment passed. She looped her arm through Mel's and said, "Let's go sit so they'll start serving, or else I'm likely to wrestle a waiter to the ground and swipe all their food."

And just like that everything was back to normal and Mel knew it was going to be okay. Joe slid into the seat next to Mel's and laced her fingers with his. Maybe they didn't see eye to eye on the handling of Cassie's situation, but Joe would never abandon her over it. It made her love him all the more.

"How you doing, cupcake?" he asked.

She squeezed his hand in return. "Never better."

"Don't worry about Cassie," he said. "We'll figure it out. I promise."

"Have I told you lately how much I love

you?" she asked him.

Joe narrowed his eyes. "Have you been drinking?"

"Yes, but I ate my body weight in crab puffs, so it's all good," she said.

She leaned her head upon his shoulder, taking a moment to appreciate him, his warmth, his strength, his humor, and his steadfastness. She promised herself she would never take him for granted. Then she glanced up to find him looking at her with an affection that was so thick she was pretty sure she could have wrapped it around her shoulders like a blanket.

"I love you, too," he said.

The tension that had been between them eased. No, the problem hadn't gone away and likely there would be more discussions, but their foundation was strong and they could handle it. Just like they could handle whatever life threw at them — together.

At that moment, Joe's aunt Rosalind walked by their table. She wrapped an arm around each of them, suffocating them in her floral perfume, and kissed both of their cheeks.

"Such beautiful babies you will have," she said. She clapped her hands together and then started to cry happy tears as she walked away after patting both of their cheeks.

Joe lifted one eyebrow and looked at Mel. "Is there something you care to share?"

"Yeah, about that . . ." she began. Then she couldn't help herself — she started to laugh. She couldn't explain it. It was just too ridiculous. She leaned forward and kissed him quick. "Not right now, but someday?"

"All right," he agreed.

Mel put her head back on his shoulder. She felt her lips curve up. Rosalind was right. They would have beautiful babies, especially if they looked like Joe. Her heart swelled with joy at the thought.

"Angie, come on! We're late!" Mel cried.

When Mel arrived at Angie's parents' house to pick her up and take her to the salon, Angie appeared at the front door still in her pajamas, looking as if she'd just woken up.

"What do you mean we're late?" Angie asked. "I just checked the time. It's only ten o'clock."

"Try looking again," Mel said. "It's ten of twelve and if we're late Mean Christine is going to refuse to do your hair and makeup."

Angie gaped at her and then at the clock

and back at her. The time thing was not computing.

Feeling compelled to use a scare tactic, Mel yelled, "Hurry up!"

"Oh my god, I overslept," Angie cried. Her brothers were scattered all over the house, sleeping on couches and floors. "Why didn't anyone wake me?"

"Because they're men," Mel said. "They're going to take three-minute showers, two-minute shaves, shrug on their tuxedos, and be ready to go. Meanwhile, we have hours of prep to begin. Let's go."

Angie blinked at her in confusion.

"Oh, for goodness' sake," Mel said. She stormed into Mrs. DeLaura's kitchen and mercifully found the coffeepot on. She poured Angie a big mug and loaded it with milk and sugar. She hurried back to the front room and thrust the cup at Angie.

"Okay, now let's go," she said.

"But —" Angie looked down at her outfit.

"No time," Mel said.

"Where are the other bridesmaids?" Angie said.

"Already at the salon," Mel said. "Good thing, too. They're stalling Mean Christine until you get there."

"Ow, Angie, watch where you're stepping," Al complained as he rolled over.

"Bride coming through," Mel said. "Move it, move it, move it."

She shuffled her feet like she was kicking up leaves instead of DeLaura brothers, dragging Angie behind her as she made her way to the door.

"How did you know I was still here?" Angie asked.

"I went to the salon first. You know, where we agreed last night we'd meet up," Mel said. "But you weren't there and all of the bridesmaids were and we realized we'd left you at the mercy of the brothers. What were we thinking?"

Angie cupped the mug in her hands. She looked at Mel with enormous eyes. Her hair was a tangled mess and she still had creases from her pillowcase on her cheek. She was wearing a baggy T-shirt over cotton pajama bottoms. By the front door she slipped on a pair of flip-flops, grabbing her purse as they hurried down the walkway.

Halfway to Mel's car, Mr. and Mrs. DeLaura came into view. They were in matching jogging suits and Mel knew they were doing their daily ten thousand steps.

"Angie!" Mrs. DeLaura cried. "What are you doing here? You should have left for the salon by now."

"On my way," Angie said.

She paused to look at her parents in the midday sun. They were the picture of a couple who'd had good times and bad, but had never, ever given up on each other or the family they'd created. She turned to Mel and handed her the mug of coffee and her purse.

"Hey, Mom, Dad, in case I forget to mention it in all the insanity later, I just want to say thanks," Angie said. Her voice wobbled a bit, as if unsteady under all of the emotion it was carrying. "You really are the best parents a girl could ever ask for and I'm so glad you're mine."

Mel felt her throat get tight, so she took a sip of Angie's coffee to try and ease it. She watched as both of the DeLauras hugged and kissed their only daughter with tears of joy in their eyes. Mel felt her own eyes get hot, and she knew that she'd better drink more than the daily recommended sixty-four ounces of fluid because the flood waters in her tear ducts were rising.

"Go. We'll see you back at the house when you're ready to get dressed," Mrs. DeLaura said.

She made a shooing motion with her hands and Angie hurried back to Mel. She scrubbed her face with her hands and sighed as she took back her coffee.

"I hope Christine has a line of all waterproof makeup," she said. "Something is telling me I'm going to need it."

Mel laughed and opened the passenger door for her. Angie slid in and Mel circled the car to get in the driver's seat. She glanced at her phone on the way. She could get them there pretty close to on time, and if they were late she'd just have to bargain with Christine the old-fashioned way.

Christine's salon was nestled in the heart of Old Town. Mel scored a parking spot down the street under a shady tree, and she and Angie hurried towards the stylist's lair.

Mel pulled open the glass door, and Angie ducked inside. The woman at the counter glanced up at Angie and then frowned. It was an intimidating frown given that her hair was wound into a huge brunette bun on the top of her head, her eyebrows had been threaded into severe arcs, her false eyelashes were so long they kicked up a small breeze when she blinked, and her lips were pursed in a deep plum color that matched the wraparound dress she wore. She was intimidation personified.

The other two women working the counter beside her, a blonde and a redhead, looked exactly the same with the big bun, eyelashes, lip color, and same colored wrap dress.

Christine liked uniformity in her staff. It certainly made a statement with three of them staring at Mel and Angie in disapproval.

"You're late," the brunette said.

"Sorry, bridal jitters," Angie said with small smile.

"Christine makes no exceptions," the redhead said.

"Not even if you're spitting up blood and possessed by the devil himself," the blonde added.

Mel and Angie exchanged a look.

"She's gotten even more hard-core," Angie said.

"No worries," Mel said. "I'll talk to her."

"No, you won't," Christine said.

Mel glanced up as Christine glided down the short staircase behind the desk that led into the salon area. Christine was tall and thin and her thick black hair was styled in the same bun as her staff. She also wore the same plum-colored lipstick and long eyelashes, only her wrap dress was different. Christine was in a hot shade of red. Just like a bride stood out from her bridesmaids, Christine was apart from her staff.

"There is nothing to talk about," Christine said. She looked Mel and Angie over in her usual ice queen way. "You're late. I do not work with clients who are late."

"I know," Mel said. "And we are so very sorry. Listen, it's my fault. Angie was depending upon me for a ride and I was late. Can you at least take care of her while I go sit in the corner of shame? It's her wedding day."

"No, that's not true," Angie said. "I overslept. It's my fault."

Christine's impossibly arched brows rose even higher, and she looked at Mel. "You lied to me?"

Mel swallowed. There weren't many people who scared the snot out of her, but Christine was one of them.

Christine moved across the floor. It couldn't really be described as walking since she moved with an eerie grace that made it seem as if she were floating.

She stopped in front of Mel. Being on the tall side, Mel was unaccustomed to looking up at people. Christine, also tall, was wearing the same shoes as her staff, stiletto pumps that added five inches to her already impressive height. Mel craned her neck to look up at her.

"Fibbed, maybe," Mel said.

Christine was so close Mel could see the individual hairs of her eyebrows, the tiny pores on the end of her nose, and the teeny tiny crack of a wrinkle on her upper lip. She felt a bead of sweat trickle down the side of her face. If Christine tossed them to the curb, she had no idea where she was going to take Angie to have her hair and makeup done. Panic began to thrum inside of her like the beat of a drum.

To her surprise, Christine tipped her head back and laughed. Mel blew out a breath. She was laughing. That had to be good, right?

She and Angie exchanged a panicked look. Mel would have relaxed except Christine's staff looked equally nervous at her laughter.

"Fibbed. You're funny, Melanie Cooper," Christine said. "Good thing I have an excellent sense of humor."

Yeah, that was the first thing a person thought of with Christine. Not.

"Come on back," Christine said. "Your wedding party is already here." She frowned at Mel. "But you owe me two dozen forgiveness cupcakes."

"Done." Mel sagged a little in relief.

"Angie!" Kaylee, her niece, called out to her and waved from the pedicure station. "Good thing you're here. Mom started to freak out."

Kaylee gestured to her mother, Angie's sister-in-law, who was under an industrial

262

hairdryer. Angie waved to her and the other bridesmaids, who were in various stages of maintenance, as Christine led them to the changing rooms in back.

"There are robes for you to change into," Christine said. She gestured towards the little closets built into the wall. "Then we'll start by managing those lashes and brows."

"What does she mean 'manage'?" Angie whispered to Mel. "I didn't realize they were having a rebellion."

Mel smiled. "You're fine. You know how Christine is. When she's done, your hair won't have any fight left in it."

"Which is why I love her," Angie said. "I'm just worried the same will be said of me."

They changed and found Christine and the redheaded assistant waiting for them. Mel and Angie sat in the two reclining chairs and Mel had the feeling she always got when she put herself in a beautician's hands: The result was out of her hands and all she could do was hope for the best.

While Samantha, the redhead, stripped the stray hairs from her face, Mel scarcely breathed. She was afraid a brow might go missing if she made any false moves. Then it was time to glue on the false eyelashes, and Mel tried really hard not to blink or pull them off. She didn't think beauty should be this much work.

Once their eyes were done, Mel and Angie moved to the hair portion. Mel's short hair required very little work. It was puffed up and shellacked into place. The one whimsical touch Samantha added was fastening tiny sparkly flower-shaped hair clips randomly on Mel's head, making it look as if the flowers had just drifted down on the breeze to nestle into her hair.

While Samantha began to work on Mel's makeup, Christine was taming Angie's thick dark hair with an intricate series of loose braids across the top of her head that trailed into waves of thick bouncy curls that ended halfway down her back. Angie had opted not to wear a veil and instead had sparkly flowers like Mel's woven into her braids.

While Christine had a mouthful of hairpins, Mel figured it was as good a time as any to talk about Elise's murder and see if the hairdresser knew any of the players. Christine's was a favorite salon to many of the residents in the Palms. She might have heard a rumor or two worth knowing about.

"Angie, did you hear that the county prosecutor is planning to charge Cassie Leighton with Elise Penworthy's murder?" Mel asked.

Angie glanced at her and Mel knew she was thinking that of course she knew, because Mel had told her. Mel darted her eyes in Christine's direction and Angie gave a slight nod.

Christine spat out the hairpins. "What? That's ridiculous!"

"Really?" Mel played dumb. "What makes you say that?"

"Because everyone knows who killed Elise Penworthy," Christine said.

SEVENTEEN

"They do?" Mel asked.

Christine gave her a look that said she was not buying what Mel was selling. Mel made her eyes big, and not just because Samantha was coming at her with eyeliner.

"I thought it was her ex-husband," Samantha said.

"See? Me, too," Angie said. "It's always the spouse, and given what she wrote about him in the book, I'm betting Hair Plugs was full of rage, and stabbing her in the back with a pen had to be a fitting end in his mind."

"It's too obvious," Christine and Mel said together.

They looked at each other and Mel felt as if Christine was looking at her with heightened respect.

"It was pretty cold-blooded to stab her with her own pen," Mel said.

"Agreed," Christine said.

"But don't forget the other victims," Angie said. "Hair Plugs could be a stone-cold killer who was out for revenge on anyone who told Elise details about his life with the Child Bride. That's the only reason I can think that he'd kill her caterer, driver, and photographer."

"*If* it was him," Mel said. "Whoever it was, they must have believed that those people gave Elise material for her book." She glanced at Christine, who had fished more hairpins out of the container on the counter. "Did you ever talk to Elise about the residents of the Palms?"

"God, no," Christine said. "If word got around that I was talking about clients, I'd lose my business. People confide in their stylists — it's a sacred trust."

Mel and Angie exchanged a glance in the mirror and then Angie asked, "Did Elise ever confide anything of interest to you? I only ask because she is deceased now, which would make your vow of silence obsolete and you could tell us who everyone thinks the murderer is."

Christine blew out her lower lip, sending her precisely cut bangs up into the air. She met Angie's gaze and then glanced at Mel. She shook her head as if she didn't know what to do with them.

"Aren't you getting married today?" she asked Angie. "Shouldn't you be consumed with that?"

"Nah." Angie waved a hand under the big apron Christine had thrown over her. "If I think about the wedding, I get throw-uppy. I mean, what if I say the wrong name, or catch on fire during the lighting of the unity candle, or trip coming down the aisle?" She shifted the apron and held up her hands, which were shaking. "Murder is much more soothing to my nerves."

"You two are so weird," Samantha said.

Christine gave her a look and Mel suspected Samantha was about to get chastised. She was wrong.

"They are weird, aren't they?" Christine asked.

When Mel and Angie both looked at her, she laughed. "What? It's true."

Mel shrugged. She couldn't really argue it.

"Look up," Samantha ordered.

Mel did and Samantha worked on her makeup with a gentle touch.

"Okay, close your eyes," Samantha said.

Not being much of a makeup girl, it was weird to feel all of this stuff on her face. Even though Samantha was keeping it light, Mel felt as if her skin was unhappy. She decided to think of something else.

"So, did Elise tell you anything of interest?" she persisted.

With her eyes shut, she couldn't see Christine, but she heard her huff out a sigh.

"Even if she did, she wrote the book ages ago," Christine said. "It's not like I can remember. Besides, anyone too close to Elise even in a professional way appears to wind up dead."

"Aw, come on," Angie said. "Consider it a wedding present to me."

"I thought doing a spectacular job with your hair was the present," Christine said.

"No, because you would do a spectacular job even if you hated me," Angie said. "It's just the kind of hair sorceress you are."

"Sorceress, huh?"

If she could see her, Mel would have high-fived Angie so hard. Praise was always an excellent way to get to Christine.

"Let me think about it," Christine mumbled. She sounded as if her mouth was full of pins.

"Okay, lips next," Samantha said to Mel.

She opened her eyes and glanced over at Angie. Her hair looked amazing. Christine was anchoring the fat braids down with pins and her delicate hands were moving swiftly through Angie's hair, tucking and pinning in a pattern that was feminine and flattering.

"Open your mouth wide," Samantha instructed. Mel did, feeling a bit like a baby bird while Samantha slathered color on her.

"Frankly, Elise liked to talk — or more accurately, complain — so I tuned her out quite a bit," Christine said.

She took the last pin out of her mouth and tucked it into the braid. She then took up the hair curler and began refining the thick curls that cascaded down Angie's back.

"There was this one time that she came in for highlights," Christine said. "She was fuming, talking about Hair Plugs and the Child Bride and how she was going to ruin them with her book. This was right after it became common knowledge that she'd sold the book to Leighton Press."

Mel moved forward and Samantha sighed as the lipstick went sideways.

"Sorry," she said, and leaned back. Samantha bent closer to repair the damage and Mel sat frozen.

"So there's motivation for Hair Plugs," Angie said. "She was intent on ruining him."

"Yes, but on that day, she also went off about this person who was stalking her," Christine said.

"Who was it?" Mel asked.

Christine frowned and her arching brows drew together in their own punctuation mark of concentration. "I can't remember if she named them."

"Anything she said may be of help," Mel said. "Was it someone she was dating, or maybe a friend?"

"Like her friend Shanna, who was married to some guy named Carl, who stroked out over the contents of Elise's book because it outed his wife's affair?" Angie asked.

"Exactly," Mel said. "Maybe Shanna wasn't as happy as she pretended to be at the signing."

"Shanna Mathews?" Christine asked. "No, she's happy, believe me — to the tune of three-billion-dollars happy."

"It's not fair," Samantha said. "How does a woman like that — she's not even nice — bag a shriveled-up old billionaire?"

Samantha moved over to Angie to start on her makeup while Christine finished her hair.

"Do you want a rich old prune?" Christine asked her.

"No," Samantha admitted. "But I wouldn't mind one in younger packaging."

"Those are rare, like Yeti," Mel said. "It takes their entire life to make their fortune.

That's why they marry women a quarter of their age when they finally make it."

"Maybe you could downsize to a nice millionaire," Angie suggested.

She looked up while Samantha did her eyes. Then down. Mel watched the transformation, thinking her already-beautiful friend was going to be stunning. Tate would lose it when he saw her. The thought made Mel smile.

"At this point, I'd be happy if I met a guy who was employed," Samantha said.

Christine fluffed Angie's big curls. They were holding well, but she hit them with a mist of fixative spray.

"Angie! Oh, you look beautiful!" Kaylee popped her head around the corner of the doorway. "Mom says we're leaving and we'll meet you back at the house to get dressed."

"Okay, see you in a few," Angie said. A look of raw nerves flashed across her face, and Mel knew from Angie's trembling lips that she was about to panic.

Oblivious, Samantha started in on Angie's lip color. She'd chosen a deep red that complemented Angie's skin tone and made her teeth sparkle when she smiled.

Angie was the whole package: beautiful, funny, smart, kind. And she'd found the same thing in Tate. They were two of the lucky ones.

Mel wondered what sort of person Elise had gotten involved with if they were stalking her. And why were they stalking her? Love? Friendship? Fame? A cut of the book profit?

"You look very serious all of a sudden," Angie said. "What are you thinking?"

"A stalker is usually someone who wants a relationship with a person who doesn't want one with them, right?" Mel asked.

"Yes, it's like unrequited love gone really, really bad," Christine said.

"What if the murderer isn't someone who's angry with Elise and her book, but rather this stalker who wanted a piece of Elise's newfound fame and fortune?" Mel asked.

"That's a big what-if," Samantha said. "But it might explain why they killed anyone they perceived being closer to Elise and her book than they were, like the driver, the caterer, and the photographer. So, perhaps the stalker was someone who wanted a closer professional relationship with Elise."

"Which disproves my theory on who killed Elise Penworthy," Christine said.

"Finally going to share, are you?" Mel asked. She leaned forward in her seat, crowding Angie and the others, getting her a frown from Samantha.

"Yes, but it's what everyone is saying," Christine said. "I was sure the killer was Mallory Cavendish."

"No, she has an alibi," Mel said. She was so disappointed. She'd been hoping for so much more from Christine.

"What?" Christine cried. "What alibi?"

Mel hesitated, then figured she had nothing to lose if she didn't name names. "She was with her 'tennis pro.' " She used air quotes so that everyone understood the relationship.

"Well, shoot, then it has to be Cassie Leighton," Christine said.

"No, I refuse to believe that," Mel argued.

"Ask yourself this: Who had the most to gain by Elise's death?" Christine asked. "As the publisher of her book and her lone heir, it has to be Cassie."

"How do you know she's her lone heir?" Mel asked.

"Everyone knows that," Samantha said. "Elise didn't keep it a secret."

"I hate to say it," Angie said. She gave Mel an uncomfortable look. "But I think Christine may have a point."

"Of course I do. And I think you need to get out of my salon and go get married," Christine said. She put her hands on Angie's shoulders and leaned down so that she could meet Angie's gaze in the mirror. "You're ready, Angie."

"I am so not ready," Angie said as they arrived back at her parents' house to find it full to bursting with DeLauras.

Joe was there, and he grinned when he caught sight of Mel. "You look amazing, but then, you always do."

"Thanks," she said. "Is it wrong that I'm counting the minutes until I can wash my face?"

He grinned. Then he very carefully kissed her, being sure not to smudge her lipstick.

"I'm off to Tate's to make sure he doesn't pull a runner," he said.

Mel laughed. "As if he would. Hey, have you been in touch with Uncle Stan today?"

"No." Joe tipped his head to the side as he studied her with a concerned look. "Any reason I should be?"

"Nope. Just wondering about the case."

"Cupcake, our best friends are getting married," he said. He put his hands on her shoulders and leaned in so that they were almost forehead to forehead. "Maybe we could shelve the murder and mayhem for a day."

Mel shook her head as if trying to dislodge

the thoughts that were bubbling up in there. "You're right. You're totally right. It's just that we were all talking at the salon and Angie said the murder talk helped her to not think about the wedding, which made her nervous."

"You two are so weird," he said.

"So we've been told."

"Tell me, on the day we get married, are you going to be thinking about murder?"

Mel laughed. She looped her arms around his neck and hugged him hard. "Only if someone actually stands up when they ask if anyone knows of a reason why these two cannot be joined. Then, oh yeah, I won't be thinking it, I'll be doing it."

Joe grinned. "And I'd help you."

He hugged her tight and planted a solid kiss on her. Mel wiped the lipstick off of his mouth with her thumb.

"See you at the church, cupcake," he said.

"I'll be there," Mel said. She stood in the door and waved until he drove away. She was going to marry that boy.

"Mel!" Angie cried her name from the second floor and Mel turned and raced to the stairs. It was showtime.

EIGHTEEN

Getting dressed while not mussing her hair and makeup proved more of a challenge than Mel was prepared for. How she wished for the simplicity of her chef's hat and coat right about now.

Angie's colors from the start had been aqua and pewter. Her bridesmaids wore varying shades of pewter in all different styles, so there were one-shouldered dresses with elaborate beading, strapless dresses with a flared skirt, and dresses with a sweetheart neckline with cap sleeves and beading along the hem. All together, they looked stunning.

As maid of honor, Mel was the lone aqua-colored dress in the bunch. To Mel, it looked like a light shade of blue, but Kim, the dressmaker, had insisted it was in fact aqua, and Mel knew that Kim had a bride-shaped pincushion in her office that looked remarkably like a voodoo doll, so she didn't argue.

The dress was beautiful whether it was called aqua or blue or green. The bodice was snug and the skirt flared. Aqua- and pewter-colored beads were embroidered along the short cap sleeves and the hem, making Mel feel very feminine, especially since she lived in jeans and T-shirts most of the time.

All of the bridesmaids wore matching low-heeled pewter-colored sandals, and as they gathered one by one in the DeLauras' master bedroom, where Angie was getting dressed, Mel felt her tension ratchet up. This was it. After today, everything changed between her and Tate and Angie. When her friends had started dating, she had been worried that things would change. They had, but only a little. Now, she suspected, big changes were coming.

Tate and Angie would be an officially recognized legal twosome. They would have kids and build a new world in which Mel was only a visitor. That was okay. She and Joe would likely do the same and she was excited about that. Still, she wanted a moment with her longtime friend just to tell her how much she loved her, how much she appreciated Angie always having her back, and that Mel would always be there for her. No matter what.

She tightened the strap on her shoes and crossed the bedroom to do just that.

"Angie, you're going to have a wardrobe malfunction if you're not careful," her sister-in-law Suzie said. "Every time you bend over, you're flashing boobage."

"What?" Angie cried. "How is that possible? That never happened in the fitting room."

"Did you bend over in the fitting room?" Suzie asked.

"No."

"Well, there you go."

"Oh, no!" Angie wailed.

Which was when Mel realized that this was not going to be their shared moment. Instead, she went into crisis-prevention mode.

"Up, up," she said. She gestured with her hands for Angie to stand.

"Oh my god, Mel," Angie cried. She grabbed her hand and said, "I don't know what happened, but my dress is showing more of me than I'm comfortable with. I'm going to end up flashing someone and it will get filmed, and I'll end up going viral like that unfortunate hat shop girl from London that we met on vacation who threw cake at her lying married boyfriend."

"No, you're not," Mel said. "Relax."

She opened her purse and pulled out a roll of double-sided sticky tape. She always carried this tape with her because it came in handy at different venues. It worked like magic to keep her cupcake displays from toppling over.

"We're going to tape your dress in place," Mel said.

Angie clutched her front. "Is that a good idea?"

"Do you have a better one?"

"No."

"Okay, then, trust me." Mel set to work taping the bodice down. The rest of the women and girls fluttered around the room, doing their last-minute preparations.

Mel figured now was as good a time as any to have a quick chat.

"Ange —" That was as far as she got.

"Oh, Angie." Maria DeLaura entered the room in cloud of lavender silk. She clasped her hands over her chest and immediately started to water up. "You are beautiful."

Mel finished fitting the last piece of tape and backed up. It was mother-daughter time. She could wait. Suzie ushered everyone out of the room, including Mel.

The bridesmaids all hurried downstairs to

fortify themselves with food and the last of the coffee. Mel always had time for a snack. She was taking a bite of her chocolate crois-sant very carefully over the sink when a man spoke from behind her.

"Well, who knew Melanie Cooper could clean up to be such a beauty?" Ray DeLaura asked.

"I did," Joe said. He entered the room, looking impossibly handsome in his tuxedo. Then he pursed his lips and gave Mel a wolf whistle while he looked her over from head to toe.

"Some guys have all the luck," Ray said. He winked at Mel and moved past her to attack the plate of pastries on the counter.

"Yes, I do," Joe said. Mel dropped her croissant and he pulled her into a careful hug. "You look gorgeous."

This. This right here was a moment that, had Mel known about it during her unfortu-nate adolescence, would have pulled her through a million dark days of bad diets, binge eating, acne, braces, and assorted other teenage horrors.

"Thank you," she said. She was pleased that she did not sound as breathless as she felt. Even after all this time, Joe could still make her dizzy.

"How's the bride holding up?"

"Small wardrobe malfunction, but we sticky-taped our way through it."

"If that's the worst thing that happens today, we can call it a win."

"How is Tate holding up?"

"Great. I don't think I've ever seen anyone smile wider. He is so ready to make Angie his bride."

Mel smiled. She could only imagine. "He wasn't singing, was he?"

"All morning long," Joe said. "Then he got panicky and sent me here to do bride recon for him. I told him I'd make sure everything was a go and then I'd take him to the church. Right now he is in the very capable hands of Marty and Oz."

"Oz?" Mel asked. "What about the cupcakes?"

"We delivered them to the reception hall early this morning," Joe said. "No worries. We've got this."

Mel forced herself to relax. A smidgen. Truly, she didn't think she'd be able to relax until the wedding was over and they were two or three drinks into the reception, but still she tried.

"All right, people," Ray called out from where he hovered over the pastries. "We have thirty minutes until showtime. Thirty minutes. If you have to use the bathroom, do it now. The limo will be leaving for the church in thirty minutes."

"That's my cue to go get the groom," Joe said. He very carefully kissed Mel's cheek. "Give Angie my love, okay?"

"I promise," Mel said. Although when she'd have a chance to tell Angie about Joe's feelings, when she hadn't even had a chance to tell her her own feelings, Mel had no idea.

It was rush, rush, rush to the limo, which was packed with bridesmaids. Mel sat next to Angie on the bench seat in the back while the rest of the ladies filled the side seats. The younger ones, who'd never been in a limousine before, giggled and chattered. Angie smiled at her family, but she had a faraway look on her face, as if she was thinking about something else.

"You okay?" Mel asked.

Angie turned to her and nodded. "I am. I feel as if I've planned everything I can for this day and now it just has to roll out however it does."

"That's very Zen of you," Mel said.

"I watched *Father of the Bride* last night with my dad," Angie said.

"Steve Martin version?"

"Of course," Angie said. "He cried — my dad."

"Aw," Mel said. She could see Mr. De-

Laura watering up. "Was it at the part where the father realizes he's been dreading this moment since the day she was born?"

"Yeah," Angie said. "It made me realize that Tate and I will be doing the same thing, you know, someday."

"Circle of life," Mel said.

"Promise me —" Angie began, but was drowned out by the stereo kicking in. Her niece Kaylee had found the music, which she cranked.

"What?" Mel yelled at Angie. She saw her lips move, but she couldn't understand a word she said.

"What?" Angie yelled in return.

They frowned at each other and then at Kaylee, who was dancing in her seat. Oblivious to their ire, Kaylee kept grooving, getting the other young bridesmaids to join in. Finally, Suzie reached across the limo and slapped the music off.

"Honestly," she said. "We're on our way to church. Settle down."

"You are no fun." Kaylee pouted.

Suzie pressed a finger to her right eyelid as if to stop it from twitching. "I can live with that."

"Oh, we're here," one of the bridesmaids cried.

They all turned to look out the window.

There it was with its doors wide open, the DeLaura family church where Angie and Tate would get married. A sudden bout of nerves hit Mel. This was it. They were down to mere minutes. She wanted to talk to Angie. She needed just a minute, but there wasn't a second to be had.

Again, it was hurry, hurry, hurry into the church, where all of their family and friends were gathered. Mel could hear the noise of the crowd right before all of the bridesmaids and Angie were hustled into a small room at the front of the church.

Angie's cousin Judi was there. She looked lovely in a floral dress that had just the right shade of blue in it. She calmly took Angie's hands and talked her through what would be happening next. A woman from the church joined them as well.

Once they left, Father Francis arrived with Angie's dad. He was a jovial priest who'd been close to the DeLaura family for years. Mel watched as he said a blessing over Angie and then told her he'd see her at the altar. Angie nodded and gave him a happy, nervous smile.

As Father Francis walked by Mel, he leaned close and said, "I expect I'll be seeing you, Melanie Cooper, for some pre-marriage counseling."

"Uh . . . I . . . um," Mel stammered.

Father Francis winked at her. "Don't be nervous. You picked a fine man in Joe De-Laura."

"Thank you, Father," Mel said.

He left and the door closed behind him. Mel stood staring at it. She hadn't really thought about it before, but this was the DeLaura family church. Of course they would be married here. She glanced down at her ring. Was she ready for that? A small smile curved her lips. Yes, yes, she was.

"Okay, it's time," Judi announced from the door. "The music is about to start. The ushers are bringing in the moms. Everyone line up."

Mel pulled herself away from her thoughts and took her place in line. Judi handed each of them their bouquets, which had been dropped off at the church by Annabelle, the florist, earlier that day.

Mel glanced over her shoulder to see Angie take her father's arm. Mr. DeLaura looked like he would burst with pride. Mel didn't want to take his moment, so she flashed Angie the hand sign that meant *I love you* and when Angie flashed it back they shared a smile and Mel took her place in line. This was it.

The moment had arrived when Angie would become Mrs. Tate Harper.

NINETEEN

The service was perfect. Angie didn't light herself on fire, trip over her gown, or say the wrong name. She did cry, however. When it came time to say her vows, she blinked and bit her lip, and in a voice that quavered with emotion, she promised to love and cherish Tate all the days of her life.

The tenderness with which Tate gazed upon his bride made Mel's resolve not to cry melt into tears that streamed down her face. Tate wiped away Angie's tears with his thumbs and looked at her as if he could not believe that this amazing woman had just vowed to be his wife.

When he slid the ring onto her finger, and said, "With this ring, I thee wed," his voice was gruff and his eyes watery. It was Angie's turn to look upon the man she loved with all of the love in her heart. Mel glanced over her shoulder at the packed church. There was not a dry eye in the house.

When she looked back, she felt Joe's gaze upon her. His warm brown eyes made her heart pound triple-time. His expression told her he couldn't wait for it to be their turn. Mel smiled at him. She couldn't, either.

They turned back to the bride and groom just in time to hear Father Francis say, "You may kiss the bride."

Tate leaned in and kissed Angie as if no one else were there. When it went on a little longer than necessary, Tony and Al both took a step in the direction of the altar and Joe cleared his throat and gave Tate a solid nudge. Tate released Angie just in time.

"I now present Mr. and Mrs. Tate Harper," Father Francis said. The guests cheered wildly as happy music pealed out of the old church organ, and Tate grabbed Angie's hand and they ran up the aisle together. Joe held out his arm to Mel and she took it, and they followed in the newly married couple's wake.

The reception was held at the Italian-American Club, a place Angie's parents had been going to for years. Mel had wondered how the upscale Harpers would react to a non-country-club venue. Well, it turned out, given that Mr. Harper was a lover of all things Frank Sinatra and that the club catered to that suave vibe, he was in heaven.

Mel saw him at the bar with Mr. DeLaura. He had his arm around him and they were crooning together as if they'd just achieved world peace, and they couldn't look happier or more relieved.

Mrs. DeLaura and Mrs. Harper were standing off to the side, shaking their heads at their men, although Mel could tell they were secretly pleased.

Mel scouted the room for Angie and found her standing amid a cluster of female relatives, showing off her platinum, diamond-encrusted wedding band and glowing like the perfect happy bride.

While Angie stood with the girls, Mel noted that Tate was surrounded by his new brothers-in-law. There was clearly some heavy male bonding going on as they all drank a toast to brotherhood and downed a shot. Al got so into it, he tried to chest bump Tate, who wasn't looking and was nearly knocked unconscious.

But there was Joe, catching Tate before he rammed his head into the wall and putting him back on his feet. The brothers were all laughing and so was Tate. Mel remembered the first time she'd met Tate in middle school. He'd been socially awkward like her, and had no friends, but when he found out she liked old movies, he busted out a horrible Groucho Marx impression that had landed her in detention for her uncontrollable laughter. They'd been fast friends from that moment on, easily folding Angie into their tiny group when she arrived as the new kid.

As Mel studied him now, she realized that he no longer wore the look of a lonely boy who wasn't sure where he fit in. Being embraced into the DeLaura family by Angie's brothers had erased that lonely little kid forever. Mel couldn't be happier for him.

She scanned the room, searching for the rest of her people. Her mother was dancing with Uncle Stan. She made a mental note to ask her uncle if Joyce had told him who she was seeing. Given Joyce's history, Mel didn't think a background check would be out of order — if Uncle Stan hadn't done one yet.

Then she glanced over at Marty and Oz. If there were two more miserable looking men, she didn't know who they'd be. They resembled two tuxedo-wearing wallflowers that were drooping. It was as if they belonged to their own personal lonely hearts club. Without hesitation, Mel went where she was needed.

She strode across the dance floor towards

the corner, where Oz stood nursing a soda and Marty a soda with some kick. She forced herself to smile as she joined them.

"Hey, guys," she said. "What's the good word?"

"Open bar," Marty said.

Mel gave him a look and he took a swig of his beverage.

She maneuvered herself in between them and leaned against the wall as if surveying the crowd with them.

"Good party," she said.

"Yeah, it's great," Marty said. "Angie and Tate look really happy."

"Really happy," Oz repeated morosely.

Mel would have hugged him but she suspected that he didn't want her to draw attention to his pitiful state. "Come on, guys, look around you. There are loads of ladies just looking for a hot guy to ask them to dance."

"I don't dance," Oz said.

"Not even with me?" a voice asked from his other side.

Oz whipped his head in that direction, causing his bangs to shift to the side. Standing next to him was his girlfriend, Lupe, and she looked beautiful.

"Lupe, I thought you had to study for midterms," he said.

"I figured I could cram for it on the plane," she said.

Oz stood blinking at her, not moving, until Marty gave him a hard shove to the back.

"Don't just stand there, dummy. Kiss the girl before she thinks you're not happy to see her," he said.

Oz sent Marty a dark look, but then turned back to Lupe and opened his arms. She stepped into his embrace and the two of them drifted away into their own bubble of giddy couplehood.

"Well," Marty said. He stared into his drink.

"Marty, what's going on?" Mel asked. "You've been weird ever since Olivia threw you out."

Marty took a slow sip of his drink as if to avoid talking.

"Come on, you can tell me," Mel said.

"I don't want to talk about it," he said. Mel opened her mouth to argue but he held up his hand in a stop gesture. "I miss her, okay?"

Mel didn't have to ask who he meant. Although no one understood the crazy relationship between Marty and Olivia in which they seemed to bicker as much as they did anything else, there was no denying that while he'd been with her he'd had a spring in his step and a smile on his lips Mel hadn't seen before or since. Mel missed his smile.

"Is it over for sure?" she asked.

"I think so," he said. "I've stopped by, I've called, I've texted, I even tried to pull her back in by using our old dating handles in an e-mail. She's not speaking to me in any format."

"Is it because your daughters are having you followed and it's just too much drama?"

"No, I hurt her," he said. His shoulders hunched and he looked sheepish. "I didn't tell her I was well-off. I let her think I was just getting by on a pension."

"Why?" Mel asked.

"Because when my Jeanie died, it was common knowledge that I was rich and all of a sudden all of these women started chasing me. Some were out-and-out stalking me. But they didn't want me, they wanted my money. When I hooked up with Liv, I wanted her to want me for me."

"Clearly, she did," Mel said.

"Yeah." Marty downed his drink.

"And it never occurred to you after a while that you should let her know you were better off than you seemed?" Mel asked.

"I was going to," he said. "Really. I just didn't want things to get complicated, but

294

then my daughters showed up —"

"And Olivia found out," Mel said.

"I don't know how to get her to forgive me," he said. "And I miss her."

"Do you love her?" Mel asked.

Marty nodded. "Crazy, huh?"

Mel glanced around the room, looking at all of the couples surrounding them. Some, like Oz and Lupe, just fit so perfectly, but then there were others, like the tall woman with the shorter man, or the younger man with the older woman, or the quiet woman with the gregarious man, who didn't seem to suit one another at all, and yet while Mel watched them she saw these couples exchange looks of affection, fondness, and love.

"No, it's not crazy," Mel said. "Unexpected, sure, but isn't that the best part?"

Marty smiled at her. It was the first genuine smile she'd seen out of him in weeks. "Yes, it is," he agreed.

The band kicked in with a slow dance, and Mel glanced up to see Tate and Angie headed to the dance floor. At the first notes of Van Morrison's "Have I Told You Lately," Mel felt her eyes water up and her throat get tight. Tate pulled Angie into his arms and they moved around the floor staring into each other's eyes as if they were the only two people in the room.

"Here," Marty said. He handed Mel a fancy handkerchief from his tuxedo pocket. "You look like you've sprung a leak."

Mel laughed and dabbed at her eyes. Joe strolled over to where they stood and slipped his arm around Mel.

"You okay?" he asked.

"Yes, they're happy tears," she said. "It's all good."

Oz and Lupe drifted back to their group and Lupe hugged each of them in a warm hello embrace. Oz looked as besotted with his girl as ever and Mel hoped that with their lives pulling them in two different directions, it didn't end in a crushing heartbreak for Oz.

She laced her fingers with Joe's, wanting to be sure of him and his presence. She couldn't imagine what she'd feel if she lost him. It would be unbearable.

Tate ended his dance with Angie by bending her over his arm in a deep dip. The photographer hired to replace Blaise was happily snapping away. Mel knew the pictures would be great, but Blaise had known Tate and Angie so well, it just wasn't the same.

"Come on," Joe said. "Let's go show them how it's done."

Mel glanced quickly at Marty. She wasn't sure he was in a good state to be left alone. He lifted his drink and waved her away.

"Don't worry about me," he said. "Go."

"Save me a dance?" Mel asked him.

"Obvy," Marty said, using slang and sounding just like Oz. Mel smiled and let Joe lead her onto the dance floor.

It was a slow song, and Joe pulled her close with her hand in his and his hand on her back. Mel put her hand on his shoulder and followed his lead, feeling at ease for the first time all day. That was, until her mother and Uncle Stan came dancing by.

"Be careful in those shoes, Melanie," Joyce leaned close to whisper. "You don't want to turn an ankle or, you know, dislodge anything." Then she turned to Joe and added, "I love a nice Christmas wedding, don't you, dear Joe?"

"That might work," Joe said. He gave Mel a cautious look. Mel felt her face get warm. Joe frowned at her as Joyce was led away by Uncle Stan.

"That was weird. Explain," Joe said.

"Oh, where to begin," Mel said. She tipped her head back to look up at him and said, "My mom has gotten it into her crazy *cabeza* that we're pregnant."

TWENTY

"What?" Joe tripped and Mel had to catch him before he fell, taking her down with him.

"I know, it's crazy!" Mel said. "I don't know how she comes up with this stuff."

"Joyce is an original," he said. Then he looked at her. "So, last night my aunt Rosalind —"

"Probably heard my mother and assumed that we're expecting," Mel said.

"Was she upset by the idea?" he asked.

"No," Mel said. "More hopeful than anything else. You know you'll always be her 'dear Joe.' "

Joe grinned and spun Mel in a slow turn. He pulled her close and kissed her quick.

"That's fine with me. She's the mother of the woman I love; how could I not be grateful to her for raising you to be the amazing woman that you are?"

"Oh my god, if you say that to her, she'll

replace me with you in her will."

"So, you're sure we're not . . ." Joe said. His gaze drifted down to her belly and then back up to her face.

"No! Believe me, if and when that happens, you'll be the first to know," she said. She studied his handsome face. "Does the idea bother you?"

Joe gave her a small smile. "Nope. In fact, just thinking about it makes me feel as if it's right."

Mel nodded. She knew exactly what he meant. She could so easily see him holding a child or two or three of his own, and she wanted that with him. It was a good feeling.

"Uh-oh." Joe's attention was caught by something over her shoulder.

"Is my mother coming this way again?" she asked.

"No, I think this crazy train is for Marty," he said.

"What?" Mel whipped her head in the direction he was staring.

Sure enough, Olivia Puckett, Marty's ex-girlfriend and Mel's longtime baking rival had crashed the wedding. Mel looked for Angie. This could go a variety of ways, from Angie being full of magnanimous marital bliss and welcoming Olivia to a less-friendly reaction that would likely involve a tackle and some hair pulling. Uh-oh.

Marty, for his part, was oblivious to Olivia's entrance until Oz nudged him and pointed at the door. Marty turned around and took in the sight of Olivia, who Mel had to admit was looking quite lovely in a royal-blue dress with her curly gray hair brushed out in waves that framed her face becomingly.

Marty put down his drink and began to walk across the room. When Olivia saw him she ran her hands over the skirt of her dress as if nervous. She sucked in a quick breath and approached him, halting just a few feet from where Mel and Joe had stopped dancing to watch, just in case any refereeing was required.

Marty didn't say anything. He stood with his hands on his hips, looking at her as if he didn't know what to make of her sudden appearance.

Olivia reached a hand out to him, but then pulled it back.

"What do you want, Liv?" Marty asked. His voice wasn't unkind but Mel knew he was hurt that Olivia hadn't listened to him when he wanted to explain.

Olivia looked him in the eye and with a voice that trembled, she said, " 'I'm just a girl, standing in front of a boy, asking him to love her.' "

Marty's jaw dropped and then he was reaching for her. He wrapped her in his arms and said, "I do, Liv, I do love you."

Mel felt her eyes go wide. Had Olivia just used a movie quote to make up with Marty?

"*Notting Hill,*" Joe whispered. "Even I know that one."

Mel laughed. She glanced up and saw Angie on the other side of Marty and Olivia with the same gobsmacked expression on her face. They shared a look and Mel raised her hands as if to ask, *What do we do?*

Angie shrugged and pointed to the dance floor. She grabbed Tate by the hand and led the way, leaving Mel and Joe to follow.

Dinner, dancing, more dinner, then Oz's cupcakes, which were amazing and made Angie cry because they had been so carefully rendered with such obvious love. The night whirled around Mel in a kaleidoscope of emotions, with bright pink flashes of happiness spotted with green sparkles of tenderness swirled with tiny orange dots of anxiety. But she needn't have worried at all. It was a perfect day.

If there was a dim spot, it was that she never did get a chance to tell Angie how happy she was for her, how much she valued her, and how grateful she was to have her in her life. It was okay, though; today wasn't about Mel and Angie, it was about Tate and Angie. Mel would find the time to talk to Angie when she got home from her honeymoon. She tried to be okay with that.

When Angie and Tate made a dash to their limousine to leave for their honeymoon, Mel stood outside under the perfect starlit sky and waved good-bye with Joe at her side and their friends all around.

Angie passed out hugs and kisses and laughs while Tate held the car door open for her.

"Mrs. Harper," he finally yelled. "We're going to miss our plane."

Angie ignored him and then her eyes went wide and she spun around. "Mrs. Harper? *I'm* Mrs. Harper."

"That you are." Tate grinned. He opened his arms and Angie hurried into them, kissing him fiercely to much cheering and applause.

They climbed into the limousine and they were off. Mel stood waving, hoping her friends had the best honeymoon even as she already missed them.

She was the last one waving when she dropped her arm to follow Joe back into the club. The music was still going and people were still dancing, milking the evening for all that it was worth.

A screech of tires sounded and Mel and Joe whipped back around to see that the limo had lurched to a stop. The back door popped open and Angie dashed out. She had her voluminous skirt clutched in two fists as she ran down the sidewalk in her heels.

"Mel," she cried. "Mel, wait."

"What is it?" Mel dropped Joe's hand and hurried forward, meeting Angie halfway. "Are you all right? Did you forget something?"

"Yes, this," Angie said. Then she grabbed Mel in a hug that strangled.

Mel laughed and then she started to cry. Angie was already crying.

"You're my best friend," Angie said. "The sister of my heart. I never would have met Tate if it weren't for you, never mind married him. Oh, Mel, thanks for being my friend all these years."

Mel choked, and not just because Angie still had her in a quasi-headlock, but because she had just said everything Mel had been wanting to say.

She pulled out of Angie's embrace and looked at her. She knew as long as she lived she would never find another female kindred spirit, bosom buddy, or bestie like Angie.

"I feel the same way," Mel said. "If it weren't for you, I never would have ended up with Joe, or opened the bakery, or any of it. I'm so very grateful that you're in my life. Promise me we'll always be best friends."

"Forever," Angie cried. "You're the Romy to my Michele."

"The Enid to my Rebecca."

"The Lucy to my Ethel."

"The Thelma to my Louise."

"Except for the ending," they said together.

Mel laughed and then hugged Angie tight. "Go. Your husband is waiting."

"Husband!" Angie jumped up in the air and then danced in place. "Okay, I'm going, but you have to make me a promise."

"Anything," Mel said.

"You have to promise you'll be careful while we're gone. Don't go investigating this thing with the Palms by yourself. Keep Joe with you at all times. Better yet, don't do anything, because I will be so worried about you. Please?"

"I promise," Mel said. She hugged Angie one more time and then gave her a gentle shove. "Now go!"

"Bye," Angie said. She lifted her skirts as she jogged back to the limo, shouting over her shoulder, "I love you!"

"I love you, too!" Mel answered. She waved and then turned back to the club to see Joe walking towards her.

He took her hand in his. "Is everything okay?"

"Yeah, Angie and I just had some unfinished business," Mel said. "Plus, she wanted me to promise to be careful, or more accurately, to stay out of the Elise Penworthy case completely."

"Can I second that?" Joe asked. He put his arm around her shoulders as they walked back into the party that was slowly beginning to wind down. "Whoever killed Elise and the people associated with her is a very angry, very unbalanced person, and you do not want to make yourself their target."

"I know," Mel said. "But Cassie —"

"Has been let out on bail and has an excellent attorney," Joe said. "You need to steer clear of this for me, for Captain Jack, and for Peanut. That poor dog has suffered enough."

"Leveraging the pets?" she asked.

"Is it working?"

"Depends," Mel said. "Do we get to keep her?"

Joe sighed. "Yes."

"Yay!" Mel was not a bit surprised. Peanut

had firmly wedged herself into their house and even Captain Jack was warming up to her. Sort of. "Speaking of the kids, are you ready to go home to our pack? I'm worried that they might have destroyed the place by now."

"Yeah," he said. "Let's go home."

The good-byes didn't go as swiftly as Mel had hoped. They never did. But when they entered their house an hour later, there were no signs of bloodshed or tufts of fur to be found. In fact, the house was eerily quiet. Too quiet.

"I don't see them, do you?" she asked.

"No." Joe sounded as concerned as she felt.

They made their way through the house until Mel heard the distinct sound of snoring. She stopped and held up her hand for Joe to do the same. He tipped his head, listening, and then jerked his chin in the direction of their room.

Mel flicked on the light and there in the middle of the bedroom floor, curled up in her favorite dark blue chenille throw was Peanut, with Captain Jack snuggled up against her.

"That might be the cutest thing I've ever seen," Joe said. "I'm a grown man and it's making my heart hurt."

"If you had a uterus like me, you'd be having spasms," Mel said.

He laughed and the sound startled the pets. Peanut jumped to her feet but it was too fast and her front legs collapsed, dropping her on her face. Captain Jack blinked at them and stretched as Peanut got back to her feet and charged at them. Captain Jack continued stretching. When he was done he leapt up onto the bed and curled up to go back to sleep. Peanut danced around their feet, demanding love.

"She's so happy," Joe said. He scratched Peanut's back right where she liked it while Mel rubbed Captain Jack's ears.

"He's never going to admit that he likes the dog," Mel said. "But he does."

"Yeah, they've bonded. I guess in the end, everyone just wants to belong to somebody," Joe said.

Mel studied her little family. It was true. They belonged to one another now and she wouldn't have it any other way.

It was three days before Mel felt as if she'd recovered from the wedding. Looking at Marty and Oz in the kitchen of the bakery, she could tell they felt the same.

"So, Lupe had to go back to school?" she asked.

"Yep," Oz answered. He was carefully boxing up some pink-and-black cupcakes he'd just finished for a birthday party that evening.

"Did you have a good time while she was here?"

"Yep."

Mel looked at Marty. He raised his hands in innocence. "Don't look at me. We're dudes. We don't talk about stuff like you girls do."

"Are you living with Olivia again?" she asked.

"Yep."

"Do your daughters know?"

"Yep."

"That's it? That's all you'll give me, really?" Mel asked.

Marty and Oz exchanged amused glances.

"If Angie were here she'd pull the information out of you or threaten to pull your intestines through your nose," Mel said. "Huh, I may have to call her."

"No!" they said together.

"Then talk."

Oz cracked first. "Lupe and I are back together. She thought it was too much to ask me to wait for her since school is taking up so much of her time, but I told her I thought she was worth it, so we're good."

"Excellent," Mel said. She patted him on the shoulder and caught his smile beneath his fringe of bangs.

"And Olivia and I made up," Marty said. "I told my daughters to call off their dogs, that I was of sound mind and that Olivia was my gal, and if they didn't like it they could learn to live without my money as I'd cut them both out of my will."

"Good for you," Mel said. "Were they mad?"

"Furious," Marty said. "But they'll get over it."

"Now, was that so hard?" Mel asked.

"Yes!" they answered together.

"All right, I am packed up and ready to ride to the Westons' house," Oz said.

"The Westons?" Mel asked. "That's the sweet sixteen party, right?"

"Yeah," Oz said. He looked pained. "My plan is to set up, get paid, and get out of there before the girls arrive."

"Good plan," Marty said.

"The Westons. Don't they live over in the Palms?" Mel asked. Both Marty and Oz swiveled their heads in her direction. "What?"

"Why do you ask?" Oz said.

"Just remembering the details of a client," she said. "No biggie. But this is an awful large party, so I'll go with you."

"No!" Marty and Oz spoke together.

"I'm sorry, what?"

"Angie and Tate made us promise to keep an eye on you and make sure you didn't do anything that might put you in harm's way," Oz said.

"And we promised," Marty said. "So you can't go."

"How is setting up for a sixteen-year-old's birthday party going to put me in harm's way?" Mel asked. "I just want to check out the neighborhood. It's not like I'm going to go door to door looking for trouble."

Marty and Oz exchanged a look. "Yeah, right."

Mel plopped her hands on her hips. "Well, I'm the boss, so guess what? I'm going."

TWENTY-ONE

"Thank you so much," Mrs. Weston said as she led them through her enormous mansion towards the backyard, which was covered in balloon arches of the same pink and black as the cupcakes. Several extra-large pink Mylar balloons of the number sixteen were anchored all around the pool area.

"It has just been the craziest day, but anything for baby girl, right?" It was clearly a rhetorical question as she kept walking while Oz rolled their cart of cupcakes behind her, following her out to the patio, where a table had been set aside to display the cupcakes.

Mrs. Weston was dressed in an adorable short sundress that showed off her toned legs and her very high heels. Her blond hair was highlighted and styled in tousled waves. She had on a chunky coral necklace and matching earrings, and her makeup was flawless, making her forty-five years look more like thirty-five.

When they reached the table, Oz started to unload the boxes and Mel took one and lifted the lid so Mrs. Weston could see the cupcakes in all their sugary goodness. She clapped her hands together and let loose a squeal.

"Oh, they are just darling," she said. "Cameron is going to love, love, love them."

Mel smiled. It was always gratifying to have a satisfied customer, but she was on information recon.

"So, have you lived in the Palms long?" she asked. Oz snorted and she coughed, covering up his noise.

"Yes, ever since my girls were born," Mrs. Weston said. "We wanted a quality neighborhood for them to grow up in."

"I can understand that, but isn't there an awful lot of scandal in this neighborhood?" Mel asked. She tried to make her face a mask of innocent concern.

Mrs. Weston made a sour expression and she gave Mel an impatient look. "Are you asking about what *that* book said? It wasn't true. None of it. I am very good friends with Mallory Cavendish and it's all lies. Sordid lies made up by that awful woman Elise —"

"The woman who was murdered?"

Mrs. Weston huffed out a breath. "Yes, well, I am sorry that happened, but when you go around lying about people and making an entire neighborhood seem like trash when really it's quite exclusive — only the best of the best get to live in the Palms, you know — bad things will happen."

"So, you think one of your neighbors murdered Elise as revenge?" Mel asked. She blinked, hoping to appear naïve and not snarky.

"No, that's not what I said," Mrs. Weston protested.

"Actually, Mother, that's exactly what you said."

A young woman with the same tousled blond hair and lithe figure stepped out onto the patio. She looked very much like her mother, but while Mrs. Weston was working hard to fake her youth, Cameron had the glowing skin and robust health of an actual teen. Mel wondered how much this annoyed her mother.

"I did not, Cammie," Mrs. Weston said. She frowned. "Aren't you going to change into the cute little dress I bought you? It shows off your figure and is totes adorbs."

Mel noticed then that Cammie was wearing baggy jeans, combat boots, and an oversized men's shirt, all of which she suspected were chosen specifically to piss off her mother. Huh.

Cammie shrugged and said, "I like what I'm wearing now."

Mrs. Weston closed her eyes for a moment, as if praying for patience. Cameron watched her and then wound her long hair into a knot that she deftly fastened on her head with a hairband she had around her wrist. Without makeup, she was still lovely but not the bombshell Mel was pretty sure her mother would have preferred.

"You are not greeting your guests like this," Mrs. Weston hissed through her teeth.

"They're not my guests," Cameron said. "They're yours."

Oz kept his head down and continued loading the cupcakes as if there weren't a mother-daughter squabble happening right in front of him. Mel took the box she was holding and joined him.

"Cammie, darling, we talked about this," Mrs. Weston said.

"No, you talked, I tuned you out, and you did exactly what you wanted to do anyway," Cameron said. "I'm not coming to this party."

As if to taunt her mother further, she picked up a cupcake from the tower that Oz had filled and then bit into it, coating her lips with the pink-and-black icing. Mel saw Mrs. Weston's fingers clench into fists. Her back was arched, her nostrils flared, and her lips were pressed into a tight line. Mel suspected it was taking every ounce of self-control she possessed not to lose her temper.

"Tina, I'd like a word with you."

They all glanced at the door to the house to see a middle-aged woman, dressed more like a typical mom in capri pants and a plaid sleeveless blouse, striding towards them. It was clear from the way the heels of her sneakers battered the flagstone beneath her feet that she was furious.

"Oh, this is gonna be good," Cameron said. She continued eating her cupcake, looking as if she was gearing up to enjoy the show.

"I'm sorry, Miranda, but I am very busy setting up for Cameron's party," Mrs. Weston said.

"Yes, Cameron's party." The woman called Miranda gestured at the decorations surrounding them. "About that, how could you not invite Rhiannon?"

"I don't feel like this is the time to discuss this," Tina said.

"Sure it is, Mom," Cameron said. She licked a dollop of frosting off of her lips. "Do explain why Rhia, who is my oldest friend, wasn't invited. I'm sure we're all fascinated to hear the answer."

Tina sent her daughter a killing glance. Then she cleared her throat and ran a hand through her hair, fluffing it in a practiced gesture.

"Fine," she said. "Miranda, I am sure that you are aware that there is a certain social hierarchy at the school the girls attend and, frankly, Cammie is in one group and Rhia is in another. It didn't seem appropriate to invite Rhia to the party. She'd just feel out of place. I was doing it for her, you know."

"What she's trying to say is that she's spent a lot of time and energy and money making sure I hang out with the cool kids, but Rhia isn't one of them, so Mom didn't invite her. She doesn't think Rhia's up to scratch, and Mom couldn't let her damage my cred with the popular girls. Isn't that right, Mom?"

"That is not what I said," Tina argued.

"Yes, actually, it is," Miranda said. She turned to look at Cameron and her face softened. "Rhia misses you." She pulled a small package out of her handbag and handed it to the girl. "She wanted me to give you this. Happy birthday, sweetie."

With that, Miranda turned on her heel and headed back to the door. She paused in the doorway and turned back to face them. "Oh, and, Tina? Go to hell."

They heard a door slam shortly thereafter.

"Well, that was completely uncalled-for," Tina said. "I mean, honestly."

Cameron opened her present. Inside was half of a heart. A sound like a hiccup burst out of her throat and she reached beneath the collar of her shirt and pulled out a pendant. Mel didn't need to look any closer to see it was the other half of the heart. Put together, they read *Best Friends.*

She didn't need to look because she and Angie had had the same ones growing up. The look of heartbreak on Cammie's face made Mel want to hug her, but she suspected that would be weird given that she didn't know the girl at all.

Cameron glanced up at her mother and her eyes burned. "Now I've lost my best friend. I will never forgive you for this. Never!"

She ran from the patio and again the sound of a door being slammed echoed in the quiet.

"Unbelievable," Tina Weston snapped. "I have done everything for that girl. I took her to the best stylist, the best personal shopper; I had her join all the right clubs and activities; I volunteered to work on committees just so I could get in with the parents of the popular kids so that she could be a part of the popular crowd, and this is the thanks I get?"

She snatched a cupcake off of the tower and shoved it into her face. Mel got the feeling she wasn't tasting the cupcake so much as keeping herself from primal screaming. That was cool; whatever worked.

Tina crossed to the beverage station, where a stack of papers sat. She fished through them and returned, slapping their check onto the table.

"The cupcakes are great. Thanks," she said. Then she disappeared inside the house. In moments, they heard her calling, with obvious fake cheer, "Cammie, come on, baby girl. Let's get you all pretty for your party."

The tower was done. Oz looked at Mel and said, "I say we make a run for it."

"And how," Mel agreed.

Oz grabbed the handles of the empty cart and led the way through the mansion back to the driveway, where he had parked their vehicle.

They climbed into the big pink cupcake truck and Oz fired up the engine and shot down the street. He drove like he was fleeing the scene of a crime, not slowing down until they were four streets away.

"That made me feel icky," Mel said.

Oz nodded. His hair flopped out of his eyes and Mel could see he was frowning. She suspected he felt yucky, too.

"Can you imagine how the poor girl who got left out is feeling?" he asked. "That wasn't right, it just wasn't right."

"People can be pretty awful," Mel said. She thought about Elise's book and how the whole thing was just one horrific example of people behaving badly, one after another.

"But to exclude someone just because you decide that they're not worthy, that's just nasty." Oz shook his head.

Mel studied him. She remembered being excluded quite a lot as a teen. She was heavyset, painfully shy, and the epitome of awkward. If it hadn't been for Tate and Angie, she'd have had no friends at all. She suspected Oz, with his goth look and love of baking, wasn't exactly a mainstream "in crowd" type of guy, either.

"I can't really blame the other mom for being so upset," she said. "She was just trying to look out for her daughter."

"Being left out can be devastating," Oz said. "Especially if it's done out of thoughtlessness, like you didn't even warrant a

319

spiteful snub."

"It might even make you murderous," Mel said.

Her heart beat hard in her chest. It hit her then that she'd been looking at this thing all wrong.

Mel snatched her phone out of her handbag. She called Uncle Stan's number at the station.

"Martinez," his partner answered.

"Hi, Tara, it's Mel. I'm looking for Uncle Stan. Is he around?

"Would I be answering his phone if he was?"

Mel sighed and said nothing. She did not want to get into it with Tara today.

"He's over at your mom's house," Tara said.

"Thanks." Mel went to end the call.

"Hey!" Tara said, stopping her. "Is this about the case?"

"Nah," Mel lied. She was not sharing with Tara before she shared with Stan.

She ended the call and turned to Oz. "We need to make a quick detour."

Oz parked in her mother's driveway. Mel hopped out and Oz came with her since Joyce was known to always have a hot pot of coffee and a snack for anyone who happened by.

"Mom!" Mel shouted as she unlocked the door and pushed her way inside.

Two people were standing entwined in front of her. Mel froze and Oz, unprepared for the abrupt stop, slammed into her back, sending her staggering forward with a grunt.

The couple broke apart and Mel felt her jaw hit the ground. "Mom? Uncle Stan? *What?*"

"Hoo boy, didn't see that coming," Oz said from behind her.

"I don't understand," Mel said. "*Uncle Stan* is the guy you're seeing?"

"Now, Mel, before you get all —" Uncle Stan began, but Mel cut him off.

"You hush," she said. "Is he?"

Joyce's hands fluttered in the air like little birds, and then she smoothed down the front of her shirt in an obvious effort to compose herself.

She met Mel's gaze and said, "Yes."

"And Charlie knows?" she asked.

"Yes."

"You told my little brother before me?" Mel asked. "Why?"

"Because we knew you'd get like this," Uncle Stan said. He twirled his hands at her.

"Like this?" Mel asked, mimicking his hand gesture. "What do you mean? Concerned? Wary? Invested? What?"

"That, all of that," Joyce said. "We didn't want to tell you until we were sure ourselves because we didn't want you to get overwrought by it."

"Overwrought? I am not overwrought."

"Not to be argumentative, boss," Oz said, "but you are yelling, which makes it appear that you are a tad high-strung about the situation."

"You hush, too," Mel said. She turned back to her mother. "Were you ever planning on telling me?"

"Of course we were. Don't be like that," Joyce said.

"Like what?" Mel demanded. "Angry that I've been left out? Of course I'm angry."

The word lingered in the air and Mel and Oz gasped at the same time and turned to face each other.

"See? It's true. Being left out does make a person angry," he said. "You need to tell him."

"You're right." Mel waved her hand between Uncle Stan and her mom and said, "This, whatever this is, is fine. Well, mostly it's fine. We'll talk about it later. But right now, Oz and I think we've made a break in the case."

Uncle Stan narrowed his eyes as he studied her. "And how did that come about?"

"By doing our jobs and delivering cup-cakes," Mel said. "Hear me out."

She went on to explain about Tina and Miranda and the big scene at the birthday party. Uncle Stan listened, but with a little wrinkle in between his eyes as he tried to figure out how a sixteen-year-old's birthday party had anything to do with his investigation.

"I'm not following," he said when she finished. "Do you think this Tina or Miranda or whoever had something to do with it?"

"No," Mel said. "They're just the ones who made me realize how being ignored could cause a person to be filled with rage just as much as being maligned could."

"Enraged enough to kill four people?" Uncle Stan asked.

Mel shrugged. "It's a theory."

"I think it's a pretty good one," Joyce said.

"So, now I do what?" Uncle Stan asked. "Cross-check residents of the Palms against people who are *not* in the book?"

"Exactly!" Mel said. "I think the killer is someone who is angry about the book not because they were in it, but because they weren't."

TWENTY-TWO

Uncle Stan conceded that it was a solid angle to work the case from. He offered to stay and talk if Mel felt that was needed, but she waved him off and told him to go back to work.

On his way out the door, Uncle Stan paused to give her one of his crusher hugs.

"So, we're okay?" he asked.

"That depends," Mel said. "Did Joe know?"

"He might have walked in on your mom and me," Uncle Stan said.

Mel's eyes bugged.

"Just hugging and stuff!" Uncle Stan said as his face turned a deep shade of red. "And I asked him to keep it to himself for now."

"Then you and I are good," Mel said. "But Joe is in for an earful."

"How about me?" Joyce asked. "Am I in trouble?"

"Nope." Mel shook her head. "You, I'm

happy for."

Joyce hugged her close and Mel heard Uncle Stan give a relieved chuckle as he headed out the door. As soon as it shut, Mel leaned back and gave her mother a minor blast of stink eye.

"But just so you know, you could have told me," she said.

"I know," Joyce said. "I do. But I didn't want to take away from Angie's wedding, and then that horrible stabbing with Elise happened. It just didn't feel like the right time."

"Fair enough," Mel said.

"Can we have coffee now?" Oz asked. "I'm dying."

"Yes, and I have fresh-made date nut bread, too," Joyce said.

Oz spun back around and bent down to kiss Joyce's cheek. "And that's why I love you, Mrs. Cooper."

Mel and Joyce laughed as he strode ahead of them into the kitchen.

"Hey, if you marry Uncle Stan, you don't even have to change your name," Mel said.

"Easy, tiger, we're just dating." Joyce laughed and wrapped her arm around Mel's waist and hugged her close. "All joking aside, are you sure you're okay with it?"

Mel thought about the ten-plus years

since her father had been gone. Who had stepped in to fill his spot? Who had looked out for Mel, Charlie, and Joyce? Uncle Stan. Not only was she okay with it, it seemed positively perfect.

"More than okay," she said. She hugged her mom back. "I think it's the best news ever."

Mel and Oz arrived back at the bakery to find Marty had it all under control. Mel retreated to her office to plan some of her specialty orders while Oz took over the kitchen to get to work on the cupcake of the day for tomorrow.

A copy of *The Palms* was sitting on Mel's desk. She stared at the retro cover, thinking how horrible it was that the written word had contributed to the deaths of four people. Whatever the motivation of the killer, anger for being in the book or not, it shouldn't have ended this way for Blaise or Elise or the driver or caterer.

She wondered if she should call Cassie and tell her the theory she'd told Uncle Stan. She knew Cassie was staying away from the shop, but if she was like Mel and thought it was only people who were angry about being in the book that she had to look out for she might let her guard down in front of someone she shouldn't.

Mel took her phone out of her purse and called Cassie's cell. There was no answer. Huh. She ended the call and decided to call the store directly.

The phone rang eight times and then rolled over to voicemail. Mel glanced at the clock. It was late afternoon on a weekday. The bookstore should be open. Maybe whoever was working the front counter was busy helping a customer. She ended the call without leaving a message. She waited thirty seconds and she called again. Voicemail again. She called Cassie's number again. No answer.

A sense of unease began to make her skin feel too tight. There was no reason for the phone to go unanswered at the store or for Cassie to leave her personal phone unattended unless something was very, very wrong. If the killer really was looking for revenge for being left out of the book, wouldn't the publisher of the book be next on their list of victims?

Mel wondered how Stan was doing cross-checking names of residents of the Palms against people who hadn't been mentioned in the book. Given that he had to match the nickname Elise used to the person's real name and then discover who didn't have a nickname, it could take ages. While it had seemed that everyone in the Palms had made a cameo in the book at least, Mel was certain there had to be some people left out. She thought back to the book signing and then she felt her stomach drop into her feet.

Janie Fulton. The petite woman with the big glasses who had lived a few houses down from Elise, whom Elise had clearly not remembered and whose name Elise had even spelled wrong at the signing. That was the sort of person who might be looking for revenge. Was it Janie — who had seemed so nice, even forgiving the misspelling — who had killed everyone she felt slighted by?

Mel was out of her chair and holding her car keys before she'd fully decided to run over to the bookstore and check on things.

Oz glanced up when she entered the kitchen. The look on her face must have registered her worry because he asked, "What's wrong?"

"Probably nothing," she said. "But I'm going to stop by Cassie's shop, A Likely Story, just to be sure."

"Why?"

"No one's answering the phone over there."

"Could be with a customer."

"Probably, but I can't shake feeling that

something isn't right," she said. "Be a champ and call Uncle Stan for me?"

"Aw, what?" Oz protested.

"Ask him to check on the whereabouts of Janie Fulton, a Palms resident," Mel said. "And tell him where I'm going, please."

"I know what you're doing," he said. "You don't want to call him and get yelled at, so you want me to do it for you. Listen, give me a second and I'll go with you."

Mel looked at the oven. The industrial batch of cupcakes he had baking wouldn't be done for another fifteen minutes. She didn't think she could wait that long. Not to mention the fact that she would never, ever put Oz in a situation where he could be harmed.

"No, you finish up here. I'm sure this is nothing, and I'm just being paranoid," she said. "But call Stan anyway, and look at it this way: I'll owe you one."

"Boss —" he began to protest, but Mel slipped through the back door, cutting him off.

Mel hurried across the alley to the parking lot where she parked her car. She slid into the driver's seat. A Likely Story was on the other side of Old Town, which was mercifully only a few blocks away. But on the chance there was something wrong and she needed to hustle Cassie to an emergency room or something, Mel wanted to have her car. Unfortunately, she had to navigate three traffic lights, a stream of tourist pedestrians, and then find a parking spot before she could get to the bookstore.

She thought about the night of Elise's stabbing. Had she seen Janie after the signing? Had the woman been lingering in the resort, waiting to get Elise alone? She couldn't remember. She vaguely remembered an unhelpful staff person in the bar when they'd been looking for Elise, but the woman hadn't looked like Janie and her name tag had read *Laura*.

On impulse, she called Christine's salon while she waited at a red light.

"Christine's, how may I help you?"

"Hi, this is Melanie Cooper. Is Christine available?"

"No," the voice said.

Mel sighed. She loved what Christine could do with hair, really she did, but the impenetrable line of defense she had going with her staff was exhausting.

"Samantha, then. Is she there?"

"This is Samantha."

"It is? Great, listen, you just did my makeup for a wedding," Mel said.

"Yes, I remember," Samantha said.

"You're the one with the skimpy eyelashes."

"Um . . . yeah, that's me," Mel said. "Do you remember that we were talking about Elise Penworthy's murder?"

"Of course I do," she said. "What bride talks about murder on her wedding day? So weird."

"Yes, we established that," Mel said. She tried to keep her impatience out of her voice. "I was wondering if Christine or you remembered the name of the person Elise said was stalking her."

"Nope."

"Okay, well, does the name Laura mean anything to you?"

"No."

"All right, how about Janie?"

"No."

"Could you ask Christine?"

Samantha made a put-upon sigh. "Hold on."

The light turned green and Mel hit the gas, cruising towards the bookstore as fast as she dared.

"She said it could have been Janie maybe," Samantha said. "But it's a definite no on Laura."

"Okay, thanks. You've been a big help." Mel ended the call as she found a spot at the corner and parked.

Nestled between a café and an upscale interior designer, the bookstore was well situated for foot traffic. Mel didn't hesitate but went right to the door, finding it locked. She stepped back. The sign on the door clearly stated that they should be open. Mel tugged the overly large handle again, as if it might open if she pulled on it differently. It didn't.

She cupped her hands against the glare and pressed her face against the glass. The lights were on in the store, but she didn't see anyone standing at the register or moving around.

She decided to check the back. Maybe whoever was on duty had just popped outside to take a break. She jogged past the interior designer and slipped down the narrow alley that separated this group of shops from the next. The access road that ran behind the businesses was for delivery and garbage trucks and was barely wide enough for those.

Mel hurried to the staircase in the middle of the building. It was empty, so there went her theory of an employee on a break. She climbed the short staircase and tugged on the glass door. To her surprise it opened. She wasn't sure if she should enter or not. She didn't want to terrify anyone who might be at work, but she didn't want to walk away if there was a situation happening and someone needed help. Dilemma.

Mel decided to sneak in and take a peek. If everything was normal, she would back out the way she'd come and pretend she'd never been here.

The back door opened into a hallway, which had two restrooms. At the end of the hall on the right was the door that opened to the offices, the workroom, and the stockroom. Mel crept to the end of the hallway. She glanced out at the store in front of her. It was empty, eerily so.

It was then that she noticed the horrible smell in the shop. She wondered if it was a gas leak. Maybe that was why the shop was closed. But why would the back door be open, and wouldn't they have closed the neighboring shops? Besides, it wasn't a sulfuric gas smell; it was acrid.

Mel couldn't place it, but she knew it was noxious, the sort that could give a person a powerful headache if they were exposed to it for too long. Perhaps that was why the store was closed, but again, why was the back door unlocked? It didn't make sense.

The hinky feeling in her belly twisted, and she glanced at the door to the offices. It was closed. During all the visits she'd made to the bookstore, she'd never seen the office closed. She pressed her ear against the wood. She could hear someone shuffling about the room, then there was a thump.

It wasn't a good thump. It was the sort of noise made when a person kicked something. Hard.

Instinct propelled Mel forward. Without overthinking it, she pounded on the door. The side of her fist met the thick wood with three solid bangs.

"Cassie, are you in there?" She raised her voice. "It's Mel. Cassie, answer me."

Where there had been shuffling before, there was now an absence of noise. It reminded Mel of how the songbirds went quiet when Captain Jack slipped out of the house to stalk them in the backyard. It was as if they thought if they made no noise he would simply turn around and go away. He never did, and Mel wasn't about to, either.

TWENTY-THREE

She raised her fist to bang on the door again. She connected once, but then the door was yanked open and her fist slipped through the open air to drop awkwardly to her waist as the smell that had been toxic before now made her eyes water.

She blinked as she took in the scene before her. Standing in front of her holding a long match was a tiny little bird of a woman, as fragile and as plain looking as a sparrow. With glasses that were too big for her face, she tipped her head to the side as if trying to figure what Mel could possibly be doing here.

"Janie," Mel said.

The horror of what she had interrupted made a shiver run down her spine. The stench was clearly an accelerant like turpentine, and a quick glance past the small woman showed Cassie bound and gagged and propped up on a pile of what appeared to be pages torn from a book. Mel didn't have to work too hard to guess which book.

Janie holding a match clinched the ugly truth. Janie was planning to kill Cassie by lighting her on fire using copies of the book from which she'd been left out. Mel thought she might throw up.

It was cold comfort that she'd been right. The killer was not someone *in* the fictionalized tell-all, but rather a person who wasn't. The killer was this petite little woman who looked like she couldn't harm a mosquito, never mind kill four people in cold blood.

Janie with an *ie* instead of a *y*. Janie, who hadn't even merited a mention in the tawdry tale Elise had penned. Janie, who clearly wanted to be noticed, to matter, to be counted, and who in her fury at being ignored had turned to murder.

Mel studied her. There was a detachment in her eyes that was more alarming than any rage she might have displayed.

"You're the cupcake baker," Janie said. "Elise liked you."

"*Liked* is such a strong word," Mel said. She didn't think being a friend of Elise's was such a good thing at the moment. "I mean I hardly knew her."

A thump sounded from behind Janie. Mel knew it had to be Cassie. Was she hurt, wounded, bleeding from an injury Mel couldn't see, while Mel stood here making chitchat with Crazy Train?

"How about we go grab a cup of coffee and you can tell me all about your years living in the Palms?" Mel asked.

"No," Janie said. "You should leave."

She began to close the door and Mel knew that she couldn't let her. She stepped forward, using her foot to wedge the door open. She peeked over Janie's head and saw Cassie, struggling with her bonds, her eyes streaming from the harsh smell that wafted up from the papers piled around her.

"Oh, Janie, no," Mel said. "You can't do this."

Janie's back went rigid. "Yes, I can. I can do whatever I want, and you want to know why? Because I'm insignificant, I don't matter, no one ever notices me. I've been able to kill them all, but no one ever suspected little Janie Fulton."

"That's not true," Mel protested. "You do matter."

"Sure I do," Janie said. Her voice was bitter. "Do you know how many times I hired that same car service? Fifteen. Do you think that driver remembered me? No. And how about the caterer? She made the food for seven of my parties. Seven. And yet she couldn't remember that I love cheesecake. And that photographer —"

"Blaise?" Mel clarified.

The look Janie gave her said *duh* more clearly than words.

"What could he have done to deserve what you did?" Mel asked.

"He was just like the others, telling tales to Elise about everyone in the Palms," Janie said. "Elise would meet up with her little spies all over town in trendy bars and restaurants, and they'd tell her everyone's dirty little secrets. Well, I knew secrets, too, loads of them. Do you think they ever included me? Do you think they ever invited me to join them?"

Mel said nothing, knowing there was no right answer here.

"They never even noticed me."

"I notice you," Mel said.

Janie blinked at her and then she let out a belly laugh. An actual laugh of amusement that shook her slight frame. It was genuine humor, which made it all the more disturbing.

"You notice me because I am not taking it anymore," she said. "You notice me because I am making everyone who slighted me, who left me out, suffer for it."

Mel saw Cassie struggling to get free.

Maybe if she could overpower Janie she could get to Cassie and get them both out of here before Janie torched the place. She took a step towards the tiny woman, but Janie lifted up her other hand. In it was a lighter. She flicked it on and held the match over it.

Mel raised her hands in the air as if Janie had a gun on her. She wondered if she blew hard enough if she could put the lighter out. She didn't want to risk it. What if she blew the flame right onto the match? The fumes in here alone might be flammable and the next thing she knew they'd all go up in a big fireball. Not how she'd ever thought she'd go. Frosting overdose? Sure. Human torch? Not so much.

"Can we talk about this, Janie?"

"No."

Mel saw Cassie frantically wriggling. She must have suspected that Janie was at her breaking point. Mel knew they were out of time. She knew she only had one shot.

"What's that?" She pointed with her left hand over Janie's shoulder. It was the oldest misdirection in the book, probably because it worked. When Janie whipped her head in that direction, Mel snatched the lighter out of Janie's hand, squashing the flame with her palm.

"Yeow!" Mel shouted. The lighter's hot metal top seared her hand, and she flung it across the bookstore.

"Hey!" Janie shouted and ran for the lighter.

Mel chased after her. She figured it was more important to keep Janie from the lighter than to untie Cassie. Janie dropped to the floor and was scrabbling after the lighter when Mel grabbed her by one foot. Janie used her other foot to kick at Mel, but she refused to let go, knowing if Janie got the lighter she would torch the place in an instant.

Panic made her heart pound in her chest. She'd been trapped in a fire once before. She'd seen what a fire could do to a person and she remembered well the burn of smoke in her lungs. There was no way in hell she was living through that again.

"Let me go!" Janie whipped around and took a swing at Mel. Her fist just missed Mel's nose.

"Stop, Janie!" Mel yelled. "It's over."

"No!" Janie cried. She renewed her efforts to kick Mel and her free foot came within a hair of smashing Mel in the temple.

A hand appeared between Mel's face and Janie's shoe and she glanced up to see Tara Martinez, who wasted no time but dropped to the ground, lodging her knee into Janie's back.

"Looks like you owe me one, Cooper," Tara said. Then she grabbed a pair of handcuffs off of her belt and wrestled them onto Janie.

Mel let go of Janie's foot and slumped to the ground. Thank god. Janie might be petite, but the tiny birdlike woman fought like a hellcat. No wonder she'd managed to bind up Cassie.

Cassie!

Mel rolled onto her side and pushed up to her feet. She raced for the office, but Uncle Stan was already there, untying Cassie and helping her to her feet. He'd removed the gag from her mouth and Cassie was sucking in great gulps of air.

"Mel!" Cassie cried her name and then staggered towards her.

Mel hugged her close and then leaned back to study her face. "Let's get you some fresh air, okay?"

Uncle Stan led the way, scouting the area outside the back door before he nodded that they could sit. He hugged Mel close in one of his big bear hugs and cupped her face.

"You just have to scare the snot out of me to keep me on my toes, don't you?"

"Sorry," Mel said. "I had no idea — just a

hunch. But at least I had Oz call you."

Uncle Stan kissed her forehead. "Yeah, that was a good play. You should brace yourself, though. I called Joe and he's on his way."

"Oh, boy," Mel said. "Scale of one to ten, how mad did he seem?"

"Eleven. I'll be back out to get your statements," he said. "I just want to make sure that Tara has that woman subdued."

Both Mel and Cassie nodded. Cassie bent over and rested her head on her knees.

"How are you doing?" Mel asked.

"Trying really hard not to throw up," Cassie said. "You saved my life. If you hadn't shown up when you did I'd have been a human torch."

"I do try to extinguish myself," Mel joked. Cassie gave her a look. "Sorry, we'll just blame that on my nerves."

They sat quietly, breathing in the clean air free of the stench of the accelerant Janie had used. Mel closed her eyes and took a second to just be grateful that she'd arrived in time for Cassie and that they'd both gotten out okay.

Two uniformed officers parked their cars in the alley and came charging towards the back door. Mel recognized Officer Lopez and gave him a faint wave.

"Uncle Stan is inside," she said.

"Thanks, Mel," he said. He studied her face. "You all right?"

She nodded and he patted her shoulder and the two officers moved past them into the building.

"I don't understand why," Cassie said. "I don't think Elise even knew anyone named Janie. She certainly didn't write anything nasty about a woman named Janie Fulton. I would have remembered."

"And that's why," Mel said. "Janie was angry not because she was in the book but because she wasn't. And apparently she was upset that Elise didn't include her in gathering her sordid tales, either."

"Oh," Cassie said. She frowned.

"Did you know that Elise was using Blaise and the others for material?" Mel asked.

Cassie glanced away, and Mel took that as a yes. Cassie was quiet for a moment and then said, "She paid them very well for any dirt they could give her about residents of the Palms. Elise had a lot of material of her own, but she wanted more. She wanted to destroy everyone who'd ever shut her out."

There wasn't much more to say. One woman's revenge had sparked a series of savage murders, including her own. The whole thing left Mel feeling sullied.

"I'm going to pull the book," Cassie said.

Mel didn't say anything. This wasn't her call.

"Four people are dead because of it," Cassie continued. "I couldn't live with myself if I published even one more copy and I'm canceling the movie deal."

Knowing that she was losing a fortune, Mel's respect for her friend soared. "I think you're doing the right thing."

"Mel!" Joe called her name as he came around the side of the building at a run.

Mel stood on the steps. She'd have run to meet him but her legs were kind of wobbly. She waited until he was within reach and then launched herself at him. He hugged her tight and for the first time since she'd arrived at the bookstore, Mel felt as if everything would be all right.

Joe pulled back and cupped her face. He looked into her eyes and asked, "Are you all right?"

"I'm fine," she said. "I promise."

"If anything had happened . . ." His voice trailed off and he kissed her again. "I can't even think about it."

"Me, either," she said. The fear that had gripped her when Janie had pulled out the lighter rippled through her again. "I'm sorry. I had a bad feeling and I had to follow up on it."

"Don't be sorry," Cassie said. "You saved my life and I, for one, am ever grateful."

"That's my girl," Joe said.

Mel looked at him and was relieved to see that he wasn't upset with her. Rather, he looked proud.

She rested her head on his shoulder. "Thanks for understanding."

"Always," he said.

They stayed at the bookstore long enough to watch Janie get hauled away and give Stan their statements. Steve arrived shortly after Joe and took charge of Cassie. Even though she was no longer a suspect, Steve considered her his client and insisted he be present while she gave her statement. Cassie seemed relieved by his presence, which Mel thought was encouraging.

When they were finally allowed to leave, Mel asked to stop by the bakery. She had already checked in with Oz and Marty and knew they had locked up for the night, but she felt the need to calm her frazzled nerves with cupcakes and wanted to pick up some to take home. Joe, her soul mate in sweets, thought this idea was genius.

She stood in the walk-in cooler packing a box of their favorites while Joe prowled around the kitchen. She had one more space to fill in her box and she wasn't sure if she wanted a Blond Bombshell or an Orange Dreamsicle. Decisions, decisions.

She heard her phone chime and popped her head out of the cooler and asked, "Will you check that and see if it's Stan?"

"Sure." Joe took her phone out of her purse and read the display. "It's a text from Tate and Angie, checking in. What should I tell them?"

Mel chose the Blond Bombshell. While arranging it in the box, she answered, "Say 'Nothing much,' " she said. "They're on their honeymoon. We can catch them up on all of the drama when they get back."

Joe began to text. He finished and tossed the phone into her purse.

"Speaking of honeymoons," he said. "I'm thinking I'd like to go on one sooner rather than later."

Mel felt her breath catch. "Are you asking me to set a date?"

"Yes."

They stared at each other and Mel nodded. They'd made a run at this marriage thing a couple times now, but this time she felt quite certain they were going to get it right.

"How do you feel about an April wedding?" she asked.

346

"Sounds perfect," he said.

"And it's only six months away," Mel said. "What could possibly happen in six months?"

RECIPES

CHAMPAGNE CUPCAKES

A light fluffy cake topped
with champagne frosting.

1/2 cup butter, softened
1 cup sugar
2 eggs
1 teaspoon vanilla extract
1 3/4 cups all-purpose flour
1/2 teaspoon baking soda
1/4 teaspoon baking powder
1/4 teaspoon salt
1/2 cup sour cream
1/2 cup champagne

Preheat oven to 350 degrees. Line cupcake
pan with paper liners. In a large mixing
bowl, cream together butter and sugar until
light and fluffy. Add the eggs and the vanilla.
In a medium bowl, sift together the flour,

baking soda, baking powder, and salt. In a small bowl, whisk together the sour cream and the champagne. It will fizz a bit. Alternately add the flour mixture and the champagne mixture to the large bowl, mixing until the batter is smooth. Fill paper liners until two-thirds full. Bake for 17 to 22 minutes until golden brown. Makes 12.

Champagne Frosting
1 cup champagne
1 cup butter, softened
2 1/2 cups confectioners' sugar
1 tablespoon champagne

Simmer one cup of champagne in a small saucepan until reduced to two tablespoons. Allow to cool. In a small bowl, cream together the butter and confectioners' sugar until thick and creamy. Add the reduced champagne plus one tablespoon champagne. Whip together until light and fluffy.

Decorate the cupcakes with the frosting using a pastry bag. Garnish with champagne-colored pearlized sprinkles.

BLACK FOREST CUPCAKES

A rich chocolate cupcake with cherry filling and vanilla cream frosting.

1 1/3 cups flour
1/4 teaspoon baking soda
2 teaspoons baking powder
3/4 cup unsweetened cocoa powder
1/4 teaspoon salt
4 tablespoons butter, softened
1 1/2 cups sugar
2 eggs
1 teaspoon vanilla extract
1 cup milk

Preheat oven to 350 degrees. Line cupcake pan with paper liners. In a medium bowl, sift together flour, baking soda, baking powder, cocoa powder, and salt and set aside. In a large bowl, cream the butter and sugar, adding eggs one at a time. Mix in the vanilla. Add in the flour mixture alternately with the milk until well blended. Fill paper liners until two-thirds full. Bake 18 to 22 minutes. Cool completely. Makes 12.

Vanilla Buttercream Frosting
1/2 cup salted butter, softened
1/2 cup unsalted butter, softened

1 teaspoon clear vanilla extract
4 cups sifted confectioners' sugar
2 tablespoons milk
1 can cherry pie filling
Chocolate shavings
12 fresh cherries with stems

In large bowl, cream butter and vanilla. Gradually add confectioners' sugar, one cup at a time, beating well on medium speed and adding milk as needed. Scrape sides of bowl often. Beat at medium speed until light and fluffy. Makes 3 cups of icing. Using a melon baller, scoop out the center of the cooled cupcakes no more than halfway down. Spoon in the cherry pie filling. Using a pastry bag, pipe the vanilla cream over the tops of the cupcakes. Garnish each with chocolate shavings and a fresh cherry on top.

LEMON-LAVENDER CUPCAKES

A tart lemon cupcake with
sweet lavender frosting.

1 cup unsalted butter, softened
2 cups granulated sugar
4 extra-large eggs, at room temperature

1/3 cup grated lemon zest (6–8 large lemons)

3 cups flour

1/2 teaspoon baking powder

1/2 teaspoon baking soda

1 teaspoon salt

1/4 cup freshly squeezed lemon juice

3/4 cup buttermilk, at room temperature

1 teaspoon pure vanilla extract

Preheat oven to 350 degrees. Line cupcake pan with paper liners. Cream the butter and granulated sugar until fluffy, about 5 minutes. With the mixer on medium speed, add the eggs, one at a time, and the lemon zest. In a separate bowl, sift together the flour, baking powder, baking soda, and salt. In another bowl, combine the lemon juice, buttermilk, and vanilla. Add the flour and buttermilk mixtures alternately to the batter, beginning and ending with the flour. Fill paper liners until two-thirds full. Bake 20 minutes. Makes 24.

Lavender Frosting

3/4 cup unsalted butter, softened

3 1/2 cups confectioners' sugar

1 teaspoon dried culinary lavender

1 teaspoon vanilla extract

1 drop purple food coloring

3–4 tablespoons milk
Fresh lavender

In large bowl, cream butter. Gradually add confectioners' sugar, one cup at a time, beating well on medium speed. Add dried lavender, vanilla, and a drop of purple food coloring, mixing well. Add milk as needed to reach desired consistency. Beat at medium speed until light and fluffy. Spread lavender frosting on cooled cupcakes and garnish with a fresh lavender sprig.

BOURBON CUPCAKES

Rich chocolate bourbon cupcake
with chocolate buttercream frosting
with bourbon glaze.

1 1/2 cups flour
1/4 teaspoon baking soda
2 teaspoons baking powder
3/4 cup unsweetened cocoa powder
1/4 teaspoon salt
4 tablespoons butter, softened
1 1/2 cups sugar
2 eggs
1/4 cup bourbon
1 cup milk

Preheat oven to 350 degrees. Line cupcake

pan with paper liners. In a medium bowl, sift together flour, baking soda, baking powder, cocoa powder, and salt and set aside. In a large bowl, cream the butter and sugar, adding eggs one at a time. Mix in the bourbon. Add in the flour mixture alternately with the milk until well blended. Fill paper liners until two-thirds full. Bake 18 to 22 minutes. Cool completely. Makes 12.

Chocolate Buttercream Frosting

1/2 cup salted butter, softened
1/2 cup unsalted butter, softened
1 teaspoon clear vanilla extract
3 cups sifted confectioners' sugar
1 cup unsweetened cocoa powder
2 tablespoons milk

In large bowl, cream butter and vanilla. Gradually add confectioners' sugar and cocoa powder, one cup at a time, beating well on medium speed. Add milk as needed. Scrape sides of bowl often. Beat at medium speed until light and fluffy. Makes 3 cups of icing. Use a pastry bag to pipe frosting onto the cooled cupcakes.

Bourbon Glaze

Glaze should be prepared ahead of time to allow it enough time to cool before adding to cupcakes.

3/4 cup bourbon
1/2 cup brown sugar

In a small sauce pot over medium heat, whisk bourbon and sugar together. Simmer the mixture until it is reduced to half, about 10 to 15 minutes. Cool completely. Drizzle over the frosted cupcakes.

ABOUT THE AUTHOR

Jean McKinlay, the *New York Times* best-selling author of the Cupcake Bakery Mysteries (including *Caramel Crush, Vanilla Beaned, Dark Chocolate Demise,* and *Sugar and Iced*), has baked and frosted cupcakes into the shapes of cats, mice, and outer-space aliens, to name just a few. Writing a mystery series based on one of her favorite food groups (dessert) is as enjoyable as licking the beaters, and she can't wait to whip up the next one. She is also the author of the Hat Shop Mysteries (*Assault and Beret, Copy Cap Murder*) and the Library Lover's Mysteries (*Better Late Than Never, A Likely Story*). She lives in Scottsdale, Arizona, with her family.